Chasing Hope

Elaina M. Avalos

Original and modified cover art by Robb North and CoverDesignStudio.com

Acknowledgments

The idea for this novel came to me on a red-eye flight from Southern California to North Carolina. The book I wrote then is not the book you're going to read today. There are quite a few passages and chapters that have been cut. I loved some of those words. I even miss them a little. But over time, I realized that what I started writing in 2005, changed with me.

Through all of the incarnations of this book, my constant supporter, grammar-checker, and encourager has been my Mom. She has read this so many times I don't know how she is still doing it. But even now, as I write this, she is checking and double-checking. If there are grammar mistakes or inconsistencies, it's not due to a lack of effort on her part. It's my fault. Thank you for your unconditional love, support, and reading this book more times than either of us can count. Thank you to Jackie, Kassi, and Keeter for reading and giving me your feedback. I am grateful that you took the time to read my book and answer my questions.

In 2006 I sent the beginning pages of *Chasing Hope* (called something else entirely then) to a writer friend. In the e-mail that accompanied his critique he said he was "brutal" but he wasn't. He was honest. His advice has stayed with me. He also said a few things about my writing that meant the world to me. They still do. He was the first person I trusted to read this and his critique has followed me all these years (in a good way). Michael Snyder – wherever you are – thanks for challenging and encouraging me.

This book is for those of you out there chasing hope in the midst of your darkest days. Keep chasing. This book is also for those of you that are waiting for some sign that it's time to start chasing dreams. This is your sign – so go for it.

"Hope" is the thing with feathers -
That perches in the soul -
And sings the tune without the words -
And never stops - at all -

And sweetest - in the Gale - is heard -
And sore must be the storm -
That could abash the little Bird
That kept so many warm -

I've heard it in the chillest land -
And on the strangest Sea -
Yet - never - in Extremity,
It asked a crumb - of me.

~ Emily Dickinson

~ One ~

Highway 306
Pamlico County, NC
September 2015

In a stroke of sheer genius, or maybe it's a sign of a quickly approaching mental breakdown, I left D.C. seven and a half hours ago and headed toward the coast of North Carolina, with the pain of a secret dream's loss, taking up the most space in my truck. Besides my personal effects and the furniture I brought into my marriage, I left everything else to my ex-husband and his Legislative Assistant.

I'm not sure what one should feel when you leave your life in a pile at the curb, but I'm damn near certain it feels about like this. What's this you ask? Doom. And perhaps a little paranoia. Definitely fear. When my marriage ended, I thought we could peacefully co-exist, like normal divorced people. You know, like the rest of America. Burns would keep our houses in McLean and Ridgemont and I would live in Georgetown. I forgot that Burns Cooper is not normal. Leaving is the only way.

On this early autumn day, it's warm with just the tiniest hint of cool swirling about. There is a promise of crunching leaves and football season floating on the edge of the breeze. I roll my front seat windows down, the fresh air providing some much needed therapy. My hair blows in every direction. I will not tell a lie, it gives me smug satisfaction to know that by the time I get to Beaufort, I'll be a hot mess. Burns would not have tolerated that. One could sum up my ex-husband in one word: controlling. Then again, I could think of a few other words and hand gestures to describe him too. On days like these, when the world is beautiful and the air is just right, I feel good. Not happy. But I feel good. I'm convinced I will never be happy again.

There's something about the wind blowing through the truck, roughing up my hair as it goes, that gives me calm in the midst of the tumult that has become my life. My hope is that leaving D.C. will be enough to get me somewhere in the neighborhood of neutrality. You know, somewhere in between agony and happy. I think I could live right there in the in-between. Charlie, my Boxer, stirs in the backseat, pushing himself into a sitting position and stretching. He barks once and then whines, just in case the message isn't clear. "Yeah, yeah, keep your shirt on," I say to him, looking in the rear view mirror. "We'll be there soon enough." I turn up the jazz - Miles Davis'

Flamenco Sketches, already filling the truck, in case Charlie decides to make a habit of the whining. He sighs with a flare, sounding more like a teenager than a dog.

He doesn't stay quiet for long. His whining increases until I say, "Fine. Hold on." I pull the truck over near an abandoned house. The house had been white at one time in its long life, but the years had added grime and mildew to its color making it a dingy grey. It has a sagging, sad front porch, covered in Kudzu. The suffocating vine covers the ground behind the house, and then climbs and winds its way up the pine trees that stretch out as far as I can see. I take a deep breath, my eyes fixated on the porch of the old house. It reminds me of me. Memories of our front porch in McLean push their way forward. With it come the sights and sounds of laughter, of William and Harper – my stepchildren, chasing each other around on the front lawn while I sat on my favorite swing, watching them play.

I am a doctor. A good one. I went to the best schools. Harvard for undergrad, Johns Hopkins for medical school, and my Meds-Peds residency was at Georgetown. The competition to get into that program just about killed me. Yet, in spite of my success, there is only one thing I've wanted my entire life - to have a family. I don't say this out loud . . . ever. There are few people in my life who understand the depth of the longing. There's an assumption that this life I made is what I wanted. But I'm not going to lie, medicine had been a way out. I didn't want for a thing in a privileged family. Scratch that, I didn't want for a single thing that money can buy.

My family life growing up had been unhappy. Dysfunction exists in all families in some form or fashion. But ours is legendary. Our household knew knock-down drag-out fights, or long periods of silence. Either way, my brother and I were raised by a woman my parent's paid to love us. So yes, medicine was my way out. My mom wanted me to stay and take over her business. My dad didn't care what I did. For my mom, medicine wasn't the type of career a "woman like me" should pursue. I went after it wholeheartedly.

Always running under every dream and hope I built my life upon, there lived this longing for a family. When friends said they wanted to be a doctor, lawyer, ballerina, or architect, or whatever else, I did too. I may have said "doctor" but under my breath and in my heart, I said, "Mom." I spent hours playing with my dolls and thinking about what my family would be like – it looked nothing like the family I was raised in. I cut out pictures from magazines, tore out recipes, and spent hours looking at catalogs thinking about my home, a home I wanted to be beautiful, happy, and warm. This is my dirty, lost secret. Women in 2015 are not supposed to admit this. We are supposed to want a career. We are supposed to leave our children with nannies or at a childcare center. If we are stay-at-home moms, society makes us feel like we're less than. But that's what I wanted.

When the opportunity presented itself to do just that, I grabbed hold. Harper, who had been three years old when we met, had this angry snarly way about her. She didn't want to be loved, touched, or held. Her father complied, lacking a basic understanding about how a child seeks to get their needs met. William was one and happy as a clam. From the moment I met them, I knew their paths were meant to cross mine. I loved them as if I'd given birth to them myself. Their mother, by all accounts, had the sweetest personality that most of her family and friends say perfectly matches William's. I wanted to raise them as she would have, totally certain she and I would have been great friends had we ever met.

When I found out I was pregnant with Katie, life could not have been more perfect. I mean, I could have had a loving husband but other than that, my life really looked like everything I'd ever dreamed. Katie was perfect. Except for her heart. She was a beautiful baby with a head full of brown hair and the bluest eyes I've ever seen. I took a lot of time off after I had her, because of her surgeries. I will never look back in regret for the time off, in spite of what many of my colleagues thought. After we brought Katie home from the hospital, after her long NICU stay at birth, I marveled at every single thing about her from her tiny fingers wrapped around mine in quiet moments in the nursery, to the way I could see myself in her. Katie didn't make a fuss about much of anything. She let you know when she needed to eat and be changed, but quietly. I love her and my step kids in a way I never dreamed possible, but hoped to experience for as long as I could remember. Six months after Katie was born and had recovered from her first surgery, I put her in her car seat and drove to the kid's school to pick them up. It had been a rare luxury as my work schedule didn't allow for very many afternoons like it. On the way home, I took them for cupcakes. With Katie in my arms, as I tried to eat a cupcake and listen to the kids talk about their day, I thought that life looked exactly as it should be. Exactly.

But my life is nothing like that now. Everything is gone, even the two-story townhouse I bought in Georgetown. I hoped against reason that Burns would wake up and see what he had done. He didn't. I shove the memories down deep, as fast as I can. Charlie and I trudge through the high grass, walking away from the parked truck closer to the abandoned house. The dog wanders to the end of his leash. He sniffs in a circuitous route as he goes. In the early afternoon dappled light, the sun's beams dance through the spindly, Q-tip like pines that line both sides of the highway. The air is filled with the smoky goodness of burning leaves, smelling like a campground bonfire. I close my eyes and let it all sink in. The last car passed by us ten minutes ago. Clearly, this is as different from D.C. as one place could possibly be.

Which is the point.

***

Beaufort, NC

Growing up, I couldn't turn down an adventure, even if that meant being brought home by the security guards in our gated community, or jumping in, feet first, into the biggest mud hole in the neighborhood. My years with Burns had buried some of that thirst. After Katie's funeral, which was nearly two years ago now, Burns left me. In one fell swoop, I lost my baby and then the rest of my family. During our divorce, I tried to get shared custody of the kids. It became my sole pursuit in the dark days of grief that followed Katie's death. Though Burns' political career came to a swift end after news of his affair broke, his friends in legal circles were in every nook and corner of Virginia. Between his far-reaching circle and his determination early in our marriage to not let me adopt them, I stood very little chance of getting 50/50 custody of Harper and William. Though I had spent the majority of their lives raising them, and thereby had the legal standing to fight for custody, power often trumps what is right and true. It did in my case.

Burns' power, though diminished during a scandal of his own making, outweighed mine. I received visitation rights after a protracted fight that went on for close to a year. For the next year after that, Burns and his Legislative Assistant played constant games with visitation. My scheduled phone calls and Saturday visits grew further and further apart. If I had to change a scheduled visitation because I was on call, Burns would twist it around to my lack of desire to see the kids – as if I'd refuse a visit offered. We are still playing that game. The kids and I lose nearly 90% of the time. We have found ways to creatively talk. But visits diminished significantly. My broken heart broke even more in that year following the custody fight. I used to think of myself as a strong woman – fearless and determined. But the grief and loss of all that I had built and believed my life was meant to be, turned me into a shell of my former self. I started looking anywhere and everywhere for something new, a new job, a change of scenery, a new haircut – I mean anything. I'd even bought a regular old truck to part with the expensive cars Burns kept me driving.

On a hot D.C. afternoon, after wandering around Eastern Market, my cell phone rang. It was Pepper Parker, a friend I met at Georgetown during our residency. We caught up on life. She knew some of the details about what happened between Burns and I because like rest of the nation, she watched it play out on cable news. When you're married to a pretty-boy Senator who became the face of the conservative movement, it happens. I filled her in on the details that the press didn't cover. In the middle of our conversation I told her that I finally faced reality. I needed to leave D.C. Pepper, never one to mince words or waste an opportunity to boss someone around, knew what my next big adventure should be. As I made my way back to my Georgetown townhouse, she told me exactly what she thought I should be doing. "So here's the deal. You were always the one that needed a new adventure. You said you want a change of scenery. I have an amazing idea."

"Uh-oh. Should I sit down?"

"Maybe? My partner moved to Raleigh and I have a medical missions trip to Uganda coming up. I could use a hand. We, I mean I, am the only pediatrician between Down East Carteret County and Beaufort. The practice provides a lot of low-cost medical care in the community. I need help. We have been through some serious crap together. I mean we have history you and me. The change of scenery will be great for you. It's quiet, beautiful, and there's absolutely zero chance you'll run into that witch Jenny.

"Huh. Interesting," I said in reply, mostly meaning it.

"It's more than interesting and you know it, dude. Think about it at least?

"Easy. I'll totally think about it. When do you need an answer by?"

Pepper replied quickly, without missing a beat, "Tomorrow. I'm not giving you time to over-think this. I know how you are. You know in your heart this is the answer. I need you. You need me. It will be perfect."

Just like that, I knew. I didn't think, pray, or waffle. I knew I had my answer. I needed to walk through this door. I hoped with all my heart the distance would bring enough healing that maybe I'd find myself again. Truth be told, though that first conversation had been three-hours long, Pepper sold me on the idea the moment she brought it up. Though the deal, with terms, timing, and the nitty-gritty details were worked out over the course of a few months, I made my decision about twenty-minutes into the conversation. And here I am, on the road to my new home and a life I didn't plan for or expect.

I took the back way this time and wound through the countryside staying as far away from the Interstate as possible. I drove through farmland and lonely stretches of pine tree forests, cut down in places and lined in perfect rows in others. I stopped somewhere after turning onto Highway 101, to pick up some cotton fluff that lined the highway. The harvesting of cotton, just beginning, had been another sign of my new world. The golden light of sun through pine trees is warming. This place is all at once swampy and forlorn and then lushly green.

As I pass Ann Street in downtown Beaufort, the water comes into view. Without the heavy tree line that had been the norm on the rest of the trip, the sun is nearly blinding on the water. Sailboats dot the creek. I turn right at the end of the road, onto Front Street. The street is nearly abandoned, though it's the middle of the day. I look at the clock on the dash of the truck, struck by the stillness of the streets, though it's nearly lunch time.

I drive a couple of blocks and then reach the front of my house. The house is a southern slice of heaven with its white paint and black shutters. It has two porches - each wraps itself around the two stories, hugging the house in the warm way a porch should. Just up the street from my house there's a small park, with a gazebo that sits out on a little point. Just to its right, a line of red, yellow, and teal kayaks line up on the muddy banks of Taylor Creek. From my vantage point, I see one woman, walking a small dog. And just as I begin to pull away from the front of the house, a car passes by. In the span of those brief few moments of observing what is to become my new world, I see two people. Crowded metros and busy city streets, overflowing with tourists and packed-in like sardines federal employees, car horns, sirens, and the sounds of construction, were my daily reality. I wanted change. But two people?

I pull my truck into the driveway behind the house and stop in front of the detached garage. "Well, buddy, we're here," I say without much emotion. Charlie sits up and looks at me, cocking his head to the right. "We're home!" I exclaim hoping I sound more convincing. He whines in reply. "Come on," I say, getting out and opening a door for him. Charlie jumps down and immediately heads for the gate that blocks the guest house and backyard from the view of the alley and the neighbors. I open the gate and Charlie charges ahead into his new domain. He wanders as I walk across the yard. I fumble in my purse for the keys to the French doors that lead into the Carolina Room. I get the door open and set my purse and overnight bag on the floor, just inside the door.

When I stand, after putting everything down, I look out through the bank of windows that are nearly floor to ceiling in the sun room. As I scan the entire yard, from one end to the other, I see a bright blue bouncing ball under a hedge of azaleas along the back fence. The couple that lived here before me had four children, ten grandchildren, and a handful of great grandchildren. They couldn't understand why I'd want a big house like this. But in today's real estate market, they didn't argue with my offer. An ache twists my heart, like it's a piece of paper, crumbled and tossed in the trash. The ache takes over as it sometimes does. The pain is unbearable most of the time but it grows in moments like these when in the midst of an everyday moment, the simple becomes complex and devastates me. I stare at the ball for a second longer and unsuccessfully push the intrusive vision of a blond nine-year-old boy, bouncing a ball against the side of the house.

That day, more than a year ago, I watched him from the window in the kitchen at our house in McLean. The rhythmic thud of the ball as it hit the wall, through a half-open Dutch door, had been all I heard over the sound of the television on the opposite counter. The ball would hit the concrete and then the wall, and then over and over the pattern repeated. I should have stopped him. But there had already been too much. I couldn't. He turned and looked straight at me, my memory of that moment as vivid and clear as if he stood there in the backyard of a house in Beaufort, NC. He smiled a wide, silly grin and waved. Even on the worst of days, William Cooper made you smile. And in spite of the death of my daughter, the signed divorce papers, impending changes, and the ring-less hand, I smiled back at him. It had been my last weekend with the kids. Burns employed what I had taken to calling the "nuclear option," as if everything we had already been through didn't suffice. Though the visitation agreement would give me one Saturday a month, once-weekly phone calls, and few days each summer, it became clear from the get-go that Burn's Legislative Assistant, would ensure that agreement would be ignored.

Though I'd been able to smile at William then, I'm not smiling now. Standing here in the afternoon light, as it spills in through the porch windows, tears run down my face, probably carrying my makeup with them. This is a fairly regular routine. I can't help myself. I wipe my face with my right hand. "Charlie. Come on, time to go inside," I say, my voice, smoky from the tears. As is Charlie's custom, he pretends he doesn't hear me. But as soon as I turn around to open the door to the house, Charlie's dog tags betray his steadfast stubbornness. As I open the door, he's there at my feet, ready to follow. "We're home, Charlie. We're home." We step inside and I shiver in the chill of an empty house. I head for the hall, searching for the thermostat. I switch on the heater and turn the heat up to 70, hoping it won't take long. "Now what?" I ask looking down at Charlie. If a dog could shrug, Charlie did. He sighs in that heavy way he does and then trots off, his nose sniffing out lord knows what. He leaves me standing alone in the hallway.

That's when it fully sets in. I'm alone in an empty house. My mind wanders in an instant, before I can stop it, to the old reality again. I would give anything, anything in the world, for the kids to come through the front door. To yell at them to stop running in the house. I'd give anything to hold Katie one more time. *Anything.* I turn and face the front door, as if I expect them to run out of my heart, and into the house. But that's about as likely to happen as their father growing a heart. Unsure of what to do next, I open the front door and walk out onto the porch. I sit on the top step and rest my elbows on my knees. Now it's my turn to sigh. I take a deep breath, hoping that it will cleanse my brain of the images that fill it and of the sounds of the kid's fighting. Or laughing. Or of something inappropriate on the television I've told them to change a million times.

But it doesn't work. The memories fill my mind and heart, until my cell phone rings to break the spell. I hit the speaker button. "Hello?"

"Mrs. Cooper?"

"Yes. Can I help you?"

"Yes ma'am. This is Tony. We spoke yesterday about your move."

"Right. What can I do for you?"

"I just wanted to let you know that the truck is headed your way ahead of schedule. In fact, you can expect them within the hour."

"That's great news. Thanks for the update."

"No problem, ma'am. I'm sure you're anxious to get settled."

"I am. I'll be here when they arrive."

"Great. Please call if we can be of any further service."

"Thank you. And I will," I say as I end the call. Things are looking up already. A house with stuff in it is better than a completely empty one. Maybe.

***

"Ava? You in here?" A knock on the front door follows. I look around the corner of the kitchen, down the long hall, to the front door. I wave until Pepper sees me.

"In the kitchen. Come in!" I exclaim, false cheer saturating my voice like thick, sappy honey. Pepper will see through me – why even bother? She always had a knack for that during our first year of residency when I tried to figure out how to juggle school, being the wife of a Senator from the Commonwealth of Virginia, and a mom. I turn back to putting knick-knacks on the shelf that overlooks the sink, and look out the large window. The bouncy ball taunts me again from under the hedge. Note to self . . . destroy the bouncy ball in the backyard. I turn as she enters the kitchen, her arms are outstretched. "Hey," I say.

We hug as she says, "Hey back. So glad you made it safe and sound."

"Me too. Me too."

Pepper pulls away and looks around the kitchen. "So wow. You've been busy.

"I can't take all of the credit. The movers were fantastic. Pretty much all that is left after they were done is hanging pictures and putting my own spin on the place. They were incredible. Thanks for sending them my way."

"No problem. I'm glad that worked out. So uh, I know you're probably not ready for jumping into small-town life but some of my oldest and dearest friends are having a welcome home party for my friend Macon, their son." I nod my head. She continues, "He just got back from Afghanistan." I hope there will be a way to get out of the invitation that is coming.

"Anyway, he got home recently and it's going to be a big to-do. Everyone will be there. And I mean ev-er-y-one. I mentioned that you were in town and the Thompsons would love for you to come. The party starts at 6:00 tomorrow night."

"Where is it?" I ask, aware that I probably can't weasel my way out of this, even though I'll give it a valiant effort. Not if I want to help run a successful business in this tiny town.

"It's next door, actually. Macon's parents live there."

"I'm not sure I'm in any shape to meet anyone at the moment," I say.

"I know you just got here but it would be good for you to get out and meet people right away. This family basically owns half of Carteret County. Plus, they're just awesome people. Come on!"

"I'll try. I can't promise anything. But I'll try. I'm not sure I have anything appropriate to wear. Most of my stuff is still packed."

"This is Beaufort. Not DC."

"Okay, well, like I said, I'll try." Although internally I'm running through my supply of standard excuses to find a way out, I know I can't. Thinking of the box of liquor sitting on the dining room table, I suddenly need a drink. Perhaps going with a slight buzz is the best way to tolerate a house filled with people I've never seen before, let alone met.

~ TWO ~

It has been a couple of years since I've been able to enjoy gardening. Everything that held meaning or had once been soaked with joy, became hollow, dried out, and empty. When I moved into my Georgetown Brownstone, I didn't even start a garden. What little yard existed there, I paid someone else to care for. After Pepper left, I walked out to the front porch and stared at the yard around me. I may have bitten off more than I can chew with this place. Clearly, I'll need a gardener. But even still, the plants on the porch alone, left by the previous owners, will require extra attention. *I must be crazy for buying this place.* Picking up a watering can that sits on a small garden cart, I fill it at the hose on the side of the house. While I'm filling the water can, or so I figured later, Charlie decides to take a little jaunt.

At least once a week since the divorce, Charlie decides that he's had enough of life with me and takes to wandering. The problem with this habit is that he's a little too exuberant on his adventures through the neighborhood. He's never met a stranger. Charlie hasn't always wandered from home. It's a recent habit. My theory is that he's searching for Harper and William. He loves me. He does. But I can't compare to those two, his faithful playmates since he was a pup. Truth be told, if I could, I'd take off after them too.

When I realize, I head after him in a slow jog, knowing that if I race after him, he'd think it a fine game and run further and faster. Charlie's a lover not a fighter so I know he won't get into too much trouble. I don't want him wandering about just the same. Though he's as innocent as a ladybug, he looks a little menacing. I hate the thought that he will scare some poor child or a new neighbor. Just past Gordon Street, I see a man jogging in our direction, a dog on a leash runs beside him.

Charlie stops his run for a minute, sizing them up. He turns and looks back at me, wondering whether I'm going to stop too. I don't. So he keeps running. The man slows as Charlie approaches. The two dogs size each other up and then, just as I'm within arm's reach of Charlie, a low growl comes from my dog and the fur on his back raises straight up. The other dog, responds in kind. Before the owner can get in between the two dogs, mine goes after his. I bridge the distance between me and Charlie, as fast as I can, yelling at him. In spite of the two dogs acting like mortal enemies, I reach for Charlie. The other owner, yells, "Careful!"

"I have to do something!" I get a hold of Charlie's collar and pull just enough to get some space between the two dogs. Somehow, I find the strength to keep Charlie at bay and then yell at him to knock it off. He whimpers a little as if he's hurt. I'm mad enough to not care. But I start to check him for injury and not seeing any teeth marks or blood, relief floods over me.

"You really should control your dog," he says. "A dog like that isn't safe to roam in a neighborhood like this. He could've done some major harm!" he says, clearly angry with me.

My cheeks burn red-hot. "My dog is one of the sweetest animals on the planet. He wouldn't hurt a fly. Maybe it was your dog. Ever think about that?" I ask, standing into an upright position and facing the voice behind me. All 6'2 of him. 6'2 of sweaty, gorgeous goodness. Wow. I grip the leash I've now clipped to Charlie's collar. I make eye contact with him and see a flash of anger in his eyes. Or maybe it's just the adrenaline. "Charlie wouldn't hurt a soul," I say again, this time, my voice lower, cracks.

"I find that hard to believe," he says, sounding smug. "Keep your crazed mutt on a leash."

"My dog isn't crazed. My dog has never done this before" I say, tears rising up in my eyes.

"Again, I find that hard to believe. He attacked Bob for no reason. All I'm saying is, keep that dog of yours tied up somewhere. You must be new here because we don't let our dogs run wild. If you were paying attention, this wouldn't have happened. This could have been much worse."

That's enough for me. The tears spill out of my eyes and run down my cheeks. "Well where I'm from, people don't talk to total strangers like they're criminals. My dog is a sweetheart. I'm sorry for the trouble we've caused. Have a good day, sir!" I say as I turn, anxious to get out of there. "It won't happen again." Silence follows me and I am thankful he didn't continue the argument.

A split second later, he calls after me, "I'm sorry. Wait a second? Please, wait." I continue to walk, ignoring his request. His feet hit the pavement in a slow jog toward me. "Wait," he says, grabbing my shoulder. I stop. "I'm sorry," he says, a new tone taking over. "Truly. Please forgive me for being so rude." I don't turn around. I wipe the tears from my face.

"I have to go," I say, turning around to face him then. The flash in his eyes has disappeared and now all that's left behind is compassion. If it weren't for the anger boiling and broiling beneath the surface of my heart, I'd think he might be a good guy. "I have somewhere I have to be. I'm new in this town, but one thing I know for sure is that accusing perfect strangers of neglecting their animals seems like something you might not want to say until you know the whole story." I say.

"I'm sorry," he says again. And then, on the edge of the breeze and barely audible above a passing diesel truck, and a helicopter in the distance, "Take care . . ."

In the few moments it takes me to get Charlie and myself back onto my property, I've calmed down only enough to stop the tears that fall far too easily these days. It's almost embarrassing how emotional I can be. "Don't you go and do that ever again, you brat!" I say to Charlie. His ears perk up and he turns his head to the side as if he's taking in every word. "You are a trouble maker. I swear. And did you have to pick someone so good looking? Of course you did."

I get Charlie inside the house and slam the door shut, as if I'm trying to make a point, to the dog. "You stay there!"

Leaving him, I stomp out to the front porch and down the stairs to the front lawn, leaning against the magnolia tree that sits on the right side of my yard. I stare out at the water, arms folded in front of me. From next door, music floats up, along with the voices of what I'm guessing are the Thompson clan getting ready for the party that will start within the next couple of hours.

"What a jerk," I say. "I mean. Really. Seems a little overly dramatic, you know? It's not like he hurt anyone. What a jerk," I say again. I fume. Anger and annoyance bubble up higher and higher, entirely disproportionate to what actually passed between the two of us. "Jerk," I say, as if saying it multiples times will make me feel better. How rude, you know? Who does stuff like that? Yell at total strangers? He was probably raised by a bunch of redneck, Neanderthal types. Men.

I pull my cell phone from my pocket and look again at the last text message I sent to Burns. "I was scheduled to talk to the kids today at 3. Please have Harper call me as soon as possible. This is the third time you've missed an appointment. If this continues, I will contact my lawyer." I didn't hear from Harper. It has been weeks since I last talked to my son or daughter. Burns never agreed to letting me adopt them. But that doesn't matter. I love them, like I love Katie. The games their father plays with me, using them as a pawn, have long outworn their newness.

You'd think he would have grown tired of it by now. But with his Legislative Assistant cheering him on, he continues the same pattern. Jenny is a child. An educated wealthy one, but a child nonetheless. I have never been in control of the response people had to what Burns did to me. The polite people of the Commonwealth hate her guts and she has yet to figure out that making me pay for the way people feel about her, will never win her friends nor will it influence anyone. Burns Cooper's political career is over and that makes both of them insanely angry.

The overwhelming urge to beat the tar out of the tree hits me all of the sudden. Instead, I sink to the ground, held up by the trunk. There's a spot made just for me here, facing Taylor Creek. I fit perfectly between two roots. I place an arm on each one, as if I sit in an armchair. I sit in the silence and wonder how it is I ever got so angry. And tired.

Above the anger, I hear a little girl's voice reach screaming proportions, "Uncle Maaaacccc! Over here!" I picture her taunting her uncle, sticking her tongue out. I think of William then. The tears, stopped up since I'd gotten away from the jerk, come back again. There are just some days, you know. The weight of being alone, as memories and losses flood over me, is intense. And the deeper my heart plunges, it seems like the world decides to measure out even more heaping tablespoons of pooh upon the pain. Someday, when the world makes sense and bad things don't happen to good people, I'm sure this will all make sense.

***

I take one last look at myself in the mirror. If it weren't for the fact that I struggle to get through each day, I'd say I look hot. I look good. Really good. For once. I smooth my lace camisole and turn to the side, looking in the mirror again. "Well . . . here goes nothing," I say to Charlie, who is sitting beside me, staring up at me as if I'm the greatest thing to walk the face of earth, in spite of our earlier kerfuffle. I step into my flip flops and head downstairs. In the two minutes it takes to get from my house to the Thompsons, I've nearly convinced myself that hot or not, I don't really want to go to a party for a guy I've never seen or met, in a house filled with people I've never met before. I'm sure no one will notice if I don't show up. There'll be a ton of people there. No one will notice. I'm sure of it. I make an about face, as I am about to step onto the brick walkway that leads to the Thompson's house.

"Ava! Where are you going? You come right back here, this instant," Pepper says from the porch of the massive house – a house filled with noise and people and happy. "Where do you think you're going," she says as she jogs toward me.

"I forgot – I forgot something," I say.

"What?"

"Something."

"Right. No chance you're leaving now, sister. Come with me. I'll give you the grand tour and introduce you to every last person you're going to need to know. So put on your best Senator's wife smile and let's do this thing," she says, wrapping her arm through mine and pulling me, not so gently, in the direction of the Thompson's house. Bruce Springsteen's "Born in the USA," plays loudly from somewhere behind the house, the sounds of 1984 surrounding me.

***

Long before I've met the guest of honor, or the host and hostess of the party, I'm convinced that I've met every last person that lives in Beaufort, Morehead City, and possibly all of Downeast Carteret County. Standing in the massive and stunning kitchen of the Thompson's home, Pepper tugs on the sweater I've now slipped on. She says, ever so inconspicuously, "He just walked in. You have to meet him. Now. Come with me," she says, pulling me away from a balding gent with a big belly and beer breath, that has been monopolizing my time.

"What's the hurry?" I whisper. "Things were getting quite serious with George. I think he was just about to propose."

"You need to meet Macon. He's finally free. Well, except for Kenly." she says, as she pulls me along. I'm so distracted by the way she's pulling me headlong, against my will, that I don't realize until it's too late, where she's taking me.

The gin and tonics I've had suddenly come rushing to my head when I look up to see the gorgeous hunk of a man who yelled at me earlier today for letting my beast ravage the town. "Oh," I say. "Oh." I look over at Pepper already confused. I haven't wanted to leave any place as badly since the afternoon I ran into Jenny at the Pot Belly in Ballston. I look up from my feet, where my eyes have been firmly planted, probably only for a moment, but for what feels like an eternity, and face him. His smile is beautiful. His eyes. Oh his eyes. They are locked on mine. I feel a little weak. Possibly faint. I want to turn away, although I don't know why. That's not really my style. He speaks first. "Nice to see you again. Macon," he says, holding out his hand.

"Ava," I say, cold.

"I see you've met," Pepper says.

"Sort of," Macon replies. "We had a run-in earlier. It involved snarling, barking dogs and my mouth, with my foot stuck in it."

"Ah," Pepper says. I stand still. Normally confident in every room and in all settings, even if I am faking it, I am awkward and uncomfortable now. I stick my hands in the pocket of my linen pants. And then I pull them out again. And then I cross my arms in front of me. "I'm sure that had to have been quite exciting. I'll avoid the formalities and just mention, Mac – Ava is the one I told you about. She's joining me at the practice."

"Great news," he says somewhat flatly.

"Thanks?" I say, quietly, unsure of his tone. "We have some great ideas for ways we can better serve the community. Some things we'd like to change up."

"This town doesn't like change," Macon says quickly in reply. "And it takes a long time for new folks to break through, especially if they make changes too quickly. Hopefully you're up for the task. It's not easy to establish one's self in a town like this."

"Well, thanks for the vote of confidence," I say. "I'm more than up for the challenge. And frankly, from what I've seen so far, this town could use a little change so people will just have to suck it up." I smile my best Senator's wife smile and then say, "Nice to meet you. And by the way, welcome home." I walk away. Hopefully there's not a mile long line at the bar, because I need another drink. Since his parents apparently own half the county, perhaps I should have been nicer. But he's two for two in the insult department.

I slip into the line at the bar they've set up in their dining room. Thankfully the line isn't bad. George waves at me from across the room. I politely smile and wave back. He takes that as an invitation and heads my way. Before he reaches me, I hear from behind me, "I'm sorry. Again. I'm not a jerk. I swear." Macon has leaned in, closer now and he places his hand on my elbow.

I look up from my feet to see my new friend George attempt to coolly play off heading in my direction earlier. I pull my arm away and turn around. I half expect him to be smiling, as if he thinks this is all a joke. But he's not. His dark brown eyes are impossible to avoid and he is undeniably sincere. "I really am sorry. Being around Marines all the time, for the last nine months, has guaranteed that the social skills my mama taught me are lacking." He smiles and in an instant, my tense shoulders relax.

"I am sure your mama did teach you well. I'll accept your apology if you promise to do a couple of things for me."

"What's that?" he asks, his broad smile showing the years and life in his face.

"Try not to make snap judgments about people - "

"Or their animals," he says interrupting.

"Or their animals," I say.

"What's the other thing?"

Without missing a beat, I answer, "When we make changes and open a free clinic, you'll come in and volunteer at least once."

"I can do that," Macon says, smiling.

"We can start over if you can meet my conditions. Until then, I'm going to have to go with my first impressions."

"Fair enough."

"If you can behave yourself, like a proper gentleman, I may be willing to change my opinion in a more expedient manner." I smile as I watch the lines in his forehead crinkle up as he raises his eyebrows. He's ridiculously hot.

"I see. Well, I'm up for the challenge. Now, what did you want to drink? My parents just waved us over," he said pointing at the host and hostess across the room. "You're going to want one with those two."

"Gin and tonic. And now I'm scared. So thanks for that."

"No problem," he says as he tells the bartender what I want, and requests another beer for himself. "My Mom is dying to meet you."

"Oh. Great."

He hands me my drink as we meet the senior Thompsons half-way between the two rooms, in the prettiest entryway of any house I've ever seen. "Mom, dad, this is Ava Cooper. Ava, this is my mom, Charlotte Thompson. And this is my dad, Beau."

I reach out to take Charlotte's hand and she embraces me. That escalated quickly. "So nice to meet you, Mrs. Thompson."

"Oh, please call me Charlotte! I'm so happy to have the Smedley house occupied again. Welcome to Beaufort!"

"Thank you," I say as I shake Beau's hand. "It's great to be here and to be getting settled so quickly."

"Pepper's mentioned some of your plans for the clinic. I can't wait to see what you do," Charlotte says.

"Well your son isn't so sure about my plans."

"Well, I love my son but he's often incorrect when it comes to downtown Beaufort. He's still mad that new buildings were built down here, and by new, I mean about twenty years old. He had a fit when they put in the bank. I'm sure if it was up to him the streets would still be unpaved and we'd be getting around by horse and buggy."

"Oh please," Macon says. "Unpaved, yes. Horse and buggy, no."

Charlotte Thompson rolls her eyes. I like her. "Whatever, weirdo."

"Hey now! Is the name calling really necessary?"

"I call it like I see it," she replies.

"Nice, mom. Really nice. Thanks."

"You're welcome, son. You are so welcome." Charlotte looks at me and winks. "So enough talk about my son. I didn't say this earlier – where are my manners? Welcome, Ava. If there's anything at all that you need, please don't ever hesitate to stop by. Beaufort is a sweet little town and though I'm sure you're well aware of this, the pace can be a bit of an adjustment so if you need a little noise and craziness in your life, the Thompson house is just the place."

"Thank you, Mrs. Thompson. I –"

Charlotte interrupts, "I'm Charlotte. Mrs. Thompson is my mother-in-law and was, as it were, the scariest woman I've ever met. It gives me chills just thinking of her. Really, sugar, please call me Charlotte."

"Understood. I had special feelings for my ex mother-in-law as well. Thank you for the warm welcome."

"We should circulate before someone starts a rumor that we're too good to talk to the people at our own party," Beau says just loud enough for me to hear. "And since you've insulted our son and my mama, God rest her soul, perhaps I should also get you some water as I believe you may have had one too many glasses of wine."

"You're probably correct, hun. Water sounds perfect," Charlotte says smiling. "Thank you for coming, Ava. Can't wait to get to know you better."

"Thank you, Charlotte. It was great meeting you both." Beau and Charlotte wave as they walk away.

"They're pieces of work," Macon says shaking his head.

"Apparently the apple doesn't fall far from the tree," I say.

"Don't tell me they made a bad first impression too?" Macon asks.

"Oh no. They're awesome. You are still on probation," I say, walking away. I leave him standing in the foyer, laughing. I'm not sure if he's laughing at me or himself. But either way, it somehow feels good to make a man laugh.

***

It's amazing what you can put your mind to when forced. Surviving the Thompson's party could be my greatest accomplishment in ages. I would never admit it to Pepper, or anyone else for that matter, but it actually felt good to be there last night. I felt good. Until I unlocked my door and stepped into a quiet house. The ache settled in then, seeping into the cracks and crevices of my heart. It does this. I try to distract myself. But some days and nights it is a pointless endeavor.

It's hard to imagine how my life could ever look again like I thought it would, when I saw visions of my future. It's certainly nothing like the life I expected when I married the dashing Burns Cooper, with his beautiful babies, who were as desperate as I, for a real family. They are still beautiful babies desperate for a family. I wanted and fought for shared custody but I lost that battle. For now, I live for phone calls that sometimes don't come. The question is . . . why? Why have I settled for something that is not what is best for Harper, William, or me? Grief, I'm sure. And yet, something about this move has awakened the fight in me. It's quiet right now, but it's growing. Perhaps it's time I turned that grief into a little righteous anger?

I climb the stairs to my bedroom slowly, Charlie on my heels. Burns has spent so much time and money on keeping me out of the picture, all to suit Jenny. Maybe it's time to step back into the fight? I've lost countless battles. Maybe it's time to win a few. I walk through my dark room, drawn to the second-story balcony off of my bedroom. Eastern North Carolina hasn't been quite ready to let go of summer. While cool, it's still the kind of night you can sit outside, as long as you have a sweatshirt. I grab a sweater from the chaise lounge near my French doors, hit play on my phone as music fills the silence, and step outside.

The town and street below are quiet. There's not a car in sight. Without lights on Carrot Island, the only lights to be seen are those along Front Street. While living in McLean offered a more suburban life, I spent my work days in D.C., and then after our separation, lived in the midst of busy Georgetown. There were rarely quiet moments like these. This town is nothing I knew I wanted, and everything I've needed.

The darkness and grief still come after me, like when I step into an empty house. But standing here in the stillness, healing and a sunrise may be on the edges of this long, dark night. For now, with Ella Fitzgerald and Miles Davis filling in the empty night around me, I plot my comeback, dreaming of my family being whole again, at least as whole as possible. In the middle of "Blue in Green," I know I've turned a corner. I may not want to face everything that lies beyond tonight. It's still going to be a fight. But it's time.

~ THREE ~

A few months later

"Dr. Cooper! Am I ever glad to see you. We've got a mess here this morning. I know everyone's usually runnin' late but not today. They're like a swarm of angry hornets in that waiting room. And -" Carol draws out the silence while raising her bushy eyebrows just long enough to make me hold my breath a second. Then I relax when I remember it's Carol. There is no way it could possibly be as bad as she makes it sound. After her dramatic pause, her words tumble out of her so fast, it's a wonder she's still breathing. "I just got a call from the Thompsons and Miss Charlotte wants you to make a house call for her grandbaby, Kenly. She's running a terrible high fever and-"

"Slow down there, Turbo. What's gotten into everyone this morning? This is the first time since I got into town that anyone has shown up for an appointment on time." My head hurts and the day has just started. Carol's accent makes my head feel like it is being squeezed between a massive boulder on one side and well, an equally massive boulder on the other side. Truth be told, it's not really the accent itself that's the problem. Jamie has the same one. It's the tone of Carol's voice that makes her twang unbearable. It's kind of like hip-hop booming next door when you're trying to sleep. It's the whine of a cat in heat. I've come to count on her and Jamie like I need oxygen, but there is no doubt she grates on me.

Carol is tall like a summer morning in the south. Long and drawn out. She gets you hot under the collar. Her hair is always piled on top of her head, like Flo from the show Alice. It's wound so tight I don't know how she lives with the thing. But perhaps this is why she whines? She wears boots every day, no matter the weather or seasons. She wears them with dresses. She wears them with her pant suits and when I ran into her at Food Lion last week it was sweats with brown boots. She's been married for forty-two years. To one man. I didn't know people still did that. She has five kids, ten "grand-babies" and more animals than I can keep track of. She's irritating, but she has a heart on her the size of California. She doesn't have to work. Her husband would prefer that she didn't. Sometimes I would prefer that she didn't, mostly on mornings like these when her voice makes me want to scream. But she stays. According to Carol, she says she couldn't stand to be in the house with him any more than she is now. He's been retired for two years she tells me. Two very, very long years. She loves him and all, but needs a break.

There's no end to her heart. Where at the bottom of the well that is my emotional life, there is often stagnation, Carol's is being fed by some unknown spring of joy. Sure, she gets worked up at the oddest moments and fights with Jamie like they're WWE rivals, but in every other way she's got what I thought I

had. As we stand just inside the back door, where she acco
I opened it, she tells me more. She gets whiny again, soundi
he wants outside.

Now would be a good time to roll my eyes. But instead,
know you've met them. And maybe Kenly. But this grandba
Miss Charlotte will be difficult to please if we don't get you
as we can. Just be prepared is all I'm sayin'. And don't keep
the others through but don't make Miss Charlotte wait. They
today either. She said they're at their beach house. And as far
everyone this morning? Your guess is as good as mine."

"I'll do my best to get over there as soon as possible," I s
promise to try, Carol isn't convinced, at least not yet. "I'll hur
Don't worry." The strain in her face disappears but she's still s
of me, blocking me from my office and my patients. "Let's get
stands there, as if she has no clue that I'm telling her to move out of the way. I
haven't been clear enough. "If you want me to get through that swarming nest
of hornets out front, you'd better move your rear out of my way."

I smile at her, hoping she'll smile back. I think I could look at her smile all
day long. If only she wouldn't talk. It takes her a moment, but eventually she
responds. Her smile is like sunlight. Rays bounce off the walls like those tiny
rubber bouncing balls you buy at the dollar store. Must come from that well of
hers. I wonder if I can get some of whatever it is that feeds her. "Sorry, Doc. I
make a better door than a window. My bum is a movin'. My man says it's big
but perfect." And then she laughs, which is second only to her smile.

"I'll be there in a minute," I say as she walks away. I stand in front of my
office door and balance my briefcase and coffee cup as I fiddle with the
doorknob until it opens. As usual, Carol has brought in some flowers from her
small greenhouse. They grace my desk with a tiny riot of color. I set my stuff
down on the brown leather love seat against the wall.

Sorting through everything I find my phone and slip it into my pants
pocket. And as is my daily custom, I hang the white doctor's coat back up on
the hall tree I keep next to the door. Carol insists I wear the coat. I refuse.
Pepper won't wear one either. Carol says patients don't respect us as much
without them. While generally I say something sarcastic when she goads me
about it, the truth is, the last thing we need to do is wear coats that are white,
starchy germ carriers - like petri dishes made out of cloth. No, thanks.

The first time I told her no, she said, "What's to distinguish you from the
rest of them?"

Jamie responded before I had a chance, "Well, the degree from Harvard
might. Or possibly going to one of the best medical schools in the country? Or
you know, maybe the residency that only eight get into every year at
Georgetown? Or maybe teaching residents that came through the program after
her?" And then, with his characteristic sarcasm, he answered himself, "On
second thought, you're right, she needs the coat." I don't wear the coat. She still
talks about it, however. One thing I do wear, my stethoscope. But I can rarely

remember where I left it each morning. Carol and Jamie are forever cleaning up after me. Embarrassing really. I don't mean to be a slob. I don't mean to be flaky either. Seems as though that's exactly what I've become.

These days it's almost as if my absentmindedness has become ingrained into my very being like my sense of humor, or the way I twirl my hair around my index finger when I'm tired, or like my obsession with coffee. I sometimes hear women joke that they lost brain cells when they started having children. I guess that's not the case with me. Or maybe it's the same problem but in reverse. I lost brain cells when my daughter died. I see the stethoscope hanging where it's supposed to - not where I last left it I'm certain. As I grab it, I stop and look into the mirror that hangs next to the closet. The circles under my eyes are dark and my skin isn't as tan and healthy looking as it once had been. My curly hair is streaked with more gray than even a few months ago.

My appearance seemed to be a thing for Burns. He thought I looked like a First Lady. He said that regularly when we talked about the future. I had it - "the look." He told me on many occasions, "You're beautiful. More beautiful than any woman I've ever known." And then he'd jump right into how useful my looks would be. I had a face people would trust. After we started dating seriously, he asked me to start straightening my hair. The curls were too much - too messy - too wild. I loved my mess of hair. I should have known the first time he brought it up that I wasn't in Kansas anymore. Even my parents weren't that bad. But now? I don't think I'm beautiful anymore. I'm not even sure I recognize myself half the time. It's like I've aged and turned into someone very different than who I was before Katie died. It's like one of those people you see at the store or in church. You know you've seen them somewhere before, but who the hell knows where. Everything that used to be me doesn't exist anymore. With one exception, I'm still a doctor.

***

By noon, I'd seen all my patients. Carol meant business about getting me over to see Kenly. At five minutes after twelve, Carol walked me out the back door of the office, carrying my white coat - she never relents, my bag, and a bottle of water, giving me instructions the entire time about how to get to the Thompsons, what to say when I get there, and how she "can't stress enough how very important this appointment is." Right. Okay. Got it. Yada, yada, yada. I try to listen. I do. But after a few months of this, I'm at the tuning her out stage of our relationship sometimes. Like today.

Driving down Highway 58, headed for Pine Knoll Shores, there is not a cloud in the sky. There's just a hint of a breeze. The thermometer on my car reads 75. It's a gorgeous day, especially considering it is winter. Both front seat windows are down. Growing up in Malibu, I have a special kind of friendship with the ocean. The air and the crashing waves revive me. The ocean gives me this sense, though often fleeting, that a hope-filled existence may be possible again. The emerald water is quickly obstructed by the growth of the coastal shrubs and trees that remind me so much of areas along the California coastline.

The strip of barrier islands, known as the South Outer Banks to locals, is bordered on one side by Bogue Sound and the Atlantic on the other. It's just a thin strip of land. I've driven down Highway 58 from Atlantic Beach to Emerald Isle a few times since I moved here. I never stop anywhere. Once I moved here, it's like all ability to try something new ended. I walk to work. I walk home. I sit on the porch. I go to bed. And then the next morning, it starts all over again. I haven't been to New Bern. I haven't gone to Wilmington or Raleigh. I haven't even been to the Outer Banks yet. In the four months I've been here, I have done whatever I could to avoid being seen in daylight lest I have to converse with my neighbors. When I have the nerve on some evenings, I plot my next steps in getting joint custody of Harper and William. Alone works for me, at least for now.

I slow down when I see a sign for Pine Knoll Shores. Carol said the small side street that leads to their home isn't far from the town-limit sign. I see it in just enough time to make the turn. Their house is straight ahead, at the end of the side street. It faces the ocean. I pull in the driveway and sit for a moment, my truck engine turned off. The house, large and modern, sits on prime Crystal Coast real estate. I close my eyes and lay my head back against the headrest. There are knots in my stomach. Nausea rises up, reminding me that the basic parts of life require extra effort now.

I'm nervous. It's not the wealth. I've been surrounded by it my entire life. I was the wife of a Senator. My parent's social circle overflowed with celebrities. I'm fairly certain my parents have more money than is right. The problem is being in a setting where I'm forced to answer questions and talk about my life. I've successfully avoided this family for weeks and weeks on end. I know they'll want to catch up. One thing is clear about the Eastern Carolinians I've met thus far . . . they're nosey as all get out. I cannot control my responses when the questions start. Something tells me that I'm meeting one of those families I will not be able to avoid from here on out since "they own half of Carteret County."

I get out of my car and walk up the sidewalk. live oak trees and more of the coastal shrubs I saw on my drive, line the winding sidewalk. The house looms in front of me. It blends in with the native plants and live oaks - like the biggest tree house you've ever seen, hidden amongst the green and brown of maritime forest. I knock on the massive oak double doors that look like they belong in an Arte de Mexico catalog and not on a house in Eastern Carolina. They're probably hand hewn. Though it's a detail many might miss, I know instantly that while they're going for an understated look, they are, in fact, extremely wealthy. That's what happens when your mother is an interior designer to the stars. I knock a second time. The door swings open and Beau Thompson greets me, hand outstretched.

"Good to see you, Mr. Thompson," I shake his hand. He's tall, and strong enough that his grip is a bit much. Goodness.

"Please call me Beau. My wife and son wouldn't shut up when we met so I didn't get the opportunity to say that when we met," he says laughing. His laugh is boisterous. It fits his size. It's the kind of laugh that originates deep in the diaphragm. It'd make your belly shake if you have one. It's the kind of laugh that makes you hope you have full control of your bodily functions. I don't laugh like that now. But I remember what it feels like. I walk with him through the entryway, into a great room with expansive views of the ocean. The beach below is visible from the wall to ceiling windows that stretch across the entire length of the room. The view and house are impressive, even to me, the ex-wife of a man that spent more money on meaningless stuff than anyone I've ever known, besides my parents that is. What I'm guessing are original paintings hang on the walls and small sculptures sit on shelves and table tops. They are modern, and well placed. It looks like something my mom would have designed for a client in Malibu or Montecito.

In the family room, a little slip of a girl is lying on the couch, asleep, with cartoons on in the background as her lullaby. As we walk by her, he stops for a moment. "That's our Kenly. She's a doll baby, she is. She came at just the right moment in time." He then points through an open sliding glass door to the deck. Charlotte sits with her feet on the deck railing, her back to us. A man, also tall, stands with his back to us, looking out at the Atlantic. Macon. Lord have mercy. I'm not sure I'm ready for Dreamy Eyes again. "Why don't we step outside where we can talk?" I nod my head in agreement. I catch a glimpse, as we head outside, of a large family portrait hanging over the massive stone fireplace. In it, the Thompson family is sitting on the beach, each wearing coordinating outfits, khakis and white shirts. Also known as the obligatory family portrait uniform. They're like a magazine ad for the perfect family. There's only one child in the sea of adults, Kenly, which is weird considering the age of the Thompson's kids.

Charlotte Thompson speaks, even though her back is to us, "It's a wonder you don't wake the dead with that laugh. I tell you what, if I had known that the serious boy I met all those years ago would turn into such a nut," she says with dramatic effect, "I would have continued to turn you down."

As she speaks, Macon turns to face us. We make eye contact. He smiles. I look away but I know his gaze is still on me. I can feel it. I can feel him. My cheeks burn. I'm blushing. Ridiculous.

"It's wonderful to see you again," Charlotte says, the teasing tone of her voice still covering her words. Her accent is more elegant than the typical Eastern Carolina twang but it's a mix. I'm not sure of what, but definitely a mix. Beau bends down and kisses the top of Charlotte's head and then his hand trails down her arm, resting on her hand. "I'm sure you remember Macon," she says.

"I do. Good to see you again, Macon." I reach out for his hand. Like his father, his hand is massive and engulfs mine.

"While I wish we weren't seeing each other under these circumstances, welcome Ava," he says as he holds my hand in his. "Thanks for coming by." He holds my hand longer than I'm comfortable with. His eyes never leave mine. It has to be hotter out than 75.

"It's no problem at all. It has been a quiet day today," I say, lying convincingly. It's the Senator's Wife Training Course I took. There's not really any training but by god do you learn how to fake it until you make it. When Macon finally releases my hand, I sit down at the teakwood table, next to Charlotte who has turned her chair to face us, away from the ocean view. She smiles and winks at me as her husband walks behind her and sits in the chair on the other side of his wife. Macon joins us at the table, sitting across from me. Charlotte is wearing shorts and a t-shirt that says "Pain is weakness leaving the body." I find this humorous and smile at the odd picture, so different from what you'd expect. Carol. It's all Carol's fault. She has me envisioning the Thompsons, after a first meeting that seemed normal, as the height of all nastiness.

With her melting pot accent Charlotte says, "By the way, welcome to our home. Thanks for coming all the way out here to see Kenly. I hope we didn't cause too much trouble in your day to ask you to come all the way out here. We stay at this house as much as we can when we have her. She loves the beach. Have you been out this way yet?"

"Yes. Well, no," I say, realizing I sound ridiculous.

"So which is it?" Beau asks bluntly.

"I've driven down this way but have never stopped. And just so you know it's my pleasure to make a house call, it makes me feel useful. I have nothing going on this afternoon. My schedule is clear for the remainder of the day."

"Since Kenly is still sleeping, we'd love to chat for a bit if that would be okay with you?" Charlotte asks and then continues before I can respond, "It seems you've done a good job of hiding since you moved here."

They sure don't beat around the bush, do they? "Well I've been busy settling in and with Pepper leaving ahead of schedule I've taken on more patients. I don't mean to be a hermit," I lie again.

"I wanted to let you know that our daughter-in-law Grace will probably call you in the morning. She knows Kenly has been sick and that you'd be seeing her today. She was much calmer than Grant about their girl being so sick, which surprises me. He's so stoic. Grace is our most sensitive Thompson. She's remarkable in her ability to understand the heart," she says, as if these are important details. "I'm no new age guru that believes in reincarnation," she continues. "I promise, I'm a good Baptist, but we have a saying in the south about babies and children who seem to know more than they ought. We say, 'that one's been here before.' But it applies to her too. It's like she's connected at the hipbone to the world because she's seen it all before. She just seems to know."

I don't think I want to meet Grace. I'm sure she's great and all that. But I don't need some physic-friends network poster child getting near the pile of steaming excrement that is my heart. Charlotte continues, "I think she missed her calling. She should have been a therapist. She's a gem."

Yeah, now I really don't want to meet her. "She sounds wonderful," I say in my, I was a Senator's wife, voice. It's a tone Ms. Grace the Pain Magnet would see through. But I'm convincing to the average Joe. I haven't lost my touch. I can pull it off without missing a beat. None of the Thompsons seemed to pick up on the fact that I'm as fabulous a liar as the man whom I learned to fake it for. After this random revelation about Kenly's mom, the three Thompsons get lost in conversation. They're cheerful people but it's different somehow than the shallow sounds of most. I see something in them I recognize. Charlotte's eyes tell me that she knows sorrow. And I'd venture to guess she knows it well. "Boys, I think we're boring the good doctor, here. She's got this glazed-over look in her eye. Perhaps we should talk about something other than our boring family?" Charlotte says.

"So Doc, have you found yourself a church?" Beau asks apropos of nothing and without missing a beat.

Why do southerners always assume one goes to church? It takes me a moment to answer. I'm trying to decide what to say. I don't want to tell him how I really feel. That I'd rather have bamboo shoved under my fingernails than go to church right now. I'd rather wade through a pool of vomit, than listen to a Pastor pontificate about God's will and goodness. It's possible that God hates me, why would I want to go to church? "Nope, I sure haven't."

"You should join us on Sunday. We go to that Baptist church on the corner there," Beau says, as if I'll know what corner he's talking about.

"Oh, that's nice of you to offer but -" I start my sentence but don't finish it because he interrupts me mid-stream.

"Well then, meet us out in front at 10:00 AM sharp and we'll escort you to the Thompson row." Beau's facial expression, a mix of amusement and challenge tell me that he knows I'd prefer not to go.

"If you're wondering which corner my nutty husband is talking about, it's the corner of Front and 5th street. It's a great church. They're a friendly bunch. I hope you'll come. Macon will be there, right son?" Charlotte asks.

"That I will. I haven't been back since I got home. You should come, Ava. It's a great church. They're not all like my family," he says, deadpanning.

"Hey. Watch it," Charlotte replies.

"Thank you for the invite. I'll do my best to be there." Beau frowns at this statement. "I mean, unless I get called to the hospital or something, I'll be there."

"Oh good, I thought that's what you meant," he says, the teasing smile returns.

"It'll be great for you to stop by," Charlotte says. "You'll meet so many folks. It's a good way to get better acquainted with the community.

Oh me, as my favorite elderly patient, Miss Ruby Lee, likes to say. It's been so long since I've darkened the doors of any church, other than the church of the bitter and angry, that is. How do you tell the owners of half of Carteret County that you're no longer certain how you feel about God? I know all about small town politics. I can't really risk saying no to the Thompsons although they seem to be nice and rather normal. You never know though. Nice and normal could suddenly turn into mean and bent on running me out of town lickety-split. "Well, thanks. I appreciate the invite. I look forward to it," I think I sound sufficiently convincing. Change the subject. Change the subject. Change the subject. "So Macon, you've been deployed to Afghanistan. What are you? I mean, what service are you in?"

He laughs and then smiles at me. He didn't wink. But he might as well have. With his eyes steady on me he answers, "I'm a Marine. Took after pops here," he says.

"He's a pilot. He's been in Quantico for a bit, but moved back here just in time to deploy." Charlotte adds, beaming with a mama's pride.

"Did you get out of the Marines?" I'm relieved like nobody's business that the subject has changed. All three look at me quizzically. "I mean, because you said he'd moved back here?"

"No. I'm a lifer," he says smiling. It's a smile that I'm certain is dangerous in other settings. My stomach drops to my feet. Flutters I forgot were possible make me remember that I have . . . girl parts.

"He's our future general. He's stationed here," Charlotte adds with pride.

"Here?" I'm totally confused.

"You really don't get out much, do you? Cherry Point. It's the Marine base in Havelock. It's about thirty minutes to the west of Beaufort. He flies Harrier jets. The benefit to being stationed here is that we're here. Well, it's a benefit for his Mama anyway." Charlotte smiles.

"I'm sure."

"This family is as snug as bugs in a rug," Macon adds. "So I'm happy to be back."

"Now all we have to do is get Charlie back here from San Fran. So, Dr. Cooper, where are you from? Where's your family?" Charlotte asks.

"Please call me, Ava," I say.

Charlotte smiles at me. "Ava it is, then. So Ava, where are you from?"

"I'm from Southern California. My family is still there."

"Where in California are you from?" Macon asks.

"Malibu. My Mom and Dad are in Malibu. I have one brother who is currently in Baghdad. But other than that, everyone is in California."

"What does your brother do?" Beau asks.

"He works for the State Department. He's been in the Foreign Service for about ten years now. He's lived all over the world. Truthfully, I don't know what he actually does."

"Yeah, that's what I hear about those State department types," Macon says with air quotes around State Department. "So when did you move to the east coast?"

"I went to medical school in Baltimore and did my residency at Georgetown. I met my ex-husband while I was a resident there. I settled into east coast living once I got back this way and didn't want to leave. I started seeing D.C. as my hometown eventually."

"How long were you and your husband married?" Charlotte asks but she sounds hesitant.

It didn't take her long. "We were married for ten years. Our courtship was a whirlwind of gifts and trips and flattery and two beautiful children who desperately needed a mom. Harper, my stepdaughter, was three when I married Burns. And William was one." I don't offer any other information. She knows anyway.

"That's a lot to take on in the middle of a residency. It says a lot about your character," Charlotte says.

"I don't know about that. I love the kids. It was an easy choice." It's time to change the subject again. "So are you all from Carteret County?" Not as much of a seamless transition as I'd imagined.

"I am," says Beau. "I grew up a little ways from here."

"What about you Charlotte? Are you from here?"

"No, ma'am, I'm from Savannah. My Daddy worked for the State Department, himself. I spent a lot of time in D.C. of course. We lived on a bit of a farm in Vienna during the school year. Our family home is in Savannah though."

"I'm sure we would have a lot of interesting stories to trade." Why did I say that? "So how did you meet Beau?"

"As Macon mentioned, he's a retired Marine. We met while I was in school, Mr. Jefferson's College," she says as an after-thought. "One of my sorority sisters had a brother that needed a date to the Marine Corps Ball. I went as a favor to her."

"You were Beau's date?" I ask.

"No. Shamefully. I went with his best friend. They were in officer training at Quantico. It was love at first sight. For Beau that is," she says laughing.

Beau cuts in, "It was love at first sight. I couldn't stop staring at her. I'm afraid I embarrassed my date and Charlotte. She was a sight to behold that night. She still is, as you can see. I bugged her for three months to go out with me. She finally relented. Thank God for miracles such as these," he says with a sincerity I recognize, but don't know experientially.

Tears rise up in Charlotte's eyes. One rogue tear spills out and runs down her cheek. She doesn't stop it. I watch her for a moment. She smiles a knowing smile. She's not smiling at me, Beau, or Macon. She just smiles. This is a love I've always wanted but have never had. "How long were you a Marine?" I ask, embarrassed that I've been admitted into this little scene and I'm desperate to change the topic, yet again.

"What was it, mom? You keep track by the hour, don't you?"

"Ten thousand, nine-hundred and fifty days, sixteen hours and forty eight minutes," Charlotte answers not missing a beat. "My husband is a retired general. It was a long thirty years. He runs the family business now. I wouldn't trade those years but I'm glad they're over."

"I can imagine. That's a long time." I have no idea what I'm talking about. This is a regular occurrence these days. I'm now certain that when you lose a child, you become stupid. Words fail. I think it's the numbness. Paralyzing numbness makes me stupid. My self-pity is interrupted for a moment when I hear the quiet voice of Kenly from the living room.

"GiGi?" Kenly says from the couch, just inside the sliding glass door, "GiGi, come here. My hands hurt bad."

***

On cue, all four of us stand and walk to the living room where Kenly has been sleeping. I pick up the stethoscope I laid down in my lap when I sat down. Kenly is sitting up. She's propped herself against the side arm of the suede sofa. She's small for her age. She's like fine china, a tiny teacup of a girl. Her hair is thick, wavy and the lightest brown possible without being blonde. She bears no resemblance to anyone in the family. And also unlike the other Thompsons, Kenly will most likely never be as tall as the others. Charlotte speaks first, "Sweetie, this Dr. Cooper. Remember I said she was going to come over and check on you?" Kenly nods her head yes. "Well, since you're up now, you need to answer Dr. Cooper's questions and cooperate with her, okay?" Kenly nods again. I step closer to the couch and crouch down in front of her.

"Hi there. How are you feeling?"

"Icky."

"Icky, huh? Why do you feel icky?" I ask.

"I hurt everywhere."

"Everywhere? Wow, that's a lot of places. Do you think you can tell me what hurts the worst?"

"My hands. And this," she says pointing to her collarbone. "This hurts bad. I try to scrunch up like this," she says shrugging her shoulders, "to make it go away. But it doesn't."

"I'm going to sit down on the couch next to you, okay?" Kenly nods again. I move the blankets that are covering her lap and I sit down next to her. "Beau, Charlotte, why don't you sit down and tell me what's been going on and then Kenly and I will get back to our conversation." Beau and Charlotte are sitting across from me on a small loveseat. Macon stands at the fire place, the family portrait above him. I let them tell me what they feel they need to and then ask Kenly to show me her hands.

"Well, there could be a few things going on here. We'll have to run some tests."

Beau and Charlotte aren't looking at me or Kenly. They're looking at each other. Charlotte reaches for Beau putting her hand on his arm. I look over at Macon. His eyes are closed, worry creating lines in his forehead and around his eyes. Beau speaks first, "What is the least worrisome of the possibilities?"

I respond quickly, "Rheumatoid Arthritis."

"Arthritis? As in what I have in my knees, arthritis?" Beau asks.

I get ready to answer and Charlotte interrupts, going straight to the point. "What else could it be?"

Beau seems eager to distract his wife. He's looking at her and then me and then back to her again. "Arthritis, really?"

"Yes." I'm relieved to get Charlotte away from the other issues at the moment. The look on her face makes me ache. I continue, "The joints in her hands are swollen, red, and warm. Her knees are swollen too but they're not as noticeable. We'll run a CBC but I'll also order a few other tests to check for auto-immune issues to include Rheumatoid Arthritis. Where are her parents again?"

"They're on a bit of a honeymoon. They never went anywhere since they were in college when they got married so we sent them on this trip. We didn't expect them back until later this week," Charlotte says.

"Do you have permission for medical treatment?"

"Yes, but we'll call them anyway. Knowing Grace, she'll want to come home." Charlotte said.

"Bring Kenly by the office tomorrow and we'll run the labs and I'll write an order for x-rays. If it's at all possible, I'd like to speak with Grant or Grace myself." I take out a card from my pocket and take the pen I've been using to scribble notes and write my home and personal cell numbers on the card. "Here's my card with my private numbers. Tell them they can call me any time. I mean that. Any time at all."

Charlotte accepts the card. "Thank you, doctor," she says, suddenly formal. "We appreciate this. More than you know. You've been wonderful." There's sadness in her eyes.

"You can come by in the morning. If you want, you come right at 8:30, I'll see Kenly first."

"Okay," she says, quiet and sad. The tone of her voice is familiar. It sounds kind of like, *what's next, what's next?* I know the tune. I've been singing it for a while now. "Thanks again."

"You're welcome. I'm more than happy to help," I say.

"GiGi, when we go to the doctor office tomorrow, can we get a smoothie from The General Store?"

"Sure thing, Darlin'. I'll get you a strawberry banana smoothie just like you like." Charlotte looks to me. "She's not eating much either. I neglected to mention that. I figure that a smoothie is better than nothing."

"It is. If they have any protein powder, have them add that in. Her appetite will improve eventually. Let her eat what she wants. Try to limit the sugar if you can. Her appetite will return to normal when she's ready. In the meantime, 'let them eat smoothies,'" I say trying to be funny.

"Will do, Doc. Thank you for your help," Beau says. He looks unsure of himself now. The earlier humor replaced with fatigue. Or maybe it's worry.

Macon is seated now, in a wing back chair in the corner. He dwarfs the chair. His long legs make it look like it belongs in a dollhouse. The worry on his face has not dissipated. This family has been through something horrible. I can see it plain as day. I've worried them. And just like that a quiet desperation fills me. I so want to give them good news once these tests have been run.

"GiGi," Kenly speaks up again, "Can we get one for Uncle Macon?"

"One, what?" Charlotte asks.

"A smoothie."

"That's sweet of you, Sugar. Uncle Macon would you like a smoothie?"

"Of course! Thank you."

"You're welcome Uncle Macon. And then maybe we can go horseback riding after that."

"I'm not so sure it would be a good idea to go horseback riding tomorrow. But, will you promise me something, Kenly?" I ask.

"Yeah," she says quietly.

"Will you promise me to get lots of rest and tell your Grandma or Grandpa or Uncle Macon if anything changes about how you're feeling -if you feel better, or if you feel worse? And then maybe in a few days you can go horseback riding."

"Okay," she says, now looking exhausted from her outburst of talkativeness. No one speaks. It's clear I need to leave them alone with their thoughts.

"Well I hate to run but I really should get going. Thanks for the invitation to church. I'm looking forward to it." I'm a huge liar.

"Yes, yes of course. I'm glad you'll be able to join us. I appreciate the effort you've made on Kenly's behalf already," Beau says.

"It's no problem, really. I'm happy to do whatever I can." At this point I'm just relieved that I can finally get out of here. This family might be getting under my skin. If I sat here longer with them, I might say more. I might say more than I'm prepared to say. The questions might continue. And perhaps, before I know it, someone will ask the question I dread. How are you really doing?

"Well, drive safe now," Charlotte says.

Beau picks up where she leaves off, "We're looking forward to you joining us on Sunday. If you can spare the time, we'd love to have you stay after for potluck. There'll be plenty of good Southern cooking there for that. If you haven't had Eastern Carolina barbecue, you really should try it. There's nothing anywhere quite like the stuff."

"Thank you," I say although I'd rather say, thanks but no thanks, I'd rather die than eat barbecue with a bunch of God fearing Southerners. "I'll check my schedule to see if I'll have time after church." Check my schedule? Right. What could I possibly have to do? I might have to take the trash out Sunday afternoon. Or scrub my toilet. My schedule?

"We'd love to have you," Charlotte says as she reaches out to hug me. "We'll see you tomorrow morning."

Macon says, "I'll walk you out." Beau and Charlotte both sit on the couch with Kenly. We step away from the living room, but I look back at Kenly one more time. She is already asleep, snoring deeply. Macon and I walk together, in step, to the front door. Macon reaches it before me and holds it open for me. An ocean breeze howls through the room. A curly wisp of my hair blows across my face. I pull it away from the sticky mess of lip gloss it is stuck to. I pull my sunglasses from my head where they've been resting. "Thanks for coming. Kenly was the only grandchild until recently. She became a Thompson, through adoption, at a very challenging time for all of us. She's kind of like our sign from God that He was out there listening. It means a lot that you'd come here and take such care with her and my parents especially. So thanks."

"You're very welcome. And listen, there's really no sense in worrying now. I know that's easier said than done. But if you can, try to encourage your parents and brother and sister-in-law to do the same, okay?"

"It's a plan. See you Sunday."

"Sunday it is," I say putting the glasses on, hoping to escape his ever present gaze.

"Bye now," he says. I turn around and wave. His smile returns and there goes my stomach again. He's easily the best looking man I've ever laid eyes on, which is saying a lot considering the man I married. He's handsome in a rugged way, a little weathered. Though not the eldest Thompson, he appears as though he should be. The massive door closes behind me, the wrought iron metal work clinking and clanking as he shuts it.

I walk down the sidewalk toward my truck. The sea oats that line the sidewalk blow in the wind. The grass sounds like tiny clapping hands. Who knew sea oats made noise? The sound is like the tap, tap, tap of computer keys or the clicking of the medicine bottle with the child proof lid, click, click, clicking in an endless circle until you hit it just right. The grass plays this tune with each breath of wind that blows through its wispy blades. It's somehow beautiful and comforting. I stand at the door of my truck. My hand, gripping the key chain, is suspended in mid-air. I close my eyes and listen. Seagulls squawk loudly. It's amazing that such an annoying noise can become so comforting.

Rolling, endless waves break at the shore. I don't have to see it to know exactly what is happening beyond the house that blocks my view from the shore. Children's voices, playing on the beach, waft up - carried on a breeze. The sounds of the beach are carried through the makeshift tunnel between the Thompson's home and their nearest neighbor. They're distant, faint melodies. In the time I've been here, they've started to become normal and familiar. It's like the way Burns talking on the phone in his study became home. Or the way Harper and Will sounded when they were arguing or playing. It's like the sound of traffic on Wisconsin Avenue. Or like the sound of Katie's heart beating on the monitor. I'm hoping these sounds will replace those.

~ FOUR ~

It really hasn't been all that long since my baby died. It hasn't. Two years seems like an eternity and not. At night, when the lights are dimmed and I've poured myself a glass of wine or some Bourbon, I think about the day that I finally met that tiny sweet thing. Her tiny hand in mine had been pressed, in a fist against me, only hours before. Shortly before my water broke, I watched my bulging belly as she dragged her hand across it. She was my miracle. Her birth changed me forever. While my step-children were born in my heart, Katie was a part of me. I never felt part of anyone.

My ex-husband sometimes used my status as the kid's stepparent against me. My own family had always been detached from my life. After a lifetime of feeling alone in my own birth family, my heart overflowed with the knowledge that a physical part of me would be walking around in the world. The day she died, her body drained of life in my arms, had been no consolation for the loss. Someone told me, I can't recall now who it was, that I would feel better if I held her before they took her away. I have trouble imagining in what world that would have been possible. I held Katie. I didn't feel better. I don't feel better.

It has been over two years since Katie lost her battle with the congenital heart defect that plagued her from the beginning. An impossible to win RSV infection took over and her body had no fight left. When she was hospitalized, I knew her chances were not good. She was in the care of the very doctors I had worked with every day for the previous seven years of my life. My own residents worked around the clock on our behalf, not wanting to leave though there was little to be done. They did it for my sake. But we all knew the truth.

Others, like the people of Burns' hometown and his staff, held out hope. I did my doctor thing and reasoned. I thought I prepared myself for the worst. Only I wasn't prepared. When one of my closest friends pronounced Katie dead, my world turned upside down. And it didn't stop then. My only consolation is that it seems as though I've finally gotten a break from the avalanche of pain that had just begun to crush me under its weight, the day my daughter died.

***

As I sit down at my desk, back in my office, I turn on my favorite all-news network and set the remote on my desk. The afternoon anchor, who kind of happens to be my best friend Jules, is chatting it up with her co-anchor. I can't really hear what they're saying. But I look up at the screen briefly. I look up just as Burns' picture flashes across the screen. I reach for the remote and turn it up. Jules' co-anchor continues to speak. I've already missed some of the story, "Our own Julianne has just broken the story. You heard correctly folks, Virginia's most scandalous Senator is going to be a father again." I drop the remote control. I stare at the TV, mouth open. Jamie and Carol are arguing in the hallway. Their voice's raise as they approach my office. I turn up the television again. Their voices trail off, probably because they can hear the television blaring. They appear in my doorway. "So Julianne," the co-anchor says, "What's the latest?"

And there is my best friend, reporting this devastating news, without telling me first. "It's true, Nate. Senator Burns has told us that his former Legislative Assistant is now pregnant. They have planned a small wedding for later this month. The Senator stated that he does not plan to reveal the sex of the baby until after the baby is born. When asked how his older children feel about this, the Senator only stated that he was certain his children were looking forward to this happy event in their lives just as he was. This reporter isn't so sure he's told his kids. Not known for his tact, Senator Burns is entirely capable of telling his kids by news report."

I stand up, pushing my chair back from my desk. I grab my phone, purse, and keys. I walk to the door, not saying a word, and wait for Carol and Jamie to move. They both look at me with puppy dog eyes. Neither moves. "Do you mind? Seriously, move!" I say when they still don't budge. They part like the Red Sea. As I walk down the hallway, I say, "I have my phone. I'll be at home." As soon as I'm outside, the tears flow. I gasp for air as I jog home. I'm having a panic attack. There's no one on the street and I'm hoping I can get there before anyone can see me. It's only a block so my chances are good. As I reach my house, I pull out my phone. I dial Julianne and listen as it rings until it goes to voicemail. I run up the stairs and unlock the door, pushing Charlie back with my foot. He's anxious to get outside. "Wait!" I yell through my tears. I dial her number again as I race through the house, dumping my purse on the floor as I go. I let it ring and ring again until it goes to voicemail for the second time. I swing open the back door for Charlie. He runs through the open door, as if he's afraid I'll change my mind. I pull the door shut and then climb the stairs to my room.

I take off my clothes, letting them fall in a pile in the center of my room as heaving sobs rack my body. I slip my arms through my red silk robe and tie it tightly around me. I walk back downstairs to my bar, grabbing an unopened bottle of bourbon. My cell phone, in the pocket of my robe, has yet to ring. I don't know who to be angrier at, God, Burns, or Jules? She may be the worst of the three. How could she not tell me about this before she broke the news on national television? I take a gulp of my drink and let it coat my throat. The tears continue, like a flood. My neck is wet, as the tears flow down my face.

Charlie barks. I don't budge. I sit down on my couch and flip on the television. They're not talking about Burns anymore. They are onto something else now. Funny how quickly they've moved on. I just heard news that turned me inside out. But they're quick to move on to someone else. Can I curl in a ball and die now? I turn down the sound so it's just barely audible. My cell phone rings. I grab it and answer as soon as I see that it's Julianne. "I tried calling you," she says before I can say a word. "I swear. I called your cell phone. But it went straight to voice mail. And then I called your office but your staff said you were making a house call. I tried. I swear. I'm so sorry, Ava."

"I don't know what to say, Jules. Should I say thank you?"

"Of course not. I'm so sorry. I had no choice. This all happened so fast. I told them I wouldn't go on air with the story until I talked to you but I had no choice, you know how they are. I'm so sorry. But you know this isn't the end of it, don't you?"

"What do you mean?"

"You are going to get phone calls and requests for a statement. You know you are. I'm just warning you. I doubt anyone will show up down there. But don't be surprised if they call. You know how Burns' constituents feel about you. This is still a story. We are all over this like a cheap suit."

"Okay," I say. I pull my legs up onto the couch and sit cross legged. I close my eyes and the tears continue their flooding of my face.

"Are you okay?" Jules asks, her voice quiet, as if she's talking to me in a room full of people.

"No. I'm not. Just when I think all this couldn't hurt worse, God finds a new way to prove me wrong. I just don't -"

"I know it hurts. I know. Is there anything I can do?"

"No. What can you do? Bring Katie back? Tell my ex-husband to take me back? Tell God to stop messing with me? What? What can you do? All I know is I was just starting to feel normal again. But apparently the unraveling continues. The unfairness of it all makes me crazy. I really can't take anymore. I've reached my limit. I mean, I'm ready to go over the edge with this one. I cannot do it. I cannot handle this, Jules. He's having a baby? With her? I mean, I – I haven't seen the kids in months and months and now this? Did I mention that I can't take anymore?"

"Would it help if I came there? I can come. I need a vacation. Let me come. I miss you. Let me find a flight and then I'll come. Okay? What is the closest airport?" Jules asks.

"Would you really?"

"Yes. You know I'd do anything for you. I am sorry about the way this happened. Please just give me some time to figure out a flight and then I'll come down, okay? What's the nearest airport?"

"New Bern," I reply quickly.

"Okay. I'll let you know when I have my flight info. Are you going to be alright if I hang up now? I am on camera again in about fifteen minutes."

"I don't know. I'll talk to you later," I say as I hang up the phone. I pick up my drink and take another gulp.

Within five minutes, I get a text message. I read it, "I won't do the report. I'm on the next flight down there. Love you." I take another drink and feel the full weight of my insanity. Now I could be costing Jules her job. Of course she might deserve it. I turn the television back up and wait for the story to air. Before it does, the co-anchor says that Jules was suddenly feeling under the weather and he's standing in for her. He gives a brief synopsis of the mess that is my life and announces that the report is a recap of "the embattled Virginia Senator's recent scandals."

Scenes from my life play out on my television. They're familiar, yet so distant. Photos from our wedding, appearances we made at The White House, and events with Senator Robertson, the man Burns had shared the Commonwealth of Virginia with for twenty years, flash across the screen. And then there are the photos of our children. The report recounts each painful step of our daughter's death, his affair, and our divorce. It's a retrospective of my life. Only it's a life that doesn't exist anymore. One by one the events portrayed, spiral down from the good to the horrendous. It may very well have been months and months ago that this whole thing came to light, but with an election within eyesight, this is a story with legs, as they say in Washington. And as long as this is American politics, this story will run from time to time until election night.

I stare at the screen as my life slowly unravels again, as if I need to see it one more time. I take another swig of my drink. I watch until the story ends with Julianne's interview with Burns. I only got a moment, a brief and fleeting moment of regret from him when the news of the affair broke originally. His pride, anger, and his overwhelming confidence in his own greatness, wouldn't allow for much more than that. The pride, his pride, is there in the smirk on his face, as he talks to my best friend about his pregnant mistress. The average person watching this just won't grasp the full irony of course. And Jules' natural chutzpah, which makes her a fan favorite, isn't out of the norm, yet her zingers are personal in this case. For that I feel guilty. Maybe I shouldn't have been so angry with her. She has to do what she has to do. Just as I do, just as I've been trying to do since my world crumbled in front of me.

After the story airs, they come back to a set in the D.C. studio with three pundits waiting to wax poetic about my ex-husband's fate in the next election. Burns is in serious trouble and has been since the news of the affair, broke. The people of the Commonwealth of Virginia do not take kindly to men who cheat on their wives. Let alone ones who cheat on a wife that is greatly loved by his constituents and that just lost a child. Burns has sealed his fate today, now that he's having a child with a mistress his constituents still don't like.

Perhaps that's the one little, itty bit of pure joy I'll get from all of this. Burns will lose everything he ever wanted politically. I'm certain of that. I stand up and walk to the back door, letting Charlie in. The air is cool. I feel the chill right through to my bones. I walk back to the den and turn the heat on. Charlie runs around me in circles as I walk through the house. "Knock it off you loon," I say to him as he makes one more round. I stop at the bar before sitting back down. I fill up my glass again. I return to my seat on the couch. Bringing the bottle of bourbon with me, I set it next to me on the couch. I pick up the remote control and begin searching for something, anything that will distract me. At least until my drink numbs my mouth and head and helps me float above the world for a little while. I stop flipping channels at TLC. It's still early enough in the day that they're running A Baby Story. I watch the final moments of an episode. Why I do this to myself I'll never understand. The tears start flowing again. I take another drink and close my eyes, hearing in the background the new mother talk about how wonderful it is to finally be a family.

I wake to Charlie licking my hand which is always a quick way to get me moving. I sit up and focus on the clock on the DVD player. It's early. 6:30 AM. "Thank God," I say out loud. After last night, I would have expected that I'd sleep through my morning appointments. Maybe God is watching over me, after all? Either that or my dog is hungry. Yeah, the dog is hungry. With each step to the kitchen my head pounds. I scoop some food into Charlie's dish and then open the door. He runs outside quickly, nearly knocking me over, and then stands on the back porch as if he's in a hurry to stand still. "Weirdo," I say, as I shut the door.

I fix a pot of coffee and stand in front of the pot, with a mug in my hand, while it brews. When there's enough for a cup full, I fill up and put the carafe back and let it finish brewing. I wander upstairs to my perch overlooking downtown Beaufort. This has become my morning tradition. While it can't possibly wipe away the darkness that led me to drink myself to sleep last night, at least it shows me some sign that the world turns.

I live in a place that just a short time ago, I had never heard of. It's an odd town. There is wealth mixed with poverty, sometimes on the same street. There are retirees mixed in with hipster millennials. I'm in a new state, alone, well except for Charlie. This is not what I envisioned when I walked down the aisle to the man I thought I would love forever. It is not in the grand scheme of dreams that I'd woven out of silken hopes from the time I'd been a small child.

But here I am, sitting on the lanai of my white house, with its long porch that wraps around both floors. I expect the azaleas to bloom like mad in varying shades of pink and fuchsia in my front yard, in a few months. Ferns hang in wire pots that hide my front windows a bit. They twist and sway when the wind blows in off the water. I have come to love this house. In these moments, when I sip coffee and let the salt air seep in, I get right near close to being thankful for the beauty around me. Even better, this house is mine. All mine. Honestly, I'm surprised I like it since it's on the main drag here in Beaufort. Tourists walk by constantly snapping photos of the grand houses. I'd grown accustomed to the privacy of long drives hidden by tall fences with alarm systems designed by security experts.

I'd also gotten comfortable with homes so large I'm fairly certain they can be seen from outer space. Burns lived by the credo of the depraved and decadent in our nation's capital. Bigger? Better. More expensive? Isn't it obvious? That's totally better. New and improved? We bought it. New Jaguar? Of course. But Back to my house. It's old. It creaks like my bones. But unlike me, it's filled with life. You can hear the memories in the walls when everything is quiet. The view of Taylor Creek and the Beaufort Inlet is perfect. I have a dock just across the street, but I don't use it since I don't own a boat. But the creek and Bogue Sound are a hop, skip and a jump away. On many days, the wild ponies on Carrot Island and Shackleford Banks can be seen from my porch. I love watching them. I saw the horses my first morning here. It has become a tradition ever since to come out here first thing in the morning. I hope to see just one of them.

That first morning here, a jolt of energy shot through my body when I got out of bed. A quiet little voice, somewhere in the back of my consciousness, whispered of what could be. It was the first day of new – new everything. The voice, quiet, like a meek child, dared against the greater weight of my memories, to speak. Albeit timid, it was just loud enough to be heard. Was her name Hope? I walked across the room, that first morning, the quiet voice of hope, whispering of this new thing. I ran my hand across the silk robe I'd hung up the night before. It, like this voice, was new. I'd thrown away every single piece of lingerie, robe, or gown that I'd bought in my years with Burns. I bought this robe after my frenzy of giving away clothing. It's red silk.

True story – I've never bought a single piece of red clothing since I'd met Burns, choosing instead the more "respectable" neutral shades that Burns preferred. I once asked if I could buy a red gown for one of the inaugural balls we attended. He said it would make me look like a whore. Yeah, I couldn't wear a red gown because it made me look like a whore. I'd forgotten that there was only room for one whore in our family. So no red had been allowed for the Senator's wife. But I'm not the Senator's wife now, so I can look like a whore if I want to. Red silk. Woven red threads. It's a miracle to me really. How is it possible that singular threads can be woven together to create a thing of delicate beauty? I picked it up that first morning, slipping my arms into it and tying it around my waist. I reveled in the newness of it all. I walked to the French doors and opened them wide. I stepped onto the balcony. The sun bright, made my eyes feel heavy and tired, like I'd had too much to drink the night before. Which I had. But I digress. I closed them for a moment. Then opened them again. I stood for a moment longer waiting for my eyes to adjust to the light of day.

It was that moment I saw them. I'd read about them before moving, but had no idea they were so close. Feral Spanish mustangs meander, every day of their lives, from one end of the island to the other. The doubts I had on my drive, the knowledge that I was going somewhere so different from anything I'd known before, began to melt away that morning. Now, when I walk or drive through town, I feel twinges of comfort. I am somehow protected within the perimeter of this tiny place, with its narrow boundaries, water on every side.

The streets of Beaufort are mostly lined with modest houses except for the stately homes on Front Street. Along Front Street, mixed in with the homes, are small boutiques and restaurants. The oldest house in the town was built in 1732. Most are modest with a roof, four walls – small yards. There's a cemetery in the center of town called the Old Burying Ground. There are soldiers from the Revolutionary War, War of 1812, and the Civil War all buried there. With the Bogue Sound behind, Taylor's Creek in front, and the Atlantic Ocean beyond, I am safe here. Confining to some, I'm sure, but welcomed by me. It's as if the town itself somehow holds me in, keeping me sane and stitching me together by the tight seams of its boundaries. When I got here there had been those first flashes of hope. Hope that I could start again somewhere new. Hope that my life could become my own again. Hope that maybe God would restore, in some small way, what was lost. But after yesterday's news? I'm not sure how I feel about Him.

***

It took every last bit of energy left in me to get out of the house this morning. Hell, who am I kidding? It took everything in me to get dressed. But somewhere after my third cup of coffee and a nearly cold shower, I did it. My heart is still in a knock-down, drag out with my head over what to do with the news I heard yesterday. The first person I expect to see at the office is Kenly and her Grandma, who owns half of Carteret County. In other words, now is not the time for my heart to win.

Needless to say, after fighting myself and the fog left behind, I'm running late. Normally it would go unnoticed. Nobody would be broken up about it if I showed up late. You know that saying slower than molasses? The folks Down East have that beat. They move slower than frozen molasses, which means they don't move for much of anything unless it involves the water. Fishing? They're on time. Doctor's appointments? Not so much. I'm learning to accept this fact. Although I'm convinced it will take some time before I stop moving at the frantic pace I'd grown so comfortable with in my old life.

The "move when we want to move" approach to life in this town is what makes my appointments run late every day. I doubt they'd care a stitch that I'm late today. The trade off to everything running behind schedule is that I have more than enough time to get through the responsibilities of running a practice. This means that when we lock the front door at 5:00 PM, I walk home, which is unheard of in D.C. and in my old life. Life moves forward. But it's not in any hurry. On a professional level this is a welcome, cleansing breath. On a personal level, I haven't figured out how I feel about the pace. My days are overflowing with time and usually filled with over-thinking. Thinking is dangerous for me most days. Yes, it's true, I have a beautiful home in a delightfully odd town. I have a thriving medical practice. What's not to love?

The great thing about this town is that I can walk just about everywhere, except to the Food Lion. You can walk in D.C. too but you have to move fast or you'll get run over. Around here I can walk like everyone else. Molasses. I love this walk. I do it every day. My commute is five-minutes, if I walk slowly. This morning is drastically cooler than yesterday. It's like an early fall day instead of winter. It's like the first day you have to wear a sweater after a long, hot summer.

I pull my sweater closed as a gust of wind blows off the water. The wind sends my hair in a westerly direction, flapping wildly toward Raleigh. I'm sure I look like the picture of grace and beauty. The sun is a bright, deep Carolina blue. It makes you believe you're alive. The words Carolina blue roll of my tongue as if the phrase itself is soft, billowy cotton. It's kind of homey and makes me feel like I belong here. It's hard not to find a brief moment of joy when you're looking at the water and the sky. The creek seems to have been sprinkled with sparkling diamond light from the sun this morning. I catch my breath as the weight of the beauty sinks in.

***

"Good morning," Jamie says from behind me.

I turn to face him. "Dude, you scared me. I'm so lost in thought."

"That's obvious. I called out to you twice."

"You did not."

"Did too."

"Really?" I ask. I'm embarrassed and feel a slight pang of worry that I can be so lost in myself that I don't hear someone calling my name.

"Yes, ma'am. I must've left the house early to have caught up with the likes of you," Jamie says, emphasizing you in the Eastern Carolina way. It comes out something like *you-a.* Weird.

"Must have," I say. "By the way, I'd say that leaving your apartment every day, at ten minutes after nine, does not constitute early when our first appointment is at nine."

"In my book, that's right on time, Doc."

"Oh yeah, I forgot. Molasses."

"Huh?"

Molasses. You're all slow. "Never mind."

"So how are you this morning? I thought about calling last night but, uh, yeah I thought maybe you might not want to talk."

"I'm good. Fine. Fabulous. I'm fine," I say.

"Fabulous? That sounds convincing," Jamie says.

"Doesn't it though?"

"Oh yeah. Completely," he says, reaching the door before me. He holds it open for me as every good, southern gentleman does

I remember my manners then, "So how about you? How are you?"

"I'm good, doc. I'm good. I'll be good until Carol starts talking. So besides the obvious, is there anything exciting to report?"

"I fixed my bathroom faucet last night." In a drunken stupor even.

"Wow. Give the girl a medal," he says winking. "I'm impressed. Hey Carol," he yells as we walk through the door, "The doc has added handy woman to her list of accomplishments. She fixed her bathroom faucet yesterday."

Carol winces, probably at the decibel level of Jamie's voice. She whines in return, "Jamie Johnston, quiet down. Can't you see there are patients in here already?" Now the patients are wincing because both of my employees are yelling. I can't believe there are patients here already. It's not even 9:00. That's twice. In a row. Wonders never cease. Carol speaks again, this time, with a toned down whine, audible only to Jamie and I, "The Thompsons are here. They said you made arrangements to see Kenly first thing? Is that right? Why didn't you tell me? I should've been prepared for Miss Charlotte."

"You talk about her like she's the Queen Mother. What's the big deal?" I ask, not sure I even want Carol to answer.

"What's the big deal? What's the big deal?" She says, raising the tone of her voice as she asks the second question.

"Yeah? What's the big whoop?" Jamie laughs when I say whoop. I can't even believe I've said it. What is this 1986?

"The big whoop," she says, "is that the Thompsons are special. And you don't just spring a thing like that on your Office Manager without fair warning. I didn't have time to put flowers in the exam room they're in or anything."

"That's sweet of you. Really it is. But it's okay. They'll only be here long enough to get blood drawn and get my order for x-rays at the hospital. They'll be gone before you know it. I don't think they're thinking too much about flowers in exam rooms at the moment. Call me crazy."

"Well, I done reckon that someone got up on the wrong side of her big, fancy bed," Carol says, clearly annoyed.

"You done reckon? Geez Carol, you give our people a bad name," Jamie says as he trudges to the coffee pot in the corner of the room. "Done reckon? Who says stuff like that? And besides, give the kid a break," he says, "She's had a rough couple days."

Carol ignores his sentiment and whines, "I do, Jamie. I say things like that. And so does my beau. It's done reckon because I say it's done reckon. I like the way it sounds. And if it was good enough for my Mama and Mee Maw, it's good enough for me. I done reckon you oughta leave me alone now," she says emphasizing done reckon.

"I done reckon you both go to your separate corners and before you go, please promise me, no more picking at each other until at least eleven AM," I say.

"I give her until ten forty-five. And then I'm back to picking," Jamie says not missing a beat.

"Ha. He's not getting more than a half-hour of pickin' free time. He don't deserve it."

"He doesn't deserve it," Jamie corrects her, emphasizing doesn't.

"Both of you. Quiet, please. You're worse than toddlers." I think they'll give me an aneurysm. One of these days, in the middle of an argument over which Andy Griffith episode is the best, how to pronounce the name of the town Wilson, or whether or not Texas Pete is a spice, my head will explode. I'm quite sure of it now. I wonder if I can fire both of them. "I'll be in with the Thompsons. While I'm in there Carol, I need you to call Carteret General and arrange for an x-ray ASAP for Kenly."

"Yes, ma'am. Will do." And then she adds, in case it wasn't clear, "Roger, that." Jamie walks off laughing at Carol's final statement. I wonder as I walk away, where Carol comes up with this stuff sometimes.

"What am I going to do with these two?" I say to myself as I reach for the door to exam room one.

My hand on the door knob, I close my eyes. A prayer floats across my mind. I want so badly to give good news to this family, after tests are run. I open the door to see Charlotte Thompson sitting in the chair opposite the door. Sitting on the exam table is Grace, I assume. She's holding Kenly. "Good morning!" I say, as cheerful as possible.

"Good morning, Dr. Ava," Kenly's sweet voice floats up over the sound of my two lunatic employees, arguing in front of my office door.

"Hi sweetie. How are you feeling today?"

"Yucky. But my mommy and daddy are home so that makes me happy."

"I bet it does." I smile at Grace Thompson. She stretches her hand out to shake my hand.

"Hi Dr. Cooper. I'm Grace, Kenly's mom. My husband and I decided to come home early after chatting with mom and dad. I want to thank you for being so reassuring and helpful when you came by the house."

"Oh well, you're welcome. I certainly hope I didn't cause too much worry by not having any immediate answers."

"No, not at all. It's just that, well it's a long story," Grace says looking at Charlotte.

I look to Charlotte and say, "Good morning." I smile. She smiles back and winks. I still don't get why Carol is so freaked out by this woman. She talks about her like she's the wicked witch of the west.

"Good morning, doc. So what's the plan for today?" Charlotte asks.

"Well, we're going to draw some blood. Carol is calling over to the hospital to set up an appointment for X-Rays."

"Can I ask what the X-Rays are for? Are they necessary now?" Grace asks.

"I believe they are. But I can certainly understand if you would be more comfortable waiting. If the blood work comes back and confirms my suspicions, the x-rays will help confirm a diagnosis. However, if you'd much prefer to wait, I will support your decision. If the blood work comes back indicating rheumatoid arthritis, for instance, x-rays are necessary to confirm. So it's up to you. Whatever you feel comfortable with."

"Well, I guess we should go ahead. Lord knows the hospital moves like molasses." I laugh. Grace smiles at me for the first time since I walked in. She's been nervous. I can see it on her face.

"Of course." I go over my suspicion of Juvenile Rheumatoid Arthritis with Grace, explaining in more detail than I did initially. "So that's where we stand," I say. "If we can get these blood tests run, we'll know what to do next."

Grace shakes her head in agreement and says, "Okay. Do you need Kenly to sit somewhere else?"

"Yep. But you're welcome to pull up a chair next to her. Kenly, I need you to go climb up into that bright red chair over there, okay?"

"Okay. I'm not scared Dr. Ava. I just wanted you to know. I'm not scared at all."

"Well that's good, because there's nothing at all to be scared about. You're only going to feel it for one quick second. It will be like a tiny prick on your skin and then you won't feel anything at all."

"I'm ready," she says resolutely. Her mom and Grandma both laugh at her confidence.

"Do you normally draw blood, Doc?" Charlotte asks.

"No. Not necessarily. Jamie does it most of the time. But I do every once in a while. It's no biggie at all."

"I'm glad you're the one that's here Dr. Ava. I love you already."

"That's such a sweet thing to say, Miss Kenly. And I love you too."

***

After I'm done taking Kenly's blood, I ask Jamie to walk Kenly out to visit the fish tank that sits in the waiting room. I want a moment with Grace and Charlotte. "I know it's easier said than done, but try not to worry too much. If Kenly has RA, we've caught it early. There is so much out there to help her and to slow the progression of the disease or even put it into a permanent remission. That does happen in young children sometimes. I know you're worried. But there's nothing good that comes from stressing out now. And Kenly will take her cues from you. You've got this," I say, to a crying Grace.

"Thank you, Ava. You are so kind. I'm so glad you're here since Pepper can't be." Grace hugs me and then steps out into the hallway. She heads straight for the front desk area. Kenly is sitting in Carol's chair, giggling at the antics of my own personal court jesters. Before Charlotte walks completely through the door, she places her hand on mine. "I know this can't be easy for you, to be someone else's rock. But my family will always be indebted to you for the love and care you have shown us already. I mean that. You're one of us now, lady." I smile as she walks into the hallway. I smile but my heart drops to my feet. This is bad. Very bad. They've already adopted me.

I follow Charlotte out of the room and down the hall. I round the corner and see Jules standing there in all her blond glory, wearing jeans and a Roll Tide sweatshirt. I'd almost forgotten she said she was coming which tells you how easily I put the real me in a locked compartment in my head. She smiles. It quickly fades when she sees my face. "Hey there," she says quietly.

"Hey. Give me a minute? You can wait in the hall there if you like and then I'll show you to my office," I say pointing just down the hall.

"Of course." Julianne walks down the hall and stands just on the other side of the Thompson contingent.

"Okay, Miss Kenly. You're all ready to go. Grace, I'll be calling you as soon as I know something. You feel free to call me at any time, okay?"

"Got it. And I will." She hugs me again, which prompts Kenly to hug my legs.

"Bye Dr. Ava! See you soon!"

"Bye Kenly," I say, and wave to her and her mom as they walk out the door.

Charlotte hugs me too as she heads out. "Remember what I said? You're one of us now."

"Got it," I say as I hug back and then wave goodbye. I walk quickly down the hallway to Julianne. "I'm so glad you're here," I say, much louder than I intend.

"I'm glad I'm here too. And frankly, I'm just happy you'll still have me after yesterday." Julianne wraps me in a big hug and rubs my back a little.

I have this feeling all eyes are on us. "Are we being watched?" I whisper in her ear.

"Oh yeah. Big time." She releases me and I turn to see Jamie, Carol and Charlotte watching us in the hallway. I look at Jamie and Carol, raising my eyebrow in as much of a Drill Instructor kind of way that I can.

"Chop, chop back to work. We've got a busy morning ahead." I watch the two of them scramble. Charlotte chuckles, and then waves again as she walks outside.

"Let me show you to my office. If you give me a few minutes to get through my next appointment, I can walk you down to my place and let you in. I will be done here as quickly as possible."

"Sounds good."

"There's a television in the office."

"Uh no. I am not going anywhere near the TV while I'm here," Jules says.

"Okay, suit yourself. The local newspaper, such as it is, is in there too," I say as I open my office door.

"Wow. Nice digs, doc. I mean Georgetown is all prestigious and crap but wow. This is gorgeous. I'm impressed."

"Thanks. I didn't decorate. I just inherited. I've been contemplating redecorating."

"Yeah, I gathered. This isn't really your cup, now is it?"

"Nope. But I'm going to run to the next appointment so I can get out of here."

"Okie dokie. I'll just make myself comfortable. No rushing for me, okay?"

"Okay," I say, as she kisses me on the cheek. "Thank you for coming," I say.

"It's the least I can do. Now scoot."

"Scooting." I walk out, leaving her in my office. Carol meets me at the door. I have the sneaking suspicion that she's been eavesdropping.

"Who is that Dr. Cooper? Why didn't you tell me we were expecting guests?"

"Mind your own business, Carol. This is personal. Focus, dearest. Focus. Did you get everything set up for the Thompsons over at Carteret?"

"Yes, ma'am, I did." She answers curtly.

Maybe I should have taken this tone with her earlier. "Thank you. Now if you'll excuse me, I have patients to see."

~ FIVE ~

At 4:30, I lock the front door of the office, looking forward to a long weekend with Jules. I'm the last to leave. Carol skedaddled lickety split today, probably smarting from my earlier admonition that she mind her own business. Perhaps I have finally found the secret to keeping her quiet. Front Street is busy this afternoon. Five cars have passed since I left. Practically a traffic jam. It's probably the weather, bringing people out of hibernation. The air is teasing us because winter has only just begun.

Jules has been at the house for a few hours now. Undoubtedly doing something efficient like dusting and mopping. The last two days have been emotionally taxing in a way I never dreamed. My head is still spinning and I've not yet had a moment, wait, let me rephrase that – I've yet to allow myself to go there. As my front yard comes into focus, I see Jules working in my garden. Charlie starts barking as I get closer. He takes off, racing at me full speed ahead, and then jumps on me. Nice to know someone gets excited to see me. Although as mean as I can be, I'm not sure why he's excited.

"Hey," Jules calls out, looking up from pulling weeds.

"Hey back. What do you think you're doing there?"

"What does it look like I'm doing? You've got weeds everywhere. I already cleaned the kitchen and unpacked the rest of your books. So I figured I'd weed a little too."

"Well. Thanks. I think."

"You think?"

"Okay, thanks."

"That's better," Jules says a smile as wide as Texas crossing her face. "So how was the rest of your day?"

"Alright. Could have been worse. I stayed busy enough I didn't have to think. That's always good, especially after the last couple of days."

"Yeah, about that. I still feel terrible. I was so afraid that this mess would be the end of our friendship," Jules stops pulling weeds and sits on the grass.

I sit on the middle step, dropping the contents of my arms into a small pile next to me. "It was tempting to let it end our friendship."

"Ouch," she says.

"Sorry. But it's the truth. The hurt – well, I can't even explain how bad it felt to find out like that. It's physical. Kind of like hot coals were burning inside me my chest and my stomach. I just - "

Jules labors a little to get up. She walks in my direction and as she does so, I notice that she's gained some weight, in her face and around her middle. I know she's pregnant and hasn't told me. The tears come before I can stop them, because my best friend is pregnant and didn't tell me and because I'm not pregnant. Julianne sits on the step next to me. "I'm sorry. That's the only thing I know to say besides please forgive me? I didn't want for it to happen like this. I'll kick myself forever."

"I forgive you, Jules. I go through my days taking care of other people's needs. This is the life I've chosen. Right now, I'm wrapped up in this family, The Thompsons, in a way I don't want to be. They're relying on me. They're relying on me and all I want to do is curl up in a ball and die, after finding out they're having a baby together. I'm not plotting ways to kill myself or anything. I just have these constant fantasies that I'll go to sleep and when I wake up, I'm either in heaven or the whole thing was some big Dallas-style dream. Yeah. That's what I want. One giant, fantastic redo."

Julianne puts her hand on my knee. Her eyes reveal all I need to know. She regrets how this happened. "I want to beat the living crap out of that man. I cannot tell you how many times I've been told to tone down a piece I've written with him in it or how badly I want to rip his head off when I see him around. I hate that you've gone through all this and are still feeling it. We left the church because I really couldn't take seeing him there anymore."

"You left?" I ask.

"Yeah. The guy tries to act like nothing happened. At first, I felt like I needed to see the kids, for you. But then I just couldn't do it anymore. We were never attached to that place anyway. You know that."

"I know. I just feel bad," I say.

"You're the last person that should be feeling bad about that! We decided to check out The Falls Church. We love it there so far, so it all worked out in the long run."

We're both quiet for a moment. I'm sure she's probably trying to figure out whether I want to talk about Burns and the kids or something else entirely. "So when were you going to tell me that you're pregnant?" I like to cut to the chase.

"How did you -"

"It's pretty obvious. How far along?"

"Four months," she says. "I'm scared that I'm this big already. Doesn't bode well does it?"

"No," I smile at her and hope she knows I'm teasing.

"Thanks. That makes me feel better."

"I'm teasing. How are you feeling? And why didn't you tell me?"

"I'm feeling okay right now. I've been pretty sick until last week. I still feel nauseous but I'm not puking my brains out now. As for not telling you, well I didn't find out until I was about to start my second trimester. We stopped trying so long ago, I just wasn't paying attention. But my not telling you can be explained by the look you gave me a minute ago. Those tears. Man. They kill me. And as if that's not bad enough as it is, then your heart spills out through your eyes and it makes me so sad and I feel guilty."

"You feel guilty?"

"Yes," she says.

"Why? Okay, dumb question. I don't want you to feel guilty. But I can't always control the emotion. I know how long you've wanted this. I couldn't be happier for you. This far out from Katie's death, those moments happen less and less but I can't predict when they will. Bottom line is I'm happy for you, kid. Sometimes though, what's missing is all I can see."

"I know. And I know you are happy for me. Thank you. John has been mad at me for not telling you. I want to be sensitive so please tell me if I say the wrong thing. Actually, I'm sure your face will tell me I say the wrong thing."

"Can we change the subject?" I ask.

"Of course."

"How did the kids seem the last time you saw them? It has been getting harder and harder to talk to them."

"I saw them three weeks ago, our last Sunday at the church. They look good at least," Jules says shrugging her shoulders. "I talked to Harper. She's pretty angry. She doesn't have much in the way of patience with Jenny, or Burns for that matter. She told me she spends a lot of time out of the house."

"Will?"

"He's Will, you know? Happy as a clam."

"Yeah. I wouldn't want things to be so bad that the kids are feeling terrible and acting out. But every once in a while, I wish that he would see that just because the kids are coping it doesn't mean it is okay to do what he's done. I'm not sure I understand the man."

"I understand him. I understand he's a pitiful excuse for a man. That's what I understand," Jules said laughing.

"Truer words were never spoken," I say smiling at Jules, thankful for her friendship. In spite of her job, which didn't always mesh well with my ex-husband's, she's been my one constant since college, besides Pepper. I've never been able to count on my parents. My brother would be there if he could, but he's got bigger fish to fry. No matter what goes on, I can't let anything get in the way of this friendship.

"Let's go inside," I say as I stand up. This after the third set of neighbors walks by the house, waving as they go.

"Friendly bunch," Julianne says, pointing.

"Either that or nosey," I say.

***

Jules and I sit at the island in my kitchen. I've poured her a glass of OJ. And me? I'm on my third cup of coffee. We were up at the crack of dawn. Julianne came to my room in a panic, after a couple of hours of cramping. After we got up, things seemed to be okay. I'm watching her like a hawk though. I came downstairs after showering and dressing earlier, to a message. Jules had answered the phone. The Thompsons, Beau specifically, wanted to remind me about church. That was all she needed to decide what our Sunday morning plans would be. So here we sit, waiting for the appropriate time to head over to the church. I can only fault myself for not hearing the phone before she picked it up. Now I'm going to church. I can think of a few things that are on my list of *would rather not.* And this is number two. But Jules has decided it would be fun. Fun! Whatever.

***

Church. I can do this. I can do this. I sing to myself over and over again in my head, as we walk to First Baptist Church of Beaufort with its white steeple poking at the grey clouds that hang low this morning. I can't do this. I can't do this. I change the words to my sing-song pep talk when I see the crowd gathered in front of the church, growing by the moment as yet another mini-van pulls up and unloads its gaggle of kids before driving off to find a parking space. "I can't do this," I say out loud.

"You can't do what?" Jules asks. Her eyes are focused on the church in front of us. "This is like a movie."

"What is?"

"This place. It's like the perfect southern town. You can't make this stuff up. Look at that church. There's even Spanish moss on the trees." We've both stopped now, watching the activity all around us as people arrive for church in their Sunday best.

From behind us I hear, "What are you two starin' at? They don't have churches up north?"

I turn around. It's Carol. "Why do you two do that? Jamie did that to me just the other day."

"What? What do you mean? I don't do a thing like that boy," she says trying to feign disgust.

"Never mind. Good morning Carol. How are you this fine day?"

"I'm just great. You going to introduce me to your friend?"

"Carol this is one of my best friends, Julianne. Julianne, Carol." Julianne reaches out to take Carol's hand.

"It's nice to meet you, Miss Carol."

"Nice to meet you too. I hope you're enjoying our fair town."

"I am. It's lovely," Julianne says.

"That it is," she says putting an arm around my shoulder and squeezing it just a bit. Then, quietly she says in my ear, "This part is never easy. But you'll see. They're good folks, except for a couple of bad apples. But I won't tell you who they are because that would be gossipin' on the Lord's Day and I cannot do that." She says it with such solemnity, I am tempted to laugh. She pauses for a moment and then says, "I'll tell you tomorrow." Priceless. She's priceless.

"Oh, looky there," Carol says as we step into the courtyard. "It's Macon! Jeepers Creepers does he get more handsome every year. He's almost as cute as my beau." Then she speaks again, before either of us can respond, "I need to get on inside. I'm singin' this morning. I'm sure Miss Charlotte will be here any minute. You're welcome to come in with me but you might as well wait here for them, because they're sure to get caught up chatting with Macon before they make it inside. Besides, they never come into the church on time. It's scandalous, really."

"You head on in. We'll see you after church," I say.

"It was nice to meet you," Jules calls after her. Carol turns around, smiles and give her the thumbs up, then walks on into the church after giving Macon's arm a squeeze as she walks by.

"She's something," Jules says, shaking her head.

"She's something, alright. Pepper did not properly prepare me for Carol and Jamie before I moved. She could have at least given me some idea. They're something."

"I like her though," she says smiling at me. "So who's the hottie?"

"That is the son of the couple I told you about. He's a Marine pilot. He's stationed here. I don't know a lot about him other than the obvious hot thing that is."

"Uh. Yeah. I know I'm married and preggers and all, but man he's one tall drink of yummy water."

"Ha. That he is," I say as we watch him. He stands surrounded by blue-haired church lady types. They are flirting with him like they're fifty or more years younger than they are. He's standing under the live oaks in the center of the courtyard. The Spanish moss in the trees is swaying in a gentle, Flamenco style, erotic dance. Macon continues to talk to the women in a way that looks as though he's interested in what they're telling him. It's something about his expression and the way he looks at them. It's clear that he doesn't know he's being watched by the likes of one crazy doctor and her pregnant best friend. But here we are.

Truth be told, I wish I hadn't ever noticed how good looking he is. I'm sure that if I exposed the crazy spectrum of emotions that reside inside me, people would have me committed. All at once, I'm attracted to this man and repelled by him. The repulsion has nothing to do with him. That's all me. It's me, because the attraction wakens my senses. I'm still not ready to reconcile that this life I lead is my life. By the way, I get that it doesn't make sense. I don't make sense.

"Earth to Ava," I hear Julianne say before I notice that she's waving her hand in front of my face. "You in there?"

"Sorry. I do that sometimes, get lost in thought that is."

"You think too much. That's your problem."

"Yeah, well - " I start to finish my sentence, in a none too polite way, as Charlotte Thompson walks up.

"Good morning Sugar," Charlotte says. My face flushes hot with embarrassment at the thought that she caught me red-handed, ogling her son. I've got to be more careful around here. These people come out of nowhere.

"Morning, Miss Charlotte. I'd like to introduce you to one of my best friends, Julianne Marcus. Julianne, this is Charlotte Thompson. She and her husband own the house we were admiring on our walk yesterday, the one with the red door?" Charlotte smiles.

"Ohhhh . . . I love your house! So nice to meet you Mrs. Thompson."

"Lovely to meet you too." She ignores Jules' outstretched hand and hugs her. "Thank you for the compliment about the house. It's our own little piece of heaven." Charlotte smiles at me as she releases Julianne from the hug.

"Macon is quite the popular gentleman," I say, pointing at him and his gaggle of lady friends.

"That doesn't surprise me a bit. He's been missed around here," Charlotte waves at Macon when he gets a free moment to look away from his adoring fans. Macon waves. I swoon. The wave draws him to us. He walks with such purpose, like he really means it, like there's nothing he'd rather do. Is he for real? As I watch him get closer, I shift my weight from one leg to the other and then smooth out imaginary creases in my silk slacks. I stick my hands in my pockets. That lasts for a second and then that too feels uncomfortable and I pull my hands back out. What do I do with my hands? Before I can figure it out, he's within arms-reach of me. He reaches for his mother and embraces her.

"Morning mom," he says.

"Morning," Charlotte says pulling away from Macon.

"Good morning," he says to me, reaching out his hand. I take it. He holds it for much longer than I'm comfortable with, as per the usual. "You have a good weekend?"

"I did. Thank you. I want to introduce you to my friend. Julianne this is Macon Thompson. Macon, this is Julianne Marcus."

"Have you ever been to Beaufort, Julianne?"

"Oh heck no," she says in that way she does that makes everyone feel like they're her best friend. "It's great to get out of the city."

"I bet. Hopefully we're not too backward for you," Charlotte says.

"I'm from Alabama folks. It's not possible for y'all to be more backward than us," she says, a giant Jules size smile making her that perfect southern belle mix of sugar and spice.

Macon laughs. He sounds like he looks, sincere. His laugh is tinged with something I don't understand. But it's real. He's real. You can see the love he has for his mother etched in his face, in the way that he looks at her. His brown eyes shine with it. I'm watching him again. He's so close now his cologne hits me and reminds me of yet another thing that draws me to him. It's not overpowering. But it is seductive.

Why seductive? Because I have a feeling that should he say and do the right things, he could seduce me. Lickety split. But he wouldn't, seduce me that is. His cologne has a fresh, crisp scent. He smells like a shower. I'm convinced that I'm warm and tingly just smelling him next to me. Truth be told, that's irritating. I'm an accomplished physician. I'm the ex-wife of a United States Senator and the griever of a dead daughter. I shouldn't be thinking about these things. Macon is facing me. His eyes are zeroed in on me like a heat-seeking missile. Heat. Wow, I feel like I'm burning up.

I've always had an aversion to brown eyed men. Burns had blue eyes. He was my type, ironically. Macon's eyes are brown like melted fondue chocolate. Sweet. Warm. Yummy. *Yummy?* He doesn't seem to be the least bit deterred at taking his eyes off of me. I think I'm mortified now. I think I might be smiling too but I'm not sure anymore because I'm going numb.

"Well it's great to have you here. I'm sure Ava has enjoyed having you around. But y'all are probably at a disadvantage here. You guys don't know as much about us as we know about Ava here especially. You'll have to stay for lunch so we can get to know you," Macon says.

"Sounds like a plan. I heard a rumor there's supposed to be some Eastern Carolina BBQ here. I can't wait. I plan on pigging out," Julianne says, patting her stomach. She's nothing like you'd expect her to be when you see her perfectly coiffed and put together at all times, on television.

I laugh at her but as I do I realize what Macon has said. "Wait. You know a lot about me?"

"Small town. Big family. Friends and family fond of gossip," he says.

"We don't gossip, Macon James Thompson. We do not gossip. We talk about other people when they're not around. That's completely different." Charlotte says apparently convinced of her argument. She looks like she's serious.

"Right, like I was saying, gossip. I heard from non-gossiping people," he said, turning to face me again, "that you might be unaccustomed to small town life. So consider this your first lesson on life in Beaufort. You're never anonymous, and everyone is talking about you. A young, beautiful, and single doctor moves into town? People will talk. I bet you've been introduced to every single son, grandson and nephew this side of Greenville. Am I right?"

I laugh again. It's not a delicate, sweet laugh. I should sound cute. Charming. I sound like a dork. "Hardly. I haven't met many people except at the office. I keep to myself." And then I add, because I sound anti-social, "I'm pretty busy with work and the house and -."

"I understand," is all he says. He speaks with a confidence that I can't relate to anymore. I used to be like this. It came with going to Johns Hopkins, Harvard and a residency at Georgetown. It came from being a Senator's wife. It came from being Chief Resident. It's gone now. I don't have it anymore. At least I don't think I do. But Macon has it. It's confidence without the cockiness his looks and his status in the community would call for. He says it again, "I understand."

How could he? How can anyone? If I don't get it than it's doubtful that he would. But he's looking at me like he understands. What is it with this family? How does one respond to the, I understand statement? Thanks? Well, it's good to know I'm not the only one to have a dead daughter, a cheating ex-husband who leaves you alone on the night you bury your child, and then to put a nice cap on it all, ensures your step kids have as little contact with you as possible? You understand? Great. Maybe you can help me understand.

Charlotte saves me. I don't know about the rest of them, but at the moment, I like her since she changed the subject. "Will you be joining us for lunch today, Sweetie?" She says to me. And then to Macon, "You'll have to introduce her to folks if your father and I get caught up in the fray, which," she says turning to me and rolling her eyes, "is likely to happen. When I get home Sunday afternoon, I tell you, I'm too pooped to pop, from all the whining. On that note, before I continue whining, I need to head on in. I need to talk to Pastor before church starts. You three come in when you're ready. We'll save seats." She puts her arm around my shoulder and gives it a little squeeze before she walks away.

"Sounds good," I say, although I feel like puking. I watch her walk away. She's tall and elegant. She walks like she's hanging on a hanger, her hips just swaying enough. I used to walk like that. Why is it that all I can think about is what I used to be? She's wearing the perfect Ann Taylor trousers. I know it's Ann Taylor because I almost bought the same suit myself. It's a navy, pin stripe. It looks better on her than it would have on me. In spite of the years she has on me, she's in better shape than I. I'm too skinny. There is such a thing as too skinny. I'm it. She walks with the same purpose and confidence as Macon. Their self-assuredness is so evident, yet there's a total lack of pretentiousness about them. I think I love and hate them at the same time. I turn around to face Macon again.

"Hon," Jules says, "I need to make a trip to the ladies' room, I'll meet you inside, okay?" she says walking off. "Great to meet you Macon, we'll have to chat later."

"Later," he says, keeping his focus on me.

"Don't worry," he says smiling at me in a way that makes my head spin, "I don't bite. I'm glad we have a second to talk before service starts."

"Me too." I'm such a liar.

"You seem upset about something."

"I - "

"Let me finish. I can tell that you don't like it when people try to get close. I can see it all over your face. But we're really a harmless bunch. So there's no need to worry.

"Okay," I say.

"Well that's believable," he says winking at me. "You sound very convincing, quite enthusiastic in fact."

"Would you like me to jump up and down, clap my hands, and give you a great big hug? Would that be a sufficient display of enthusiasm?"

"That would certainly do the trick." His smile widens.

"Well I'll get right on that," I say as I make a motion with my arms that I'm about to jump.

He laughs a deep, belly laugh, much like his father's. "Okay, okay you called my bluff. No need to jump up and down in this crowd. They'll commit you. So," he says, as I resume my normal stance which means I don't know what to do with myself. "Mom said you haven't done much in the way of sight-seeing since you moved. I'd be happy to show you around. Things will be quiet for me the next week to ten days for me. I'm always up for a little sight-seeing."

"Thanks." Thanks? What do I say now? Thanks but I can't traipse around town with a hunky pilot who wears cologne that makes me remember that I'm a woman.

"Maybe after Jules heads home?"

"How about I pick you up next Saturday, late afternoon. It'll be your first intro to Eastern Carolina living. How does that sound? We can take a quick tour of Beaufort by car and then I'll take you to where the real action is."

"Oh, well, uh." Brilliant. I've never been so eloquent.

"Come on. It'll be fun. I promise. And like I said a minute ago, I don't bite. What do you say? It's supposed to be even more beautiful later this week. It's hard to believe Christmas is around the corner. We can grab a bite to eat."

"I -"

"Come on. I dare you," he says.

"You dare me?"

"I dare you."

"I don't know. I've got some things-" I say, trying to find an excuse.

"Things? Like what? Laundry? Vacuuming? Maybe some grocery shopping? You can do those later. You need to get out. It will be fun. I promise. What could it hurt? What's a few hours? Really, I promise, it'll do you good." What does he know about what will do me good?

"You seem to say 'I promise,' and 'I understand' a lot. Why is that? You hardly know me. How do you know traipsing around for a few hours when I could be folding laundry and vacuuming will be good for me?" Did I really just say that to him? Macon laughs at me. Not with me. At me. Then he looks at me square in the eyes and smiles, his eyebrows raising. If my heart weren't already in tiny pieces, it would melt. Melting chocolate. His eyes warm me from the inside out.

"I say I promise a lot because I know what I'm talking about. I'm confident that you need dinner in Swansboro. Give it a shot. What have you got to lose?"

Nothing. I've got nothing to lose. "Okay. I'll do it."

"Wow, Doc. Once again, you sound so enthused. It's not torture. Just a walk and maybe a few antique stores if that's the kind of thing you like, and then dinner of course."

"I'm sorry. I –"

"You don't have to apologize. I'm teasing. You don't have to explain either. I understand," At that, Macon reaches out and lightly touches my shoulder. "Why don't we head in? It may take me a minute to get through the gauntlet," he said pointing to the line of church attendees lining the walkway and standing in clusters near the door.

"Okay," I say, still dizzy from his touch.

"You don't talk much do you?"

"No," I say and then laugh. Macon laughs with me. "I'm a real chatterbox, aren't I?"

"Shut up, will ya? Let a guy get a word in edge wise, once in a while."

"Okay," I say smiling. I'm smiling? Smiling at a man?

***

As sermons go, the Pastor's wasn't the worst I'd ever heard. There weren't any annoying platitudes and a bunch of BS about how everything happens for a reason. There couldn't possibly be anything worse to say to someone who has faced devastating loss, which is probably the reason I've avoided church and Christian types for so long now.

If everything happens for a reason and God somehow, by default, wills whatever happens, even evil, I'm not interested. But, woven into the service today there were some moments, though brief, when I thought his words might fit in with that hint of peace that surrounds some of my days now. Probably not though.

***

"Who is that piece of work over there?" Jules asks, pointing to a tiny bird of a woman wearing the brightest pink suit one has ever seen.

Macon answers from behind me. He's been caught up with well-wisher after well-wisher, all of them determined to give him a squeeze or thank him. He's finally been able to fill a plate and sits down at the picnic table, beside me. "That is the illustrious Miss Hattie Robertson. You may not get to meet her today because she is far too important around here for the likes of us. But, you'll meet her soon enough. She's the mayor of one of the small towns nearby. She's as crazy as her outfits."

"She's not crazy, Macon. She's . . . eccentric," Charlotte replies.

"Right. Crazy as the day is long," Macon says.

"Maybe a little. But aren't all good southern women a little crazy?"

"Oh yeah," Jules replies. "Loud and proud, baby." Everyone laughs.

"I look forward to meeting her," I say. "Wait. Is that Hattie Robertson as in the Virginia Robertson's? I feel like I remember hearing Blaine had a sister in North Carolina."

"Those are the ones. I guess you would know them, " Charlotte says.

"Yeah, you could say that. I mean, I don't know Miss Hattie but I remember Blaine talking about his sister. Weird. I had no idea she lived here."

"She has for most of her adult life," Beau speaks up. "She wasn't a big fan of her older brother's way of running the family business after her father passed, so she moved to Beaufort to teach. She met her husband shortly thereafter. She never had any children so her niece is as close to it as possible."

"Huh. Campbell?"

"Yeah," Macon says in reply.

"Oh I know her alright. The world is a small, small place," I say before trying to find a way to change the subject. I look up at Jules, pleadingly. Maybe she'll take the hint. I don't want to go down this road because we'll end up at my husband. Scratch that, my whoring ex-husband.

"So if I only have a couple days left here, what are the one or two things I should see?" Jules asks, flawlessly. I love her.

"Hmm. Good question. Maybe Shackleford or Cape Lookout?" Beau answers. "What do you think, love? Good options?"

"Cape Lookout, definitely. If you can get out there tomorrow, the weather will be perfect. The ferry is just over yonder - just a couple minutes from Ava's," Charlotte answers.

"What do you say, hun? Should we do it?" Jules asks.

"Why not?" I say in reply to Jules. "I mean, it's not like I have a job or anything."

"Oh look who's a comedian. Come on. Can't you play hooky?" She asks.

"I'm kidding. I asked Carol not to schedule any appointments. We'll be closed tomorrow."

"Good. I think we both need this little day trip. You especially," she says pointing at me.

"Gee, thanks."

"No problem."

"So what have you thought of the church so far, Ava?" Beau asks. Why does he always seem to go back to this?

"I enjoyed it. Thank you for the invitation," I say without emotion.

"You don't sound convincing," he says in reply.

"You're right. But that's about all I've got for you on that topic. I am not sure I have much useful commentary - other than the Pastor seems very knowledgeable but not annoyingly so. So he's got that going for him. But other than that, I'm not the best judge of church stuff these days."

"You don't have to be," Macon says quickly. "So for your trip to the Cape, there isn't any food service so you'll want to pack lunches. The bathrooms aren't open right now and I would definitely take sunscreen, a light jacket or a sweatshirt, and obviously towels and something to lay or sit on," Macon says changing the subject, much like Jules had earlier. I owe them both.

"And don't forget a bag for shells," Charlotte adds. "This is a great time of year, before the tourist season hits, to find some pretty awesome treasures. You are going to have a blast!"

"Thanks for the tips - both of you. I am looking forward to this. I need something to look forward to. Lord knows I don't have enough of that in my life these days." With that, our picnic table turns quiet. I realize Macon is watching me. I look up from my soda can, which I've been playing with to avoid making eye contact, lest the conversation take us back in the general direction of my ex. He smiles when I look up. I look down, overwhelmed by the attention he gives me, but wanting more just the same.

I look up again. He's still watching me and still smiling. It's a crooked smile. It's the kind of smile that makes a woman think he could get whatever he wanted from you, but may or may not try. As Anne Shirley said, "Well, I wouldn't marry anyone who was really wicked, but I think I'd like it if he could be wicked and wouldn't." I wish I could smile back. But I don't think it's in me. I wonder if, or when, it will again.

~ SIX ~

In the still of an Eastern North Carolina morning, when the world has yet to awaken, you almost wonder if you've stumbled upon a sliver of heaven on earth. There's something in the air – a pungent earthiness that connects you to the way the world should have been. As the sun rises, the living, breathing water awakens too. If I sit long and quiet enough on my balcony, I can see the birds slowly begin their hunt on the water. For a few fleeting moments, the Jumping Mullet break the glassy water and then dive below again before the boats start churning the waters up too much to see their dance. The wild ponies appear one at a time, from wherever it is they sleep, and begin grazing.

Even though many days are a struggle to get through, these are the moments when the faint whispers of hope are there around every corner. I'm still in the duck and cover phase of grief, especially after hearing about Burns and his Legislative Assistant's baby. I'm not entirely certain when or if a time will come that I can stop waiting for the next hammer to fall.

Now there's this family that has weaseled their way into my life. Today I hope to have lab results in my hand that will tell me whether or not Kenly has a likelihood of cancer, a possibility I avoided discussing with them because I want desperately for it to not be what Kenly is facing. With all my heart, I want to give them good news or at least better news than cancer. If bad news awaits, I don't know how I'll get through telling them.

***

"So what's the word doc," Charlotte asks, holding Grace's hand. Grant, Kenly's father, is standing against the sink in our largest exam room. I expected a full house this morning. Now that I've met Grant, I can't keep them waiting much longer.

"Well, as I was anticipating, I believe Kenly has Juvenile Rheumatoid Arthritis. On a positive note, it's possible that this is something that Kenly may not deal with her entire life. There are times when RA in children is not a lifelong diagnosis." No one looks relieved.

"So, what does that mean? What do we do next?" Grant asks.

"Kenly needs to see a Rheumatologist for the confirmation of my diagnosis and a treatment plan. There is one in New Bern that I would refer you to first. I asked Carol to schedule an appointment. They were able to get you in this afternoon. Will that work?"

"Yes, of course," Grace replies.

"We can't thank you enough for the effort you've made to make this as easy on us as possible," Grant says.

"You're quite welcome."

"Thanks, Ava," Grace says standing up. She reaches out for me. I hug her. "I don't know if I could handle this without you. Thank you," she says again. "I guess we should go get Kenly and try to explain what's going on."

Grant picks up where Grace leaves off, "Speaking of our little wild woman. This may be a dumb question but, do you have any tips for how we can explain this to her?"

"Great question. The most important thing is for you to be honest with her. First of all, she already knows she's sick, right? Some parents make the mistake of talking about it as if it's not actually happening to the child. That said, just explain that she is going to go meet another doctor and that he may have more questions for her and more tests. And then see where it goes from there. If she says, okay and drops it, so do you. You take your cues from her."

"Makes sense. Thanks."

"No problem."

"We'll be in touch, right?" Grace asks.

"Of course."

Charlotte, who has been extremely quiet throughout the visit, hugs me as soon as Grace lets go and walks out with her husband. "Thank you. Thank you for taking good care of my babies," she squeezes me and then looks me in the eye. "You are an exceptional woman. Don't you forget it," she says as she walks out. Even though the diagnosis is better than what it could have been, it still makes me ache inside. Maybe I should give up medicine? I don't know if I can do this anymore. It's impossible for me to remain impartial and at a distance. It's what happens when you lose a child. Your heart breaks into a million more tiny little pieces when you see another family hurting. I don't know if I can do this anymore.

***

I used to think in the early days after Katie's death and the end of my marriage, that I'd never notice another man. I didn't think I'd be attracted to anyone again. That is, apparently, not the case. And now I'm hours away from spending an evening with a man that is easily, the hottest man I've met in ages. I can't stop thinking about the lines in Macon's face or the smallest little cleft in his chin. There's something about the imperfection of the lines that takes him to a new level of hotness. Manly. He's manly. There is history in those lines. They are there for a good reason. It's probably what makes him say things like, I understand. Although, I highly doubt he understands my life. He may understand in a general sense but he doesn't really get it.

Nonetheless, there's depth to him. I saw it first in that family portrait on the wall at the Thompsons. Macon's heart pours out of his pores. He oozes confidence. But there's just something genuinely good about him. Well that and hotness. Even now, I kinda want to run my finger down the little valley in his chin. But after a day at work and phone call, that I still can't wrap my brain around, I can't deal with his touristy, let's show you the area, while I'm all hot and stuff, plan. I'm not even sure I know what way is up right now, after the last two days. My stomach is tangled in knots and my chest hurts. In the last hour,

I've alternately considered driving myself to the ER or taking a Xanax. I'm not sure I can handle Macon, on top of what lies ahead for me as of yesterday morning.

***

Friday morning, Pepper called me from Uganda and asked if we could talk. I should have known trouble would be close behind. "What's up?" I asked, as I sat down at my desk.

"I had an e-mail from Carteret County DSS late yesterday evening my time, so I called them. I just got off the phone with them again to confirm a few additional details. They have a baby in their custody, she's three months old. She's being released from the hospital. Well, not until they find a home for her but they're desperately trying because she's ready. She has spent all of her life in Greenville, in the NICU. Alone. There was a foster family originally lined up for her but they have decided that her medical needs are too much for them right now. She's waiting for one last heart sur-" Before she says anymore, I shake my head no, as if she can see me. I know where this is going.

"No," I say before she finishes her sentence.

"Just let me finish. It would be temporary until I get back, if they haven't already found a family for her. They asked me first but obviously I can't. Would you be willing to take her? Until I get back?"

"I can't - I mean, how can I possibly? This makes no sense, Pep. I -"

Pepper interrupts me, "You can. It would only be for a little blip of time."

"I'm not a foster parent. Don't you have to be licensed?" I asked.

"Well yes. But this is an unusual situation. She's medically fragile and there is a significant shortage of foster parents in the county in the first place. They started with me since we see most of the foster kids that live in Morehead and Beaufort. There's a way to work with them on that. It's not the norm by any means, but it's possible."

"What is the diagnosis? What is her name? Where is her family?"

"PA," Pepper says.

"You're kidding, right?"

"No. I'm not kidding. But she's stable. And they anticipate that a heart transplant will not be necessary. Her third surgery is scheduled. As for her family, her mother is an addict. While on parole, she got cleaned up during her pregnancy but apparently continued to drink. A week after the baby was born, and while she was still in the NICU, she was pulled over for DUI and possession. Obviously, they believe the alcohol led to the PA. She has no one, Ava. There is no family to take her. They've tried that route. The father is in prison and his parental rights were terminated in a hearing a few weeks ago. They anticipate TPR for the mother to follow, soon. The mom has other kids and they've all been taken from her, too."

"What's TPR? And what is the baby's name?" I ask.

"Her name is Hope. TPR is termination of parental rights."

"Hope? Hope." Ah, the irony. "When would I need to bring her home?" I ask, not even certain why I'm asking the question. I can't do this. I can't.

"Next week. Sooner rather than later. When I get back, I can take over. We can do this together. We're a team after all."

"I don't have anything ready. I don't even know how I'd have the time to get ready. The house would need a major cleaning. I mean, my house is clean, but not baby with weak immune system, clean. I'd have a ton of shopping to do and I still have patients today," I say, panicked though I haven't said yes.

"It will all get done. I've already talked to the church and they're gathering up supplies as we speak. Knowing the Ladies Guild like I do, I have a feeling there won't be much to buy. Their goal is to bring things to the office by this afternoon, as long as you're agreeing. We need to give DSS an answer today."

"Today?"

"Well, actually . . . now."

"Tell them I will," I say, unable to fathom how I'll do this.

"You will?" Pepper asks.

"Yes. Now make the call before I change my mind."

"Thank you, Ava. Thank you. I'll update you after I hear from the Ladies Guild. But I have a feeling you won't need for anything."

Except my sanity. Because clearly I've lost mine for saying I would do this.

***

When I got home earlier, I sent Macon a text and said I couldn't go out with him on Saturday after all because I didn't feel well. He didn't put up much of a fuss. That made me happy and miserable at the same time. See, crazy. I'm crazy. I'm pretty sure that if he pushed the issue a little and wanted to spend time with me, I'd say yes. But going out with crisp, clean, smelling like a spring morning, Macon Thompson, is more than I can handle right now.

I've been on the phone constantly after my conversation with Pepper - between the Ladies Guild at First Baptist and the county. The church had this thing all figured out from the beginning. Within hours of my first conversation with a social worker, I had plans to meet up with a few of the ladies, to pick up my first round of baby stuff. They took the keys to my house on Friday afternoon and right then and there, set up Hope's room - crib and all - though she'll sleep in a bassinet in my room for the time being. They told me more baby gear would follow Saturday and they weren't wrong. I have everything I could possibly need, except for a car seat.

Now that the house is clean and Hope's room has some semblance of order to it, I am sitting on the front porch, staring out at Taylor's Creek. There are a few horses on Carrot Island in my view. They're grazing, lazy. In the water there are about ten sailboats docked, smack dab in the center of the creek, up and down Front Street. It's the perfect kind of weather for a nap. The truth is . . . I'm exhausted. Probably more so than I have been in ages. I can't tell if it's from the lack of sleep or the additional fear and anxiety that has become my new companion since I said I would take Hope.

***

"Well, look at you sleepy head," I hear his voice through the fog. Macon speaks again. I still haven't opened my eyes. Maybe I'm dreaming or better yet, dead. Maybe his voice is beckoning me from the great beyond. Come with me, Ava Bennett-Cooper. Touch my chin and enjoy my cologne forever.

"Ava, are you awake?" No dream. He's really here.

"I'm a-wake. I think." I say, telling myself as I speak.

"Have you been drinking?" He asks with urgency but no judgment.

He doesn't waste time. "No. I'm not drunk. Just exhausted. It's been a long two days. And I haven't been sleeping well anyway."

"Well either way, it's not good. You don't look well," he says. No judgment but I hear something else. He's concerned. "Have you eaten anything today?"

"Today? And by the way, thanks for saying I look like crap."

"Yeah, Ava - today. Have you eaten anything today at all?" Now he sounds pissed. Why is he pissed at me? He's the one intruding upon my evening.

"I had some cottage cheese this morning."

"When this morning?"

"Earlier," I say. I'm so smart. I smile now.

"How much earlier?" He's not smiling.

"You ask a lot of questions, don't you?" Maybe I can stall him. I sit up, facing him.

"How much earlier?" He asks again this time with more force.

"It was this morning," I say.

"How about you be more specific?" He asks as he crouches down in front of me, one hand on either side of me. His huge hands gripping the edge of chaise lounge. His right hand grazes my left knee.

"Crap, Macon, what is this?" Now it's not cute.

"Just answer the question, Ava Cooper."

Ava Cooper? He looks at me like I'm in trouble. When he has kids, they won't get away with anything. "It was around midnight." He looks at me like I just murdered his puppy. Why does he care when I ate? He moves his hand the short distance from the chaise to my knee and keeps it there for a moment. I think I might faint, which, truth to be told, could be the lack of food and sleep. But it's probably just him.

"I'll be back in a few minutes," he says. He stands up and as he does, he frees the chunk of hair that's plastered to the dried slobber on my cheek. Okay, maybe I had been sleeping. I swallow the dodge ball sized lump in my throat. He looks at me for another second and then walks away. I catch a whiff of his cologne.

"Why does he have to wear that stuff?" I say to the squirrel that is running across the other end of the porch. "He smells like April." It's perfectly lovely.

***

What is he doing in there anyway? In my house? He's been in there for like a half hour or maybe it's an hour? I don't know. I'm going to lie down again. My wooden screen door slams shut as I lie down. "Sorry," Macon says apologetically. He's carrying a tray with a plate, fork and napkin. "I made you some scrambled eggs. I don't know if you eat scrambled eggs. But you're going to now," he says with enough force, I'm afraid to protest. "I've got coffee brewing. I'll go back and grab that in a second. How do you like it?"

"Black."

"You need to eat all of this," he says handing me the tray.

"Yes, sir," I say like I'm five.

"I'm going to toast a whole wheat bagel and slap some peanut butter on it. You'll eat that too," he still looks like I've done something torturous and sadistic to that puppy before killing it. "I'll be back in a minute," he says staring at me. I'm frozen. "Eat," is all he says pointing at the plate.

"Okay." I pick up the plate and take a bite. I am, in fact, hungry. To a normal person that would be a no-brainer.

The door slams again as he heads inside. "Sorry. I'll have to remember that."

I'm wondering why he thinks he'll have to remember not to slam the door. Because he's not invited here again, like ever. "It's okay. I do it all of the time. It's either me or the wind. I guess I should fix it, you know?"

"I can fix it for you before I leave tonight."

"Tonight? I don't think so. You'll be leaving a lot sooner than tonight." Did I say that out loud?

"Yeah, we're still going out. We'll have dinner on the water and then I'll bring you back later tonight. I'll fix the screen door before I leave." A few minutes later he returns with a bagel. "Now eat, we have plans," he says.

"I thought I told you I wasn't feeling well." Now I sound pissy.

"You did. I just don't believe you. I hope you're a better doctor than you're an actress." I'm staring at him now, dumbfounded. "What?" He says. I think he's amused. "Did you think I believed all that waa-waa I don't feel good, crap? Give me a break."

Now I'm not only pissy but I'm mad. "Who are you to say whether I feel sick or not?" I obviously didn't try out for the debate team in junior high, high school or college.

"How many times do I have to tell you to eat? Chop, chop." He leaves me alone sitting, going back into my house for Lord knows what - probably to pick out my clothes.

***

I'm mostly recovered from my earlier state. Being walked to your shower by a guy that's a helluva a lot taller than you with massive Terminator arms will do that. He shoved me into the bathroom. Well, maybe not shove. But he sort of shoved me. The water, already running, is cold. He shut the door and then yelled through it, "Don't turn on the hot water. Take a cold shower. Put your robe on and then come out."

"*O* - kay." I said under my breath sounding like a 15 year old talking to my father. So I took a cold shower as commanded by Macon. He'd found my robe lying on the floor of my room and laid it across the sink when he'd gone in there to start the water. Macon knocks on the door the second I turn off the water and speaks again, this time quieter because the water is off. "I heated up a towel for you. It's on your dresser. I'll step out of the room."

I waited to hear the sound of my bedroom door close and then opened the bathroom door. On my dresser, were two folded towels, so warm they were almost hot. Tears poured down my face. Burns wouldn't have considered doing something so simple. I pick up the towels and walk back into the bathroom, slamming the door. I dry my face of the mix of tears and water and then dry the rest of my body telling myself with each rhythmic motion not to cry. I pull my robe on, slipping my arms through the red silk. Not exactly warm after the shower I'd just had. But it's better than nothing. I tie the sash tightly around my waist. Macon speaks through the door. Why was he in my room again?

"I'm here again. I found some clean clothes in the laundry room so I brought them up. I set some jeans and a sweatshirt out for you. I'll be waiting downstairs and-"

Before he could finish his sentence, I jerk open the bathroom door and let it slam into my bedroom wall. "You know, I'm perfectly capable of dressing myself." In that one instant Macon lost the you tortured and killed my puppy look and now looks like a man. A man that thinks I'm the cat's meow. His eyes followed the form of my body. Although I'm sure he probably wished they hadn't. Because by the time he reached my eyes, he looked a little embarrassed, which made me feel like a jerk. There's only one reason Macon Thompson is behaving this way, or he wouldn't be embarrassed for his humanness. For a reason that makes little, if any sense to me, he cares.

"I know you are, Ava. I'm sorry. I've been a little overbearing, eh?"

"A little?"

"I'm concerned." He says and then looks down at his feet. I look at his feet too. He's wearing flip-flops with brown straps that seem to melt into the tone of his skin. I don't think Burns owned flip flops.

It's the first time I've noticed what he's wearing. I follow the line of his long legs. He's wearing jeans, no holes but worn. Lived in. They hang on him in this way that only a man with a body like his, could pull off. I have trouble focusing my thoughts when I look at him. He's wearing a pink polo shirt. There are only a handful of men that can pull that off. Macon is one of them. I almost feel sorry for him now. I haven't exactly been nice. "Thanks for warming my towel."

"You're welcome."

"And thanks for bringing me up some clean clothes. I'll be down in a few minutes." He looks up from staring at his feet and smiles. It makes me ache inside.

"Okay. I'll be waiting on the porch."

~ SEVEN ~

After a quiet dinner on the water, in Swansboro, we wandered down the street and through a couple of open stores. The weather, perfect in every way, demanded we stay outside and made me wonder all at once when winter would make up for being so docile. We walked down to a small gazebo and sat in chairs, facing the White Oak River. We were quiet for a couple of moments before Macon ventured into scary territory. "So what's up with working yourself to exhaustion, until you fall asleep in a drooling, snoring mess and hardly know where you are when you wake up?" He asked. Straight to the point.

"I freaked out a little," I say.

"Why?"

"Do we have to talk about this?"

"I think so. I don't think you do enough talking. Just an observation."

"There's just a lot on my plate. I'm still trying to navigate my way through this grief mess and hearing that my ex is having a baby with his Legislative Assistant sent me over a little cliff. It has brought up a lot of stuff."

"Legislative Assistant?" Macon asks, raising an eyebrow as he does.

"Yeah. My husband had an affair, with his Legislative Assistant. Her name is Jenny," I say with air quotes. "But I prefer Legislative Assistant. It has a nice ring to it, especially when I'm feeling extra bitter."

"Ah. Gotcha."

"You haven't heard the story?" I ask.

"I can't say that I have. I know you were divorced after the death of your daughter but that's about it."

"I'll spare you all of the gory details. Meanwhile, he is not following the court order regarding visitation with my step kids and that doesn't help.

"I can see why the ugliness of the grief feels more real right now."

"Exactly. So while I'm trying to pull myself out of the mess which was getting a little easier after a visit with Jules, and our amazing day trip out to the Cape, Pepper asked me to do something I still can't believe. I'm not sure I have it in me. But I'm stuck now."

"Stuck with what? What's going on?"

"I'm fostering baby. She's medically fragile and the county struggled to find a home for her. She's ready to be released from the hospital. She has some weight to gain and some other milestones to reach before her next open heart surgery. Pepper asked because she's a pediatrician and sees so many foster children at the practice. But with her trip . . ."

"So she asked you?"

"She asked me."

"And you said yes?" Macon asks, eyebrow raising again.

"I did. I don't know why. I don't know if I can handle this."

"I'm sure you can. One, you're a doctor. Two, maybe it's just what you need right now."

"It's more complicated than that," I say, thankful unexpectedly, for someone to talk to about this. Usually emptiness and quiet fill in the void around me. Frankly, all that quiet may be too much. "She has PA - Pulmonary Atresia. Which basically means that her pulmonary valve didn't form correctly so blood doesn't flow to her lungs as it should. The treatment and prognosis depends on severity. In her case, open-heart surgery. In -" I say and then stop. Tears form in my eyes and I look away from Macon, out to the river. There's a beauty to this evening, as the sun slowly starts slipping down in the west. It's impossible to not see it. And yet, speaking these words into the warm, salty air is the reminder that life is ugly underneath all this beauty.

"What is it?" Macon asks, his voice growing quiet. He reaches out his hand and places it on mine. "What's wrong?" He asks, as tears now flow down my face.

"Katie? Katie-"

"Your daughter?"

I shake my head yes. "Katie had PA. I don't know all of the details about Hope's medical prognosis. We expect to have all of those details on Monday when I go to Greenville with her social worker and Guardian Ad Litem. Katie died of an RSV infection that was just too much for her little body and heart to handle. Katie would have had a heart transplant if we had kept her alive. How am I supposed to do this when I haven't yet wrapped my brain around losing my sweet girl?"

Macon's hand remains on mine. "I don't have an answer for that. I'm not sure you want one." I shake my head no. I'm starting to think he does understand, somehow. "I mean I don't have an answer, but I do."

"What do you mean?"

"There usually aren't answers to the questions that plague us when it comes to loss, grief, and finding our way out, into the sunlight. I don't buy into the, *everything happens for a reason,* BS. I never will, after what I've seen. But I do know that in the moments when it is easiest to retreat and hide, it's usually the exact time to face it head on."

Growing uncomfortable with the direction of the conversation, I pull my hand away from Macon's and quickly get out of my chair. I stand against the railing, looking out at the river. He could be right. But it doesn't make me anymore ready to deal with this situation. Macon didn't get up when I did. I realize I'm not always the nicest person these days. But sometimes, I just can't deal with these conversations. I turn around to see him stand up. He doesn't seem the least bit fazed by me. "Should we keep walking?" he asks.

"Yeah, sounds like a good plan." We walk around the rest of the small, historic downtown, following the sidewalk past a restaurant or two and several shops. We cross the street and head back in the direction of his truck. I stop in front of children's boutique. I stand there, glued to the scene playing in front of me. Like all of the other times, I am witness to a life I thought would be mine, tears bubble up from that place I keep hidden. A young woman is standing on just the other side of the window, inside the store. She's pregnant. Looking ready to burst wide open, she's in the waddling, exceedingly uncomfortable stage of pregnancy. Her husband is standing across from her, holding a little girl with brown curly hair. He's laughing at his wife. She looks like she's talking a million miles a minute, with her hands gesticulating wildly. She is acting irritated but her eyes are laughing. She puts one of her hands on her fat belly. She points to the antique looking rocking chair in the window. Her mouth moves and forms the words, *"But I want that one."*

He laughs again. "Okay," he says. The husband turns toward the sales girl behind the counter and speaks. There. That's settled. They've picked out a rocking chair. I want to be that woman. That's when the tears decide that they'd rather not hang out in my eyes anymore. I turn and look for Macon, hoping he's found himself something entertaining because I don't want him to see this. He's watching me from a couple paces ahead of me. I turn back to the scene in front of me. I'm trapped. There's nowhere to go unless I walk away from Macon and the happy, pregnant couple. So I guess I should walk away. I do an about face and head off toward Highway 24, which is steps from the boutique. I take off in a jog, anxious to be by myself again.

"Ava. Wait." He calls after me as I look at the oncoming traffic. I stop in the middle of the highway and then keep going once cars have past. I walk to the small park beside the river. Tears stream down my face. I can't control my emotions, how am I going to take care of a sick infant? Macon reaches me within moments of me sitting down and crouches in front of me, his hands on either side of mine just as he did earlier in the day. He brushes the tears away from my cheeks, probably smearing foundation and blush together with the black of my mascara. This small moment pushes me to react. I suck in a deep breath as if Macon has just slapped me. "Don't," I say. And then again, "Don't."

"Don't what?" he asks.

"Don't touch me. Don't try to help me. Don't pretend you care. And don't ever tell me again that you understand me. Got it? Just don't," I say, looking away from him, at the river.

Macon responds forcefully, "I know you may not realize this now, but someday you will. But uh here it goes . . . you're not the only one on earth to suffer. You're not the only one that understands and has felt the deepest, darkest grief imaginable. And you're certainly not the only one to want to die because it's easier than to face the pain. But here's the deal with that, there comes a time when you're so bogged down in the grief that it becomes more comfortable to you than letting go. And that, my dear, is where you're at. I know it like I know my shirt is pink. Why am I wearing a pink shirt, by the way?

But that's definitely where you're at. It's written all over you from your head to your feet."

"What makes you think you know me so well?" I ask him in a tone of voice that resembles a snarl, my normally well-hidden anger finding its voice.

"I recognize the symptoms," Macon says looking me in the eye.

"You don't know anything about me."

"I do though. I just wish you would recognize that you're not as hidden as you think you are. I see right through you. Right through you," Macon says, his voice softening ever so slightly.

I stop crying as the anger takes over. My hands grip the wooden bench. My knuckles turn white because I'm holding on so hard. "You don't know a thing about me," I say. "Whatever it is you think you understand you don't. So if I were you, I would stop offering unsolicited psychoanalysis because last I heard you're a Marine, not a therapist."

"Touché. You have me there. A therapist I am not. But I know what I'm talking about. So I would encourage you to think about what I've said."

"Are you for real? Like seriously. Are you for real? Maybe you've grown too accustomed to people following your orders, but I am not one of your soldiers that you can order around. You've been doing it all day and I'm over it," I say, my face feeling hot and probably turning bright red.

"Marines," Macon says standing. "Not soldiers."

"What? What are you talking about?"

"You said soldiers, but Marines are Marines. It's a proper name. Capital M. Marines are not soldiers," Macon says seriously but with the slightest twinge of a smile.

"Whatever. My point is my point. You can't just waltz into my life and decide you know who I am, what I'm about, and what's happened in my life."

"You think you've escaped notice here just because you wanted to? Did you really think you could come here and go unnoticed?"

"Well, I…"

"Did you?"

"That's not really my point. My point is that you think you know, but you don't. There's nothing more patronizing than telling someone like me that you understand what I'm going through. So just don't do it, got it? In fact, don't talk to me about anything, ever again related to what I should or should not do. Don't try to understand. Don't pretend to understand. Because someone like you could never understand my grief."

Macon looks away. I stand up, determined. I'm determined now, more than ever, to keep him at arm's length. When Macon turns back around to face me, something has changed in his face. His confidence is gone. And with that, I know I will regret the tone I've used today, for a long time. Even still, I look him square in eye and say, "Take me home."

"Okay. If you want, you can wait here and I'll go get the truck and bring it around."

"Fine. Whatever." I can't believe his nerve. Why is it that people think they have the right to tell you what and how you should be feeling and how you should be dealing with pain that they can't understand? Who does he think he is? *Mr. I'm a Marine so I can tell you what's what.* Unbelievable. I knew I should have stayed home.

***

"I just need to make a quick stop," Macon says with his eyes on the highway.

"What?"

"I need to make a stop. It's on the way back home. I promised Mee Maw White I would. I know you want to go home but I promised."

"Fine. Whatever," I say in fine passive aggressive mode.

I watch outside the passenger side window as we reach Cape Carteret. Macon turns off Highway 24 down a winding two-lane country road and before I know it, we're deep into the woods, loblolly pines line the road and stretch as far as I can see. Macon pushes a pre-set button on his stereo as I begin to construct a way to avoid going inside when we reach this Mee Maw White's house. Country music fills the cab of his truck.

Macon turns off the highway onto a gravel road. After what I guess is about a mile, he turns right onto another dirt road. There's a slight clearing in the tree line. I see the faintest glimmer of water across a field and through the trees. A creek comes into view moments later. Outside of my window is horse pasture with a barn in the distance. Macon stops at a wooden gate that stretches across the dirt road. He gets out of the truck and walks to the gate. I am struck yet again by how . . . hot he is. He opens the gate, swinging it back toward the pasture side of the road. He turns to face the truck and he catches me ogling him. He smiles and looks down. I turn my head to the pasture. Note to self: remember how to check a guy out on the sly.

Macon gets back in the truck, quietly. He pulls forward, slowly driving down a dirt road that needs some work - large potholes like land mines require him to drive much more slowly than we had been. I can tell we're almost there though. The tree line has thickened again but I see a house in the distance. There's no way in hell I'm getting out of this truck. But what do you want to bet she's just as pushy as the rest of them and I'll have to get out? Macon pulls up in front of a white plantation-style house with an absolutely massive front porch - complete with ferns and ceiling fans. The ceiling of the porch is painted a light blue something I've recently learned is often called haint blue. More common in South Carolina, but still found here, there's something about it that instantly calms me.

The house is white, with black shutters. The house is beautiful. There is a sidewalk that leads from the long driveway to the front of the house. Macon drives right up to the sidewalk. It's then that I can see who I would guess is Mee Maw White. She stands up from her seat on the swing and bounds down the steps as if she is a teenager. It's then that I remember that Macon hasn't been home for long. Somehow I'm guessing this won't be a quick stop.

I wonder why she wasn't at the church Sunday to welcome him with the rest of the crazies. We park and within seconds he's unbuckled his seatbelt and made a b-line for Mee Maw White. As Macon turns back to the truck, just steps from Mee Maw, he looks back at me and mouths, "come on." I obey his order though I don't know why. I climb out of the truck and walk to the reunited pair. Mee Maw pulls away from Macon and says, "It's been too long, Macon Thompson. Too long."

"It has, Mee Maw. It has. It's so good to see you," he says as he takes the tiny woman in his arms and gives her a bear hug.

Mee Maw interrupts the moment and says in a voice I'd be sure to hear, "Is this the crazy one you told me about?"

They pull apart and Macon replies, "This is Dr. Ava Cooper, Mee Maw White."

He says this as I reach his side and stick my hand out to shake hers. "Lordy," is all she says looking at my hand. Lordy?

Macon speaks up first. "Uh, Mee Maw is not a big fan of touching people's hands."

"Ah, I see. Well, I do apologize. It's so nice to meet you," I say wondering where they make southerners. This one broke the mold.

"Well it certainly is nice to meet me," she says laughing and then continues, "I don't shake hands but you can curtsy and kiss my ring if you'd like." I stare at her outstretched hand. Is she for real? Somehow the look on her face suggests she is. She sticks out her arm again and shakes her hand a little as if to say, "Well?"

I make a move to kiss her ring and she pulls her hand back and laughs. "You're a serious one, now aren't you? I'm just teasing, Child," she says in the distinctive Eastern North Carolina drawl that makes "child" sound like a two-syllable word.

"Oh, I see," I say. "Funny."

Mee Maw White looks at me, the humor drained from her face and says, "Ah, I see. Well. Come along." I don't know what she sees, but this is getting old. What the hell is wrong with these people? I follow behind Macon and the old lady as we climb the steps of the house and make our way to a small parlor just inside the door. There are pictures all over the room, some in frames on tables and shelves, others hanging on the walls gallery style. I sit down where directed by Mee Maw's pointing finger. Macon sits next to her on the couch. She pats his knee, "I'm so happy to see you, Marine. This deployment has made me sick with worry for some reason."

"Well, I thank you but there's no need to worry over me. Everything went well. But I do thank you for your worry and prayers."

"Well, you know it's my pleasure," she says squeezing his hand. And then, looking at me, says, "Macon and I go way back."

"Oh," is all I can say.

Mee Maw rolls her eyes, and says, "Well, my dear, I made you sweet tea. Come with me to the kitchen and I'll get you some. Crazy," she says to me, "would you like some?"

"No. Thank you though," I say, my voice strained just slightly as I try to fight back tears. I'm not crazy. Or maybe I am? That's probably why I want to cry. I watch them get up and walk down the hallway. Muffled voices float down the hallway. Their laughter and chatting leaves me suddenly overwhelmed. I get up and walk around the room, looking at each picture, wondering who the people in the pictures are in relation to the Thompson family.

I make my way slowly around the room until I reach a group of pictures on the wall with a tall blond in the center picture. She's brushing a horse. A small child is standing in the dirt next to her. He's about two, looking at the camera, with a devilish smile. He's wearing overalls and boots. I'm drawn to his face. I look for a moment longer and then notice the baby carrier just to the left of the two, under a live oak. You can't see much but a pink blanket covers her. I look at the other pictures and in each, the blond is featured prominently. She has a tender, serious look to her.

I am taken by one picture in particular. She's standing in front of a red ribbon, stretched across a dirt lot, from the business on its right, to the business on the left. It looks as though she's about to cut the ribbon, on a ground breaking, scissors in hand. I take a step closer to get a better view. It's then that I notice who is standing off to the side. Macon. Charlotte. Beau. Grace. Grant. They're all there. A sick feeling eats at my stomach.

The pictures reveal to me a world I don't have the courage to ask about. I know this in an instant. I frantically begin searching the pictures in the grouping next to it and settle on the one that will make me eat my words. I know it already. It's Macon. He's laughing, while lifting the toddler boy, to his shoulders. The blond is walking just a couple of steps ahead, pregnant. She has a ring on her left hand. I can't describe the urge I have to see Macon's left hand as well. I step closer and squint. A ring. He's wearing a wedding ring.

Before I can move back to the couch, Mee Maw White's orthopedic shoes clomp back down the long, hardwood hallway. I don't have time to step away. But I don't want Macon to know what I've seen. Mee Maw White rounds the corner as I make a rather stupid attempt to get myself to the other wall where there are old black and white photos. As I make a mad dash, I trip over a stack of books and fall headlong to the floor. Mee Maw has already seen me. Now I've not only been discovered but I've made a total idiot of myself. Par for the course. "Macon, dear, before you come back, be a dear and get me an ice pack from the freezer, will ya?"

I hear Macon call out from just the other side of the wall, "Sure thing." The old lady just saved Crazy. She says in a quiet voice, "Hurry now, get up. Now is not the time for Macon to know you've seen those pictures up close. I'll cover for you. But you're going to have quite a lump on your knee so we need to get some ice on it."

"Okay," is all I say, embarrassed and horrified by how rude I've been.

Mee Maw White reaches me more quickly than I expected. She reaches out and brushes a curl from my eyes. "Don't assume you know, just as you don't want others to make assumptions about you. He's told me you were unconvinced that he might have any insight into your life." She says this thing that makes my heart ache even more and then smiles just ever so slightly, "Her name is Caroline and she was my grandbaby."

I look up when I see a flash of movement out of the corner of my eye. Macon. The sick feeling returns. I am a horrible person. "What's the ice pack for?" he says, sounding chipper, as he often does.

"Crazy," Mee Maw answers without skipping a beat, "tripped over my stack of books over there," she says pointing off in a direction opposite of where I actually fell.

"Are you okay?" Macon asks. His eyes are filled with concern once again. He's so protective. I deserve to be laughed at but he's not laughing.

"I'm okay. But I think I'll have a nasty bump on my knees and my hands are already feeling bruised. But that's what I get for being such a klutz."

Macon takes my hands, examining them as if he's the doctor. "Sit down," he says. He's protective and extremely bossy. But I sit just the same. He hands me the icepack and I place it on my knee. There's a bump popping up already.

Mee Maw replaces her softer tone with me, in Macon's absence, to the old one, "That'll teach you a lesson. Watch where you're walkin' next time."

Macon laughs. It's the first time he's reacted to her snide remarks. "Give her a break," he says in my defense. "She's got a lot on her mind."

"Yes, of course she does. But most people don't forget how to walk when they have a lot on their minds," she says with a Cheshire smile stretching across her face.

"This is true," Macon replies. "But our girl here is a special case. She's prone to this type of thing."

"Uhm . . . hello people? I'm sitting right here. Why do you insist on making fun of me as if I'm not right here in front of you?"

"Ah, see, it's to get you to talk. Otherwise it appears as though you're a mute you get so quiet." Mee Maw is apparently proud of herself at this last comment as her grin stretches even further this time.

"Okay, okay. Enough of that. You've had your fun at my expense. Thank you for the icepack. Thank you for the mean jokes, Mee Maw White. And now, Macon, I would like you take me home. I have some things to get together before a medical meeting with Hope's specialists. And then I meet her. It's a lot to prepare for."

"Of course. I got what I came for," at this Macon holds up a plastic bag and jug he'd previously sat on the couch. "Sweet tea and Persimmon cookies. Now I'm good to go. So thank you, Mee Maw."

"You're so welcome, baby doll. You know I love you like one of my own. Don't be a stranger," she says as she takes him into a bear hug.

"I love you, too Caroline. I love you too. I'll give you call next week sometime. I want to come out and ride."

"That would be wonderful!"

"It was nice to meet you," I say instinctively stretching my hand out and then withdrawing it immediately.

As we walk to the front porch, she responds, "It was nice to meet you too, Miss Ava. Don't be a stranger." She says this and then squeezes my shoulders.

I head down the stairs slowly. Macon still stands on the porch with Caroline White. I hear her say ever so softly, "Take care of her Macon."

His only response? "Done."

***

"Carol? Would you come in here?" I say as she passes by my open office door It's early Monday morning and I've been desperate to talk to her since Saturday evening.

"Yes, Ma'am. I'll be right back. I'm just going to put these flowers in the exam room down the hall." I don't know how I'm going to bring up the subject but I have to. I've been so mean to Macon. If his wife and children are in those pictures, they're gone now. And regardless of how or what happened, I think he does understand.

"What's up Doc?" Carol breezes in, nearly shouting in her whiny way.

"Would you shut the door for me? I need to talk to you about something in privacy."

"Uh-oh. Am I getting fired?" Carol asks, her face turning bright red.

"Why would I fire you?"

"Well. I, uh . . . I don't know. I just thought that maybe you might be mad at me for sic'ing Macon Thompson on you."

"What do you mean?" I'm angry in an instant and I don't even know what she's talking about.

"I told Macon at church that I thought that you needed a friend and that maybe it would be good for you to get out a little. I figured he'd be the perfect person to help you out of your shell. Because, well, anyway, I just thought he would be," she says in a tone I am not prepared for. Carol's voice is uncharacteristically quiet. She is worried about me too.

"No. No, I am not firing you. But that is sort of the reason I wanted you to come in here."

Carol interrupts my train of thought. "I'm sorry, Dr. Cooper. I know it's none of my business but I wanted to help. I didn't mean anything bad by it."

"I know. I appreciate that you wanted to help. But I need you to explain something for me."

"Sure. What?" Carol asks, her face showing some relief.

She really did think I would have fired her over the Macon thing. I probably need to work on my tone with Carol, and a few other people, apparently. "I know this might seem like a gossipy kind of thing to talk about but I need you to know that I have my reasons for needing to know."

"O-K," Carol says pronouncing each letter slowly and as a question.

"Is Macon married?" I ask, fearing the answer.

"He was."

"Was?"

"He was married."

She offers no further details. I suppose it's a protective reflex. "He has children?" I fear this answer more than the first.

"Yes."

Yes? So where are his children? I ask to myself. Carol interrupts my thoughts quickly.

"Well. I mean. No."

"He doesn't have children?"

"He does. He did."

"He did?"

"Yes," Carol says averting her eyes and looking at the paisley pattern of her pink skirt, following the curves of the pattern with her fingertip.

"What happened?" I'm desperate to know what happened and yet, don't want to know.

Carol continues to look at her skirt. Her finger has stopped tracing the pattern. But she's yet to look at me. This is most definitely a story I'm not ready to hear. But I must. "Dr. Cooper, this is a long story. There are a lot of moving parts. I can't explain it all now, especially since you have to get to Greenville" she says still looking at her skirt. "But I can tell you a few important details, the most important ones," she says looking up at me.

"Okay, so?"

"Macon married Caroline Parker when she moved back to Beaufort from New York City. He was older than her by a handful of years but not enough that they hadn't known each other coming up. When she moved back here, she had an infant son. His name was Christian. She didn't really plan on getting involved with anyone and a lot was expected of her."

"What do you mean?" I asked.

"The Parkers, Whites, and Thompsons are true, blue money here. The Parkers have always ruled the roost though. Caroline might as well have been born a princess. That's why a lot was expected of her. Anyway, everything was set against them, which is part of the long story, but they married anyway. Christian might as well have been Macon's son. You never would have known he wasn't his child by blood. They had a daughter about a year after they got married. Her name was Grace Charlotte Parker, after Grace and Charlotte Thompson."

"What happened to them?" I wish she would just get to the details.

"They were killed," she says, in matter of fact way.

"Killed?"

"Yes. Tragic car crash. Killed Caroline and the baby instantly. Christian was taken by East Care to Vidant. He died five days later."

"My god." I don't know what else to say. Nothing else is appropriate.

"There are other details but that's the most important thing you need to know about Macon." She stops for a moment and then continues, "This is why I wanted you two to spend time together. He understands, Ava Cooper. He understands. Jamie and I are here whenever you might need us but there are so many things I could not possibly understand about your losses. But Macon does. And by extension, so does the rest of the Thompson clan."

I hate that there are tears welling up into pools in my eyes. Regret over the way I spoke to Macon? Sadness because of his loss? My own pain revisiting me? I'm not sure. All I know is I have hurt the one person in the last two years that can understand me. "May I ask," Carol interrupts my self-analysis, "where this came from? I'm assuming he didn't tell you else wise you'd know the answers already."

"We stopped at Caroline White's house yesterday. The two of them wandered off to the kitchen and I started snooping around looking at the pictures." I feel ashamed to admit my snooping to Carol.

"Well it's no wonder. There are pictures everywhere at the White farm. Does Macon know that you know?"

"No. I guess I should talk to him about it though?"

"Are you asking?"

"Yeah, I guess I am asking." I don't want to talk to him about it but I've been so unkind.

"Yes, that would be something I would recommend."

"He doesn't have problems talking about it?" I ask because I'm certain he must. I certainly do.

"He did at one time. But it has been some time now and he's quite open about it."

"Okay. Thank you for clearing that up for me." Thank you for clearing up that I'm a horrible, horrible person.

"You're welcome. I should hurry back to the front. I wouldn't trust Jamie to handle the front desk if my life depended on it. He'll just make a mess."

"You really are too hard on him," I say. "You should lay off a little."

"You're probably right. But I wouldn't give him such a hard time if he didn't give me so much ammunition," she says as she gets up out of the leather chair in front of my desk. "He gives me oodles of it," and then laughs at her own comment as if she's just told a hilarious joke.

"Okay, okay, back to work. Thanks again."

She waves me off as if to say "no problem," and heads out of my office. She is chiding Jamie before she reaches the front desk. They exhaust me. I'm not sure they realize how they sound. Then again, they must. I've told them so many times. In some ways, I suppose I'm thankful for the bickering. Listening to them helps me realize I can have other emotions besides sorrow. Like irritation, maybe? I pick up my cell phone and call Macon. Each ring that he doesn't answer is a little like torture. Just as I'm about to give up hope, he picks up.

"Hello?"

"Macon, it's Ava."

"I know. I'm just surprised to hear from you." There's not even the slightest hint of anger or irritation in his voice. "What can I do for you?" His voice is gentle, which is another reminder that I have been horrible.

"I wondered if we could talk. Maybe on my way back from Greenville?" I say sounding like an eight-year old that is in trouble and flinching from the impending tongue lashing.

"Of course. Anytime is good. I'm back to work so there's a chance I could be there. But I'm not flying this week so my day is pretty open."

"I can call you when I leave Greenville and then maybe again when I hit Havelock. Does that work?"

"It does. Keep me posted," he says.

"I will."

"I'll be praying for you. I'm not very good at saying that. Sometimes I think I don't pray enough. But I know it won't be easy so . . ." He says, his words trailing off.

"Thank you, Macon. I appreciate it. I'm not very good at praying these days either. I'm scared as hell but suddenly very anxious to see this tiny human being."

"I can see how you might feel like that. Are you sure this is a good time to meet up?"

"Yes," I say quickly and matter-of-factly.

"Roger that," he says.

I laugh. It reminds me of Carol and Jamie. "Roger," I say in return. I think I'm funny. Roger to the Roger.

"Roger," he says again. He thinks he's funny too. I can hear his smile. I don't understand why he doesn't hate me.

~ EIGHT ~

While we wait for Hope's cardiology team, I am sitting next to her social worker and guardian ad litem, while they talk about the East Carolina University football team. They grow silent after constantly chattering for the past half-hour. In the silence, I say, "What is it with doctors making people wait?" The both laugh. "Note to self," I say, "Don't make patients wait."

Before either can comment, a receptionist steps into the waiting area of the cardiologist's office area and ushers us into a small conference room. On the far side of the room is a line of doctors, and I'm guessing at least one nurse. We are introduced to each person. When we get to the silver-haired doctor sitting at the head of the table, he stands and reaches for my hand. "Dr. Cooper. Great to meet you. I've heard a lot about your great work in D.C. I'm James Pierce."

"Please call me Ava. It's great to meet you, too."

"Shall we begin?" Dr. Pierce asks. I sit quickly praying I can stay focused and not let myself wander into territory I can't return from. The last time I sat down with a pediatric cardiologist, he told me that he didn't think my daughter would live through the day. "We are happy that a home has been found for Hope. She is a special girl. There's a lot of spit and vinegar in that tiny body. Holly here," he says pointing to a woman in her mid-thirties, "is one of her nurses. She will take you over to the NICU when we're done and can fill you in on all of the details we don't cover here. But I know we're all on a tight schedule so let's get right to it."

At that, we dive into forty-five minutes of medical details that I'm certain will leave the social worker and GAL, with spinning heads. I ask the questions. They ask none. Besides being a doctor, I've been here before. It's the same song and dance we went through with Katie - with one minor difference; Hope has a significantly better chance at a full and normal life than Katie did. I receive honest, technical answers, from the entire team. Hope has had two surgeries so far. They have been successful, but one remains. Though she is not out of the woods, they're very positive about her prognosis. What this cardiology team can't tell me is how my own heart will survive caring for this tiny one who still has a long road ahead.

"If this doesn't hold, clearly a transplant is our next step. Obviously we don't want it to get that far. To be honest, the length of time it has taken to secure a foster home for Hope may have been a blessing in disguise. She is much stronger than she would have been had she gone home a month ago. I have high hopes, for Hope," he says smiling, "that her last surgery will be successful and a transplant won't be necessary. Do any of you have any further questions?"

The other two shake their heads no. I reply, "I don't either. You have been very thorough and with my background in this territory, I think I have a very clear picture of Hope's prognosis and what lies ahead. Thank you for taking the time to meet with us. As you can expect, I will be in touch. At the first sign of infection, we will get in the car and get here to Greenville. Do you expect I can bring her home this week?"

"Absolutely," Holly says. "Today if you would like."

"I'm not ready today. But I can come back up tomorrow. I do have a house full of baby gear, but I planned to buy her car seat this evening. Does tomorrow morning work?"

"Of course. Whatever you need. We are all so thankful for you. Shall we head over to the NICU now?"

"Yes, lets," I say hoping my voice isn't shaky like I think it is. "I need to meet this little firecracker," I say, meaning it for the first time since Hope's name began tossing around in my head and heart.

In the soft light of the NICU, I pray again. This may be a trend. The beeping of monitors are as familiar as the sound of my own voice. We step up to the sinks inside the double doors. I show the social worker, Nina, and the GAL, Toby, how to wash their hands and forearms. After washing and drying, we move through a second set of automatic doors. A baby's pulse ox monitor sets off an alarm, bipping its notice to the nurses. The nurses don't move in the direction of the baby. Nina and Toby grow nervous. I'm not. I can see the baby's vitals are normal. She was probably just moving. "She's okay," I say. "She's just wiggling and it causes her pulse ox monitor to respond. They can see her vitals so they know all is well."

The social worker, Nina, says, "Oh man. This is a lot to take in. You are the perfect person to bring Hope home," she says sincerely.

"Well thank you," I say, suddenly overwhelmed by the weight of what I'm doing here. I continue following Holly until we reach Hope's open crib and my heart drops to my feet. She is next to a second nurse's station which I hope means she's gotten a little extra attention. She is a tiny little bird – so much smaller than Katie had ever been.

I step up to her crib. She's sleeping. While she is on monitors, in preparation for my visit and her impending discharge, her central line has already been removed, which I already knew. I reach into her crib and lightly touch her hand. Her brown eyes open wide. I smile, I cannot help myself. I reach for her hand again. She curls her hand around my forefinger.

"She is precious," Nina says. "So tiny. I've seen pictures but you just don't realize how small."

"Would you like to hold her now?" Holly asks.

"Oh yes," I say, all doubt and fear quickly slipping from my heart. The nurse unhooks her from the monitor and steps away. I reach into the open crib and take Hope in my arms. She watches me like a hawk, alert and focused.

"Would you like to sit?" Holly asks.

"I think so." She walks away to grab a rocking chair. I don't take my eyes off of Hope and she hasn't taken her eyes off of me. Holly pushes a rocking chair up next to the crib and I sit down.

"I think you two are a match made in heaven," Holly says.

"Yes, definitely," Toby says. "Like it was meant to be." I heard Toby say it but I try not to react. Somehow the thought that this sweet baby had to be born with a heart that could kill her, to parents who gave up their rights to her, and both sit in prison as we speak, is sickening to me. Not to mention the fact that I had to lose my daughter and have barely talked to Harper and William, let alone seen them, while dealing with an embarrassing divorce. Meant to be? No. I can't live with the thought.

They both crouch down, one on either side of me. "So sweet," Nina says.

Toby reaches out and touches her foot and smiles. "I think I'll head back Down East. I think everything is good here."

"Me too actually," Nina says. "I'll stop by your house the day after you bring her home. I'll be in touch about timing."

"I think I'm bringing her home today."

"Really?" Nina asks.

"If you guys don't mind," I say to Holly, "I'll go to Babies"R"Us and buy the car seat and bring her home today. The house is ready. Her room is ready. I just didn't have the car seat."

"Of course. We would love to send her home today. It's long overdue."

"I am not ready to go just yet," I say. "I'm not ready to put her down."

"I understand," Holly says.

Toby says, "Thank you, Ava. This has needed to happen for far too long. This is a great day for Hope. I will be in touch soon," he says.

"Sounds good."

"If your plan is to take her home today, then I will be by tomorrow," Nina says. "I will call when I have a better sense of my schedule."

"Thank you," I say, my eyes never leave Hope's. She has fallen asleep in my arms. I forgot how amazing it is to hold a sleeping baby. It's possible I'm in love already.

***

Wandering the aisles at the store, I've found myself filling up my cart. The ladies at the church had gone to tremendous lengths to fill a nursery with everything imaginable. But holding Hope, my mommy abilities kicked in, and while almost all of the clothing was in wonderful shape, though hand-me-downs, it's almost all too big. I'll be working on beefing her up but most of the clothes will be too big for a little while. I had help setting everything up. People who have never met me have signed up to bring me meals so I don't have to worry about cooking. Every time I looked for an excuse, as to why I couldn't do this, someone found a response and then some.

From the moment Pepper brought this up, I've been pushed and pulled headlong into bringing this baby home. I have gone kicking and screaming. Until I held her. Hope and I? We need each other and I knew the moment our eyes locked. With clothes, a mirror for the back seat, and extra crib sheets piled on top of the car seat, I walk to the checkout line, anxious to return to the hospital.

While I wait, I send Pepper an e-mail telling her what's happened. I hope she's up to read it. She'll be so happy that Hope is coming home today. I write and send the e-mail quickly, hitting send as space clears on the conveyor belt.

***

Driving a medically fragile infant home, two-hours, by yourself, isn't the brightest idea. Every peep, every time she stirs, I want to pull over. But I keep driving Highway 43, praying as we go.

"Charlie is going to be beside himself," I say, quickly looking into my mirror at the tiny one in my back seat. "He is going to adore you, Miss Hope. He misses the kids so much." Hope stirs again. I smile, seeing her stretch in the mirror that lets me keep an eye on her though she's rear-facing. My heart fills with a joy I haven't experienced in a long, long time. Thinking ahead to getting the baby home, I start a mental list of everything I need to do still – least of which is calling Carol to take her up on the offer to stay with the baby, at my house, until we work out nanny details.

As my list grows, my cell phone rings through the truck's hands-free device. I look to the stereo face that tells me who is calling. Burns. As quickly as the joy filled the air around me, it's gone in an instant. I answer, monotone, "Burns."

"Ava. Your last text threat seemed a little over the top. The kids haven't been interested in calling or texting you. That's why they weren't available."

"You're a terrible liar, Burns. I know better than that. Give me a break. I expect to hear from the kids this week."

"You will. But I called for another reason," he says.

"What could that possibly be?"

"I'm having some problems," he almost sounds sincere.

"Yeah?"

"Yes. The kids and Jenny – they're constantly fighting with her. Fighting about everything. It has been like this for a while but it got really bad after I let Miss Ellie go."

"What?" I ask, furious in an instant.

"I let Ellie go."

"Why the hell would you do that? She has been with the kids since day one – literally. Why would you do that? You're removing everything important from their lives, why wouldn't they act out?"

"I had no choice, Ava. Her relationship with you led to issues between her and Jenny. I know that rubbed off on the ki-."

"No! Don't say another word," I say my face hot with anger, and my voice growing louder. "This is about Jenny. I know Ellie like I know myself. She would not have behaved unprofessionally no matter how she may have felt. This is about your Legislative Assistant's childishness and immaturity." Hope stirs and lets out a little cry.

"Was that a baby?"

"Yeah. So here's the deal, I talk to the kids today at 7:00 PM. I will talk with them about making better choices. But you need to deal with your Legislative Assistant. This is not about the kids. It's about her."

"Will you ever stop calling her that?" He asks. Why he cares isn't clear.

"Not a chance," I say, without missing a beat.

"I will have the kids call at 7:00," he says.

"Good. I have to go, Burns. Do not forget this call tonight."

"I won't. Bye."

I end the call before saying another word. As soon as the call disconnects, I hit the call button on my steering wheel. My hands free device responds and I ask it to dial a number I know by heart. It responds, "Dialing Ellie." I wait for the ring and hope she'll pick up, though if I were her, I might not. She answers after several rings. "Ellie! How are you?"

"I'm good, Ava Love. It is wonderful to hear your voice."

"Why didn't you tell me that Burns fired you? He should be glad I live so far away. I am furious."

"It's okay. I mean, it's not. But what can I do? Jenny is not a good person. To say the least."

"They're two peas in a pod."

"Well that's true."

"Are you doing okay?" I ask. "Have you found another job?"

"I'm okay. Really. I saved well. I haven't found another job. I'm trying to stay positive by looking at this as an extended vacation."

"Well I guess that's a good way to look at it. Is there any chance you would be willing to come to NC for a job?"

"What kind of job? And yes, I probably would. There's nothing keeping me here if I can't be with William and Harper."

"A nanny job. Working for me."

"What? How?" She asks. I smile.

"It's a long story but I'm taking care of an infant for a while. Her name is Hope. She's just gotten out of the NICU. She is doing well and her prognosis is good but she has some health needs that made it a challenge to find her a foster home. Her parent's parental rights are basically already severed. There are no family members to take her. The county asked Pepper but she's doing the medical missions trip. She asked me to take Hope. The county believes that her chances for finding adoptive parents would be better if she was a year or so from her last surgery and doing significantly better physically. Their hope was that Pepper, as a doctor, would be a good place for her while her health improves. So now I have her."

"How old is she?"

"She is three months old. Oh you will just crumble when you see her! She is the tiniest little thing. At the very least, maybe you can come on down and visit. I have plenty of house and even a casita, over the garage, if you wanted privacy. It didn't occur to me to ask you about being Hope's nanny until I said it. I called because I wanted to check on you and see if you wanted to visit. I'll cover the cost of your plane ride down here."

"Really?"

"Yes. Please come. Even if it's just a visit. I would so love a familiar face down here. Charlie will be ecstatic to see you, too."

"I think I will take you up on that offer. I would love to see you. I saw some of the photos you posted, it's beautiful. The water and sea air might do me some good. When should I come? I'll drive by the way."

"Anytime, Ell. You can come anytime."

"I will leave tomorrow then, if that works?"

"Absolutely. I can't wait to see you," I say.

"Ditto. When you get home, send me your address. I'm going to get to packing!"

"I love you, Ellie."

"I love you two, Sweetie."

***

I made a couple of other phone calls along the way. I talked to Carol, Jamie, and Pepper called as I got closer to Beaufort. It made the drive go faster with a sleeping baby in my back seat and anxious energy bubbling up the closer I got to home. Pulling into the driveway a few hours ago, I realized how odd my life is, the twists in this road, taking me to unexpected places.

With the baby swaddled in a wrap against my chest, and jazz playing softly from inside, I've quickly settled into mom-mode. Getting Hope to eat consistently may yet be a challenge. She is an excellent napper, however. I rock on the porch as the sun begins its descent. Hope's heart beats against mine. I close my eyes and enjoy the moment, already letting hope seep in a little further. Footsteps on my brick driveway wake me from a nap I've apparently taken.

Macon! I completely forgot to call him. "Hello!" he calls from the gate. I use the universal signal for "shh" and he says, "Oh, sorry," as he quickly approaches. "Well, I was going to give you a hard time about not calling me but I can see you're otherwise occupied. Who is this?" he asks, pointing at Hope's barely visible head.

"This is Hope. I am so sorry for not calling. I forgot. I totally forgot. I went to Greenville, as you know, to meet with Hope's doctors and before I knew it, I was shopping for more baby gear and then putting this little firecracker into a car seat and driving her home. So sorry."

"No apologies are necessary. But I did want to check on you just in case. Mind if I sit?"

"No. Thanks for checking on me. Do you have a minute? Since you're here, maybe we can talk. I called you for a reason."

"Of course. I have all the time in the world. Well, sort of. Dinner is at the folk's house in an hour. But other than that I'm free."

Hope stirs and finishes her mini-stretch with a sigh. The contented sigh of baby is like the first night of summer. There's so much promise ahead in a summer with a clean slate and months of fun ahead. When you're a kid, it might as well be the best thing in all the world. There in that spot next to my heart, this tiny one wants for nothing and there is so much promise ahead. I look down at her and smile, forgetting for a second that Macon is there. How easily I slip into this role I've wanted my entire life. "So, where was I?"

"Well you hadn't said anything yet. I can come at a better time. Your focus doesn't need to be anywhere else than right there in your arms."

"No. That's not necessary. Well," I say swallowing hard. "I need to tell you something. Plus, I owe you an apology."

"An apology?" Why?"

It's then that I notice, truly notice, the way that he's looking at me. If I didn't know better I would think he is falling for me. "Well, see, I uh wanted to say that I am really sorry for all of the things I said to you on Saturday. I behaved terribly. I acted like a mean, thoughtless, rude child. I was wrong. I'm sorry for being so horrible."

"Thank you for the apology. It's not really necessary but it means a lot to me. But I think I interrupted you. You were about to say something else."

"Yes, well the thing is, while we were at Mrs. White's house, I was walking around looking at pictures and I saw a photo of you." I watch him. He turns his face away with his eyes focused on the creek, not me. It's not that he's lost the confident air that he usually exudes. It's that I've finely placed the far off look that I sometimes see in all of the Thompsons.

"And?" He asks quietly.

"I saw the pictures of you, Caroline, and your children. I didn't know right then of course, who everyone was. But Mrs. White told me when she came back from the kitchen that your wife's name was Caroline. I asked Carol for more information. But I just want you to know that I didn't ask for gossipy type reasons. I saw your wedding ring in one of the pictures and it made me feel so bad when I saw it and realized . . . "

I stop talking and close my eyes. I start crying. I can't help myself. When I open my eyes, I continue, "I am so sorry, Macon. I said such horrible things to you. You are the one person that actually can understand what I've been through. And what's worse? What's worse is that what you've been through is so much worse than what I've been through. I am a horrible person. I'm so sorry for being so ugly," I say.

"Ava," Macon says trying to get me to look at him. "Listen to me, it's okay. I know you hate these two words but, I understand. I understand all of this. I know why you reacted like you did. I know why I came across as a know-it-all without explaining where I'm coming from. I know that you don't mean to lash out. I've been there. I've been in exactly that spot. By the way, we shouldn't get ourselves into a pissing match about whose pain is worse. We've both endured the worst possible pain and that's all the credentials we need to understand each other."

I look down, away from Macon. I'm conscious in that moment, as a breeze picks up and rustles through the pine tree next to the porch, that he smells better than any man should. It's possible that I want to smell that smell for the rest of my days.

"Thank you for being so understanding, and kind. I don't deserve it. But thank you."

"You're welcome. So now you know my story, or at least the main details."

"Yes. I know the important details. I'm sorry that you've been through this, Macon. I am so sorry."

"Please stop apologizing."

"Okay," I say as if that's the end of the story. I know I'll run through my rotten attitude over and over quite a few times, probably too many times, until I've sufficiently forgiven myself.

"Now that we've cleared that up, what is your plan for Miss Hope during the day?"

"Well, for now, until I can find a nanny, it's Carol. She volunteered. But the good news is, my step kid's nanny, Miss Ellie is coming down for a visit, tomorrow. My ex fired her so she has some time on her hands. I hope she will consider staying and working for me. I have that casita over the garage. Or she can find a little place of her own. She has been with the kids forever. My ex hired her before Harper, my stepdaughter," I say, based on the question on Macon's face, "was born."

"That would be pretty amazing if it all worked out. Why did your ex fire her, by the way?"

"His Legislative Assistant. She's the reason. Ellie is good people. Among the best I've ever known. She loves the children fiercely and has been there for them through everything, including losing their mother, sister, and now me. This is just pure spite. And not surprising in the least."

"Your ex's new wife seems like a pretty nasty person."

"Oh she is. Not sure what happened to her as a child, but it must have been bad."

"What in the heck does your ex see in her?"

"Dollar signs?" Macon laughed out loud. "Her daddy's connections? Who knows? Sometimes it still shocks me. Burns never really knew how to be a husband. He worked. He paid for stuff. He worked some more. He wanted a partner in his political life. I think he thought he got that with me. In his mind I looked like someone he should marry. My parents are rich, I went to all the right schools, and I knew how to work a room. The only problem was that I didn't really care about any of that. Which I told him. Over and over. Somehow it didn't quite sink in. I didn't go to every event with him. I didn't entertain as much as he wanted me to entertain. I worked. Hard. I raised two kids. I didn't have time to be a trophy wife, too. He needed a trophy wife. So he found one."

"Wow. Well, his loss," he says, winking at me. I smile. I cannot help myself. He's good at taking a dark moment and lightening it up. "I mean that by the way. Maybe someday I can say his loss is my gain?"

I smile again. I don't know what to say. I'm a little rusty in this department. I look down as Hope stirs and I remember . . . now is not exactly a good time for any type of romance in my life. "Maybe so," I say, unsure of how to handle a moment that brings up competing emotions.

Before I have to stumble around for something else to say, my cell phone buzzes from the side table. I reach for it when I see it's Harper's cell phone number. "It's Harper," I say to Macon. I answer quickly lest I miss her. "Hi Sweetheart. How are you?" Macon stands up and mouths bye, as Harper quietly says she's fine. We both wave at each other. He lingers a moment, holding my gaze longer than any man should. That eye contact thing he does makes my head spin.

He smiles and says quietly, "See you soon." He turns and walks down the stairs before I can say a word. I turn my attention to Harper, hoping desperately things aren't as bad as I fear. With Macon gone, I hit the speaker phone button.

"Are you sure you're fine, Sweetie?"

"No. I'm not fine, mama."

"What's going on? Are you alone, alone?"

"Yes. Dad & what's her name are gone. Some party or something."

"Who is there with you?" I ask.

"This new chick they hired to watch us. She's not bad. But she's not Ellie."

"I know. I just found out about that today. I'm so sorry. I might be able to talk him into hiring her back."

"Don't bother. He won't listen. I don't care about that anyway because I don't want to live here anymore. Mom, I want to live with you. Will does, too."

From close by, Will says, "I do, Mommy."

Mommy. I haven't heard that in a while. He's a big kid now he says. It's been mom for the past year or so. "I want you both to live with me, too. More than anything."

"Then take dad back to court. We can't stay here anymore. We can't. Please?"

"Every day that you're not with me is a horrible day. I miss you both and want nothing more than for you to be with me. Can you give me time to work through some things with my lawyer?"

"I don't think I can wait," Harper says.

And then William, "Me either. We can't do it," he says.

"You can do it," I say, though I ache speaking these words in the air.

"Are you saying you won't?" Harper asks, angrily.

"No. I am saying until we can get a different Judge, and start over, you can do it."

"Okay. So you're going to keep trying?"

"I want you two to live with me every single day possible. So yes, I'm going to keep trying. Of course I am."

"Okay. Just making sure."

"How is school going?"

"It's good," Harper says.

"William-Boy, how about you? How is it going?"

"I like my teacher. He's pretty cool," he says.

"That's great news. What else is going on?" The kids take turns chattering back and forth. Now is not the time to tell them about Hope. Maybe soon. But not now.

"Kiddos, it's getting close to that time."

"We know," Harper says.

"Before you go I wanted to mention something. I know this is very hard. But you have to try with Jenny. Please be respectful. If she's saying something that is hurtful to you, maybe find a way to take some deep breaths and ask to be excused. But do it respectfully, okay? Even if she upsets you, she is still an adult and you need to make sure you're respecting her. Got it?"

"Mom, we do. She's lying. Dad told us what she's been saying. We aren't doing what she's saying. We aren't being bad."

"Are you saying you're not arguing with her at all?" I ask.

"Well sometimes. But I argue with you sometimes."

I laugh. She can be stubborn alright. "You have a point there. But you're saying that you're not fighting often – like maybe all the time?"

"No way. Does that even sound like us?"

"No."

"Yeah, exactly."

"So why is she saying that, then?"

"Because she wants to get rid of us now. We're cramping her style, Mom. She wants us gone. The more she bugs Dad, the angrier he gets and the more he defends her and yells at us for literally for no reason. Or for some stupid made up offense."

"Why . . . I mean, what could she possibly?"

"She's a horrible person, Mom. That's the only reason you need to know."

"Just promise me you will be as good for her as you would for me and Miss Ellie?"

"Promise."

"Promise," Will echoes.

"I love you both. Forever and ever. And ever."

"We love you, Mama. We can't wait to see you again."

"I can't wait to see you two crazy kids."

"Love you, Mom," William says into his sister's phone.

"Love you, too Baby. I will see you as soon as humanly possible."

"Toodle-oo," Harper says. And then like she sometimes is known to do, she ends the call before I answer. Throughout my phone call and talk with Macon, Hope has napped. She's a champion. I take a deep a breath. Maybe hoping to cleanse Burns and Jenny from my psyche. In an instant, I'm convinced like never before that moving here had been the catalyst to getting back the fight I lost the day Katie died. I'm ready for the fight now.

~ NINE ~

I hardly slept a wink last night. This is what comes from having a baby with a heart condition sleeping in a bassinet attached to your bed. But for our first full day together, we didn't do half bad. Hope is not fond of being out of my sight. She wants to be held constantly. I can't say I blame the girl. After spending the first few months of her life in an incubator, without the love, affection, and physical contact that the average infant has, I would feel the same I'm certain. She met the right woman because I don't want to put her down.

Ellie is a few miles away. She called from Highway 70. Charlie has no idea what's in store but he can sense my anticipation. He runs around me as I walk through the house, like he knows something big is at our doorstep. Hope, as per our usual so far, is going with me everywhere I go. I don't know who loves this more at this point. The person that came up with these wraps deserves some kind of award.

Hope is the quietest baby I have ever met. Until I put her down. And then she's fire and brimstone. You do not want to test this one, or she will light your world on fire, she will. That's a great sign. She has to have some fight in her to get through this recovery. It has been about ten minutes since Ellie called. I step out to the front porch with Charlie in tow. From my rocking chair, I unwrap Hope knowing that Ellie will want to hold her the second she sees her.

Like clockwork, Ellie pulls up in front of the house, ten minutes later. I wave as she steps around the front of her car and walks toward the house. She waves back, her million dollar smile outperforming the sun on the creek. "Charlie," I say to my snoozing, oblivious dog, "It's Miss Ellie!" His ears perk up. He picks up his head from the tiny spot of sun on the porch and sees her. I've never seen that dog get up so fast from a nap. He tears across the yard, tail wagging.

Charlie jumps up when he reaches her, practically knocking her over. I don't say a word because I know she's better at controlling him than I am. "Now you listen here you turd, just because you haven't seen me in some time does not mean you get to act like a hooligan. You sit down right this instant!" Charlie obeys because he rarely sasses Ellie. I'm another story. "Stay," she says, commandingly. "That's more like it, Charlie boy. Now how are you?" she says scratching his head. He looks up adoringly.

"Hello there! I am so glad you are here," I say reaching for her. We go in for the biggest hug we can with the baby in my arms.

"My girl. Oh how I've missed you. You look . . . so much better than the last time I saw you. How are you, Sweet Stuff?"

"I'm okay. I'm actually okay."

"I can see Charlie is still three gallons of crazy in a two gallon bucket."

"Always. But you seem to have him under your spell already."

"Well are you gonna let me come sit on that porch of yours or are we going to stand around here on the driveway all day?" she asks, teasingly.

"Of course. Follow me." After Ellie drops her purse on the porch, she sits down in a rocking chair.

"Phew. How is it that driving makes one so tired? Now do I get a proper introduction and story about the Missy there."

"Yes, ma'am. This is Hope," I say walking over to Ellie with the baby. "I know you want to hold her. I don't even need to ask."

"You know me well," she says, taking Hope into her arms, cradling her. One look at her and I know Ellie isn't leaving anytime soon. Thank God. "She is a tiny little Miss, isn't she?"

"Yes, very. While you hold her, why don't I go in and get you something to drink. What would you like? Sweet tea, lemonade, or water."

"Got anything stronger? I could use something . . . adult beverage like. It's 5 o'clock somewhere, right?"

"It's 5 o'clock here, Miss Ellie. How about a glass of a ridiculously expensive French wine to celebrate being together?"

"Oh yes. That would be perfect." I leave Ellie on the porch with Charlie already napping at her feet and holding the sweet surprise that is Hope, in her arms.

In the kitchen, I reach for two wine glasses. I crouch down in front of the wine refrigerator and try to make up my mind about what to open. It's a special day. It calls for a special wine, like Louis Jadot 2014 Clos de la Roche. I'm not saying I took it from Burns when I left, but I took it from Burns when I left. It's the perfect way to celebrate having Miss Ellie, a part of home, and as much a part of my kid's lives as me, here. I grab it from the refrigerator feeling somehow victorious over Burns, as if taking a $250.00 bottle of wine somehow makes up for everything he's done. He probably doesn't even know it's gone with a wine cellar that is the envy of many.

I have a sudden urge to tell Ell where it came from. I uncork the bottle and put it and our glasses on a tray. I take a wheel of Brie from the refrigerator, suddenly excited to have someone in my home to enjoy two of my favorites. It's a reunion. One that I didn't think I'd see for quite some time. I prepare the Brie and put it in the toaster oven. I return to the porch with the wine and glasses.

"Well I wondered if you got lost," she says, rocking the now sleeping Hope. "She's a sweet little doll," she says.

"That she is. Let the wine sit for another ten minutes or so. I'll be back with a snack."

"I can't wait!" Ellie exclaims, always a fan of the goodies I whipped up, when I had time to do it that is.

My cell phone, left on the counter in the kitchen, is in mid-ring when I return to answer it at the last second, "Hello?" I say, half expecting no one to be there.

"I didn't think you would answer but I'm so glad you did."

"Hi Charlotte. What's up? Everything alright with Kenly?"

"Yep. She seems to be doing better at the moment. We are waiting for a second appointment with the rheumatologist to go over the additional labs and find out what her treatment plan will be."

"Good. So what can I do for you?"

"Macon mentioned that your step kid's nanny would be in town. We thought we would invite you all to join us for dinner at the Pelican Inn. I'm not sure if the baby is okay to be out in public and all. We know she has special medical needs. Would you like to meet us?"

"I think that sounds perfect. Hope will be fine. I won't be dragging her all over the world but dinner out will be just fine. What time?"

"We were going to walk down at 7:00. We have a reservation shortly thereafter. We plan on sitting outside. The weather is still perfect. It's bizarre."

"We'll be ready when you get here," I say.

"I can't wait to see you and meet that baby," Charlotte says, sincerely.

"I am looking forward to it, too. See you in a couple of hours," I say as she says goodbye and hangs up.

I pull the Brie out of the toaster oven and spoon fig preserves over the top. I carry it out on a serving tray. It's a good day. For the first time in ages, I am looking forward to a social event. So this is what it's like to start living again? Ellie has poured us both a glass of wine, expertly, with the baby undisturbed. "You are a pro," I say, watching her settle back into her chair.

"Oh I am! What have you brought me? It looks scrumptious."

"It's Brie and fig preserves. Let me have Hope and you can dig in," I say as I get the wrap set up again, tying it around me.

"Well that would have been a convenient contraption back in the day I was raising my own babies," she says. "Heck, it would have come in handy for Harp and Will." She expertly leaves Katie out of the mix. I notice it and swallow hard. Katie is always there in the spoken and unspoken.

When I've finished getting the wrap ready, I take Hope back and somehow, though it still surprises me, I expertly place her in the wrap. It seems as though I've been doing this my whole life, but really I've never used one before yesterday. I credit the moms of YouTube for my baby wearing abilities. In the few days before bringing Hope home, I watched more of those videos than I care to admit. I sit down with Hope and reach for a plate, serving myself some cheese and crackers. "Being hands-free is going to come in handy. Never mind the fact that this munchkin is overdue for some serious snuggling."

"Yes, she sure is. So tell me about how this happened. But before you get to that, what's the plan for dinner? You know me."

"We had an invite from new friends of mine. You will love them. Dinner at the Pelican Inn at 7:00. It will give you chance to see our lovely downtown. Sound good?"

"Perfect. Now tell me about Miss Hope so I can go freshen up.

***

The golden-pink light of the sun making its way down in the West is a comfort to me now. The warmer weather, though Christmas is days away, has brought the town out in full force. They pass by, with us hidden on the porch: retired couples, young families, joggers and bike riders, eking out what's left of this warmer weather. This town is like a postcard for the perfect life.

Laughter and conversation from a crowd, before I see them, tells me that the Thompsons are on their way over. Kenly is skipping ahead of the pack. She stops at my fence and turns around to look back at them, her hands on her hips. She's the boss. "Hurry up, Uncle Mac! What's taking you guys so long?" I am self-conscious already and I haven't even seen him yet. I scan the group looking for Macon. Yep, still hot.

"Good evening!" Charlotte Thompson exclaims.

"Good evening," I say. Miss Ellie and I stand up and head down my long driveway.

Macon, pushing a stroller, of what I'm guessing is the newest and second Thompson grandchild, makes up the caboose of the long line of Thompsons. He waves, smiling. When Charlotte and Macon reach the tiny boss-girl, they step inside my fence.

Miss Ellie, characteristically to the point, "There's a whole mess of ya'll."

Charlotte laughs. "I know. We're overwhelming. We don't deny it."

"I'm Ellie Hanover," Ellie says offering her hand to Charlotte. "Thank you for the invitation to join you."

"Charlotte Thompson. And we won't expect you to remember this but this is Macon. That's my husband, Beau, that's Grace and Grant – they live here in town." Grace and Grant wave in reply. "Charlie is our California-living son, and our son Carter, and his wife Elizabeth live in Durham with their little man, Noah. And Pierce and his wife Taylor live in Wilmington." They all wave as she says their names.

"Well it's lovely to meet you all. But there's no way I'm remembering names."

"It's okay, Miss Ellie. I hardly remember their names," Macon says, holding his hand out to shake her hand.

Kenly, not one to miss out, pipes up. "I'm Kenly. GiGi forgot about me. But she shouldn't have. It's nice to meet you," she says, confidently.

"It's nice to meet you, Kenly!"

"Shall we head that way?" Beau asks. As if it were a command and not a question, everyone starts moving again.

"Dr. Ava," says Kenly, in a perfect eastern NC accent, "You will sit next to me, okay?"

"Well I . . . "

"Resistance is futile," Macon says. "She is not a woman to be trifled with." Kenly grabs my hand.

"Please? Pretty please?" She asks.

"Of course I will sit next to you."

"Good call," she says, apparently completely serious judging by the look on her face.

We make our way through town, the laughter and conversation of this way too happy group has picked up, presumably right where it left off. They're in the middle of conversation and story I don't really understand. But whatever it is, it's hilarious to them. Kenly is holding my hand. I have a new best friend. We're just ahead of Macon and the baby. Ellie is already deep in conversation with Charlotte.

I walk in silence, overwhelmed. I try harder than I have in recent years to not let it show. I like them, even if they are weird. The restaurant is on the far end of downtown, not that this is saying much considering you can walk from one end to the other in ten minutes flat. The Pelican Inn is in a grey-blue building that looks much smaller than it actually is. Long before we reached it, I can smell what I already know will be some amazing seafood.

With us all seated, I have a hard time deciding what to order so I order a few things – wanting to try a little of everything. Everyone else seems to have their favorites. After ordering, I realize they're all staring at me. "What?" I ask. "Do I have something on my face?"

"That's a lot of food for one little lady. You gonna eat all that?" Beau asks.

"Every last bite." Eyebrows raise in response. "Kidding. I kid. I'll try a little of everything and take home leftovers. Everything looks so good. I don't want to choose."

"I can relate," Charlotte says. "I'm a fatty at heart."

At the other end of the table, Beau begins telling a story. His voice, like the man itself, is big and booming. He's not fat, he's just a mountain. Good thing we're on the deck, alone. Truth be told, I'm not really listening. My thoughts are focused on Taylor's Creek, the gentle breeze blowing through the patio screens, and the baby in my arms. Still lost in thought, the Thompson clan laughs at the end of Beau's story. I smile and Senator's Wife Fake Laugh, something I've perfected over the years.

No one notices that I have absolutely no idea what the story is about or why we're all laughing. Ellie on the other hand is looking straight at me from across the table. She has that look. It's the one I've gotten to know quite well over the years. She always knows when I'm faking. She winks at me - also an Ellie thing. It's like she's saying, "I see you. I get you." Unlike others who think they know me, she actually does. I look down at my plate, thankful she's here.

The Thompson clan, as per the usual, continues with their stories – side conversations are happening all around me. If it weren't for the fact that I just met them a few months ago, I'd say this is the family I've always wanted. Looking around the table I try to remember names and who belongs to whom. The baby, Noah, belongs to Carter and Elizabeth, who live in Durham. I study Grace for a minute. She is beautiful and nearly the exact opposite of Beau Thompson in every way. Soft spoken to his booming voice and tiny compared to the giant. Yet, the two of them are garnering the biggest laughs at the table. They're two peas in a pod.

Grant, her husband, looks most like Macon, just enough they could be twins, but he's thinner and shorter, probably 6'0. The other Thompsons at the table are Charlie, who looks more like a So Cal surfer than a southern boy from a wealthy family. Pierce and his wife Taylor, though they live close-by in Wilmington were not at Macon's party so tonight is the first time I've met them.

How I got myself in the middle of this crew, I have no idea. But here I am. I force myself to focus on them. The conversation has turned slightly serious as they discuss some local politics and the upcoming congressional election. I pray they don't draw me in but before I know it, Pierce goes for it. "Ava, with your background I bet you have opinions on the upcoming election. What are the chances the underdogs can oust the incumbents – including right here in Eastern NC? Maybe you can convince everyone at this table that's not happening here anytime soon."

"I'm not much for talking politics at dinner, with people I don't know."

Macon speaks up without missing a beat, "You know us. "

"Well technically. But I don't know your politics. Nor do I know who you know." I say, wanting to get out of this conversation as quickly as possible.

"That doesn't matter," Macon quickly retorts. "This family doesn't exactly dictate what others are required to believe, so what we think doesn't matter too much. But I guess after being married to a Senator I wouldn't want to talk about this backwoods district and its politics, either."

"Hey now. We're not backwoods. And let me remind you this is where you were born and where you live now, buster," Charlotte says.

"Backwoods . . . relatively speaking that is," Macon says.

"It's backwoods," Charlie says.

"This is a wonderful place to live. It is not backwoods."

"Didn't say it wasn't wonderful, Mom. But you have to admit, things can be pretty screwy here sometimes," Macon says.

"Okay, maybe they can. I'd still rather live here than anywhere else. On that note, what do you think Ava? Do we get a reprieve from the old white men that have been running the show?"

"Hey now!" Beau says, laughing his belly-jiggling laugh.

"I think your local Congressman's days are numbered," I say. Maybe now they'll drop it.

"Really, now?" Pierce asks. "Huh. Interesting. I don't know."

"He has a lot of powerful friends," Beau says.

"Exactly," Pierce says.

"And enemies," Taylor, Pierce's wife, replies, over their babbling son, Noah. The baby has been passed from person to person since we sat down.

"Exactly," I say. "I honestly believe his days are numbered. I'll buy you all dinner if I'm wrong."

"It's a deal!" Kenly says, as if she has been in the middle of the conversation all along. Everyone laughs.

Macon musses Kenly's hair, "You nut. You never turn down an opportunity for chow, do you?"

"No, Sir, I do not." Half the table laughs. "Well it's true," she says. She is a girl after my own heart. Before they dig into the next conversation, servers arrive with the food. Everyone focuses their attention on dinner and I'm thankful the last conversation didn't turn personal. Political talk inevitably leads to, "so what's up with your ex-husband?"

***

The walk home grew quiet, quickly. With everyone's bellies full, it's no wonder. Half of the party has wandered off to the wine bar downtown. Charlotte and Beau push Noah's stroller - his parents having joined the others downtown. Kenly, too pooped to walk, is carried by her Dad. Macon has chatted with Ellie, just ahead of me, quietly, the whole way back. Hopefully not plotting against me. When we reach my fence, the hugging and see-you-laters begin. Charlotte and Ellie, already best friends, have a coffee date planned for Saturday. In such a short period of time, my life has been woven into theirs. I haven't had much of a say in the matter. Macon gives his mom a kiss on the cheek. "I'll see you on Saturday," he says. She waves to us as the rest of them head next door.

"That's my cue," Ellie says. "I'm exhausted. I'm on breakfast duty." Ellie puts her arm around my shoulder and gives me a squeeze. "It was wonderful meeting you, Macon. I hope to see more of you," she says shaking his hand.

"It was great to meet you, too." Ellie kisses the top of Hope's head. Awake through dinner, she's snoozing again. I watch Ellie walk away, awkwardly wondering if I'm supposed to say something to Macon.

"It made my parents happy to have you join us. Thanks for coming."

"I had fun." Did I really just say that?

"Good. I don't think you've had much fun in recent times, have you?" He's closer to me now. His cologne hardly noticeable before, is all I can think about now. "Maybe you'll consider letting me change that? Maybe have dinner with me sometime?"

Looking away from the street which I've been staring at, hoping to avoid eye contact, I catch his eyes intently fixed on me. There's an entire conversation happening in his eyes. "I'm not sure what to say."

"You could say *okay*? Or maybe *that sounds like a lovely idea, Macon.* Or you know, *eww.* I don't know. Maybe just say something."

"Thanks for caring about whether or not I'm having a good time?"

"I guess that's better than nothing?" He asks to my question.

"Sorry. I'm not sure what to say. I have a lot going on. I don't think I can even begin to think about dating or whatever you mean by dinner," I say, smiling. I sound like an idiot but I'm kind of amused by my own weirdness.

"I meant a date. I know you have a lot going on - now more than ever," he says, reaching out and touching Hope's tiny head, just peeking out over the top of the wrap. "Maybe just think about it?"

"I will think about it."

"Can I at least be off of probation? I think I deserve at least that much?"

"Okay, we can agree on that much. You're off. For now."

"For now?" Macon asks.

"Yeah, we'll see how it goes from here out," I say, as I step across the sidewalk onto my drive. Maybe he'll take the hint and mosey along.

"You're a hard sell, Doc. But I'm game. Whatever it takes," he says holding my gaze a moment longer. "Whatever it takes."

Without a word and with just a wave, he turns around and heads back to the main part of town. Probably to join his siblings at the wine bar. I watch him a moment longer before walking up my driveway to the porch. Hope lets out a cry and I look at my watch. I unwrap us both from our contented little cocoon, before she really goes crazy, which is bound to happen if she catches the slightest hint I'm not listening.

"You're like an alarm clock. Right on the nose for your next bottle." In the kitchen, I prepare a bottle, while trying to soothe the now very cranky 3 month old, that is newly attached to my hip, or rather, chest. Not yet ready to turn in, I grab a blanket from the living room and head out to the porch. It has become my second living room. I spend hours here, maybe hoping the night air will clear all of the cobwebs that have taken up residence in my mind.

October 2013 - Ridgemont, VA

The moon, silvery and just shy of full, is the kind of moon you shouldn't witness by yourself. But I'm by myself. I put my feet up on the small table in front of me, closing my eyes, hoping the tears will stay put. For the briefest of moments I am certain that willing them back has worked. The back porch of our home is bathed in the mystery of moonlight. The stars, with little to no competition, out here so many miles from town, are bright and fill the sky with thousands of pin-prick lights. This is the kind of night that's meant to be shared with the one you love, not witnessed alone.

Conscious of the beauty and pain co-mingled, the tears fall. How does such beauty exist on such an ugly day? An owl hoots from a tree nearby. I lift my glass up to toast him. *Hoo-hoo,* he says again. "Good question. Who? Who would leave their wife alone on the night of their daughter's funeral?" I take a drink of the whiskey in my glass and as it settles back -- the amber peace swirls, leaving a coating of the thick, throaty liquid on the inside. I stare into it for a moment and then close my eyes and rest my head on the back of the chair.

Images of the day fight their way to the surface, as do the questions. The questions began the day Katie died. Her last week in the hospital had been overwhelming. One moment she seemed to be doing better and I would let hope step in. The next, one of my residents intubated her. Within minutes Katie died. I called a few hours later to tell my parents their granddaughter was dead. This is a conversation no parent should ever have. Especially with parents like mine. That last week happened so fast. Things had been difficult for the previous six weeks. We had been in and out of the hospital. Burns' constituents and colleagues, our neighbors in Ridgemont, and my colleagues at Georgetown, were there every step of the way.

Pink Ribbons had even gone up all over town, even at the courthouse. The personal investment everyone felt in our daughter is the cursing and blessing that is small town Virginia. A prayer vigil had been arranged at the church in Ridgemont. Our church in D.C. arranged for regular visitors to Children's National. So much happened in such a short amount of time that there had been no time to process and certainly no time to ask the questions I needed to ask.

My entire world changed in an instant. Nothing that had been before Katie died, remained. And the sting of that ache is worsened tonight. Clouds, blowing in from the west, begin to cover the moon. The bright night, slowly gets darker and somehow colder. I shiver and tighten my jacket around my body. The whiskey in my hand and the never-ending questions, are my only company. Harper and William, asleep in the house, are the only justice and beauty left in the world now. They don't remember much about their mother. They were young when she died. William was just a baby really. My love for them is no different than the love I have for Katie. And though there is an ever widening, gaping hole in my heart, at least I have Harper and Will.

I take another swig of the whiskey and let it burn. In the days since Katie was pronounced dead, my emotions, as one might expect, have wavered from one end of the spectrum to the next, uncontrollable like the ocean. There is, in one moment, relative stillness. It's easy to see what swims there beneath the surface. Willowy bits of seaweed, shells, and rocks tumble along in the current. And then in the blink of an eye everything changes. The softly breaking waves turn, on a dime, to something almost sinister and wild. Perhaps I'm not the wild one. But grief is. It's unrelenting and dangerous, taking the most perfectly normal days and carrying them in a rip current that is impossible to fight.

Present Day - Beaufort, NC

Little did I know that night had only been a beginning. For the better part of my adult life, I had been Burns' girlfriend, fiancée, and wife. I was his partner in everything. We had it all planned out. When Katie got sick, I was just months away from giving up medicine, at least for all intents and purposes. I was quitting so Burns could run for President. I had been completely content and satisfied with the idea that I'd be a mom to my kids and a D.C. kind of wife. My parents were proud of me, maybe for the first time ever.

As far as they were concerned, I finally had the life befitting their expectations. When all of that went up in flames I didn't know what to do with myself. I became mired in my own grief, unable to see the path ahead. Holding Hope puts so much into focus. I've always looked for adventures around every corner. I've always jumped headlong into whatever fight or challenge stood in my path. The grief and losses wiped the drive right out of me. Until now. Now the memories are lighting a fire.

~ TEN ~

November 2013 - McLean, VA

"Mom! Mom! Come here. Quick!" Will's voice carries through the house, from the kitchen. The television is just barely audible above the click, click of the keys on my laptop. "Hurry!" he says.

I high tail it to the kitchen suddenly worried. "What in the world? Is it necessary to yell?"

"Yeah. Dad's going to be on the news. They just said. I don't really know what it's about but they said it was next."

"Okay. Well, thanks for letting me know. Why are you watching the news?"

"I was just flipping channels and saw him."

"Well why don't you go get your skateboard and go outside, okay? You've been inside all day. Go do something." I say, squeezing his shoulder.

"I'm going to. Can I take my skateboard to the tennis court?"

"Sure," I say, against my better judgment. As I say it, Ellie walks in, her arms full of groceries. Her eyes are just visible above the brown paper bag. I knew my husband would have a cow if he knew I let Will play on the court. But there's something sitting in the bottom of my stomach – something bad. I want him in eye sight. And if he goes anywhere else, I won't be able to see him.

"Thanks Mom!" he says as he walks out. He reaches into the grocery bag as he goes and grabs the tortilla chips that are sticking out. "Hi Miss Ellie! Bye Miss Ellie!" He slams the kitchen door. I watch him run across the grass, in the direction of the tennis court. He stops shy, choosing to play in the dirt instead.

Miss Ellie speaks up, watching him just as I am, while she pulls groceries out of the bag. "Lord have mercy, I do not know where that boy gets his energy. Whenever there's a teacher workday, I start to have an anxiety attack wondering how in heck I'm going to keep him busy all day," Miss Ellie says laughing and shaking her head.

"I know the feeling. Trust me. I know the feeling." I turn and face the television, remembering that sick turning of my stomach. Burns' face flashes across the screen as a mid-day news talk show begins. A democrat strategist, one unfamiliar to me, is the guest. My finger, inches from the red button, could shut out what I've already begun to fear will be bad news. But the urge to turn it off is suppressed by the even greater weight of the sick twist of my stomach, nearing a cramp. The anchor introduces the strategist. Chris Findlay.

The guest and anchor talk shop – most of it unrelated to my life. The anxiety tempers a bit but then, suddenly, Findlay goes in for the kill. "Listen, I'm the last person to say that the personal sex lives of our politicians matter . . ." *Whoa, where'd that come from*, I think. "I mean during the Clinton years, I was the first person to say that doesn't belong smack dab in the middle of our public discourse. If they get the job done, they get it done. Who cares about their sex lives? However, the problem comes in when these supposed men of God, family centered and the morality police for the rest of the world, on the right . . ." and that's when I tuned out for a moment. Heat, red hot, rises to my cheeks. I know my heart rate increased.

The host of the show takes the bait of course, because that's how they've planned it, "Anyone in particular you're talking about?"

"Well look at Senator Cooper for instance," Ellie takes several steps in my direction. She places her hand on mine. "The man has set himself up as the paragon of virtue. He's sat in judgment of others on matters of personal morality, called for the resignation of those who have certain marital indiscretions, on the other side of the aisle of course. And maybe worse? He thinks *his* view of the world and *his* religion is the only way."

The host interrupts for a moment, "Where are you going with this?" I step closer to the television, away from Ellie.

"I'm getting to that. Senator Cooper has his eyes on the White House. We all know that. It's no surprise. And yet he's vehemently and with malice ripped his opponents to shreds who engage in behavior no different than his own," his voice is dispassionate but resolute.

"Are you saying that Senator Cooper has had extramarital affairs?" asks the host of the show. As if she doesn't know what he's about to say.

"Yes. That's exactly what I'm saying. This guy has had a long line of mistresses stretching back to his first marriage. He's arrogant enough to believe this will go unnoticed and that he'll get away with it forever. Well, as long as he's going to talk out of one side of his mouth and carry on like this in his private life, I think it's time we all see what this man really is."

"There are stories that circulate about nearly every member of Congress. We've all heard the rumors. But how can you be sure this is true?"

"Listen, they're not just rumors. This guy spent the night of his baby's funeral with his mistress. That's just sick. Who does that? I don't care what he really does in his personal life. And I mean that. I'd be a hypocrite if I did care. What I care about is integrity. If you're going to claim to be the paragon of virtue and behave like this in your personal life, it needs to be exposed. I don't care if I lose everything I have by unearthing this."

"What specific proof do you have?"

"I have pictures. And I have sources that have corroborated the rumors and the pictures that surfaced several months ago."

I stand motionless, staring at the television, no longer hearing the words but seeing photographs of my husband splashed across the screen with the young woman I know to be one of his Legislative Assistants. Jenny. Ellie says from behind me, "Ava?"

"Miss Ellie. I need you to pick up Harper from school immediately." I look out the large window over the sink and watch Will as he sits down on his skateboard. "Take the kids to the country. Please? I know I gave you the afternoon off. But we've got to get the kids out of McLean before the press shows up. Please be careful. I will call you as soon as I can. Do not let the children watch television, okay?" I say, with perfect control. I turn back to her now, "Please run upstairs and get Will's book bag. I will go get him in the car."

"Yes ma'am," Ellie says rushing from the room.

I step outside putting everything I've just heard and seen into a small box in my head. "Hey bud," I say, maybe a little too enthusiastically.

"Hey," he says a little dejected.

"What's wrong?"

"I'm still not very good on this stupid thing," he says, smacking his board.

"You'll get better. That's what practice is for right?"

"Yeah." His voice is deflated. "I know."

"So uh, bud . . . how would you like to take a few days off school and spend some time in the country with me and Harper?"

"Really?" A smile stretches across his face. "I thought you had to work."

"I'm going to take some time off. I think it's a good idea if we play hooky. What do ya say?"

"I say that my mom is freaking awesome." I laugh as he jumps up and hugs me. "Do I need to pack?"

"Nah. I'll do that. I'm sending you, Harper and Miss Ellie there now. I'll be down in a few hours okay?"

"Okay," he says, shrugging.

"Why don't you hop in the car now? Miss Ellie will be down in a minute with your book bag." A moment of confusion crosses his face. But true to form, he shrugs his shoulders, picks up his skateboard and runs toward the car. I follow him and watch as he climbs into the backseat, sliding across the leather seat to his favorite spot behind the driver. I shut the door and walk around to his side of the car. I open it as he buckles his seat belt. "Be good, alright? And I'll see you later tonight."

"Okay mom." His blonde hair, matted with sweat to his head, makes the fissures in my heart that appeared the moment Katie died, crack just a little deeper. I kiss his cheek. "I love you," I say.

"I love you too, mama." I kiss him on the cheek again after tousling his hair. His sweaty, playing outside, all-boy smell follows me as I shut the door and turn toward the house. Miss Ellie is inches away with the book bag and a small overnight bag.

She smiles at me in the only way she knows how. It's her *it's going to be alright*, smile. I've gotten that particular one a lot over recent months. Just above a whisper she says, "Please don't panic my girl. Please. We don't know the whole story yet."

"We know enough. I will call you soon. Promise me you'll keep the kids away from the television. This will be all over the place shortly."

"I promise. Please call me soon."

"I will," she says as she walks to the Land Rover. After watching them drive away, I walk back to the house, steeling myself for what's to come next. Charlie is waiting at the threshold, smiling and completely unassuming. I walk through the house and draw all of the blinds on the first floor, already worried the press will be swarming within moments.

I return to the kitchen as a breaking news alert begins. It will surely be a constant crawl along the bottom of the screen for the next twenty-four hours. "Virginia Republican Senator and champion of conservative family values accused of extra marital affairs . . ." I grab the remote and flip the channel from each cable news network to the next. They've all picked up the story in one form or another.

I change the channel back to my favorite all-news channel. The story is running on the crawl and the afternoon anchor is already pouncing. Even the friendlies are out for a kill. I lean against the counter for support, my cell phone in one hand, the cordless phone resting on the counter next to me.

"Our sources have indicated that the Senator and his team were unaware this story was about to break. Cooper was on the Senate floor today delivering a speech on health care reform. We have footage just in to us, from our man on the Hill, of what we believe to be the moment he was informed." I know my husband, his ambition, and every light and dark place in his heart. I know him like the back of my hand. Though hope is quickly fading, I hope to see something in his face that tells me this is all an elaborate rouse on the part of the liberal media and an overzealous operative. The anchor, known for his sense of humor and charm says, "Let's get this show on the road," when the clip doesn't immediately play.

The clip rolls. And there it is. Burns Cooper is standing in the chamber, orating to perfection, as usual. He looks up at something off camera. Panic spreads, in a mere instant, across his face. I am sure no one else noticed this look. A millisecond later, he's returned to his confident, steady self. The staffer, a young man named Zach, on his first job out of college, just became a face that will be splashed across every paper in the country tomorrow morning. He walks hurriedly past the few seated and straight to the Senator. He hands Burns a message. Zach waits for him to read the white, folded piece of paper. Burns closes his eyes for a split second. When he opens them, they're filled with defiance. He nods at Zach which is his cue to exit. I hoped for a look of sorrow. Remorse. Anything. But defiance? That I did not expect. He returns to his speech as the clip fades to black and returns to the anchor.

"Well would you look at that folks? He didn't seem a bit phased, now did he?" I sink to the hardwood floor. The guests that have now joined the anchor are already talking over each other. I can't see the television any longer. The island in the middle of the kitchen, blocks my view. But I can hear it all. The pontificating begins. The last thing I hear before both of my phones start ringing again is the voice of someone my husband has known since she was a small child. Someone I have known as long as I've known my husband. The anchor quiets the other guests and says, "Let's give Campbell Robertson, who may have some insight, the floor.

***

Maybe if my husband had been your average, run of the mill politician, this would blow over within twenty-four to forty-eight hours. However, Burns Cooper had made himself the party's leading voice for conservative values. The comparisons to Ronald Reagan have only fueled his national platform. He is just a few months shy of announcing his run for the Presidency, something that we have been planning for years. He's just shattered every hope he's ever had to be President. Far worse than that, and what I am not certain they can recover from, is that he's now opened us up to a second wave of devastation. As if Katie's death weren't enough.

Burns' national platform and platinum-plated image is the stuff of dreams. But it's for this reason that what they've begun to put in place today are so measured and could, on first appearance, seem extreme. His political enemies are numerous. His smile and good boy persona, with that distinguished silver hair and pretty boy handsome, attract attention from the national media.

He's a story. And by extension, so are we. His speeches make the national news. Our vacations or social events appear in the society columns. Our homes have been featured in magazines. Katie's death had been followed by the news media as if he had already been elected President. The outpouring of support had been a soothing salve. No. Burns Cooper is no run of the mill politician. He is a celebrity. They will go through our trash. They will try to take pictures of the children at school. They will follow us wherever we go. I suspect it's only the very tip of the iceberg.

***

I unplugged the house phones. They were ringing off the hook. My Blackberry has been burning up with emails and calls. I called the hospital to let them know that it would still be a few more days before I returned. I didn't have to explain much. They knew without asking that I would have to take a few days off. Guilt surged for leaving my colleagues in a bind yet again. But there would be no way I could go back right now. It would be a mess. I called my mom about an hour ago. She was going into a meeting with a client and didn't have time to talk. I didn't press it. I've long given up trying to fit into my parent's world. She'll find out eventually. Somewhere in the midst of the news, L.A. style, after the Hollywood crap they all live for, my mother would hear the news. I emailed my brother, in Khandhar, about an hour ago as a head's up. He would call when he could, I knew.

I sit at my kitchen table. Waiting. Though I know I should turn off the television, I can't bring myself to do it. It might do Burns some good to be confronted with it when he walks in the door. They've been saying the same things for the last two hours anyhow. There's nothing new to report. Not a soul can testify to other affairs. But apparently everyone in the world but me suspected this affair.

Julianne, currently sitting with her co-anchor, passes along her well wishes to me and the kids, for which she'll probably get in trouble for later. I hate when I'm the news and my best friend is reporting it. It has always been a struggle between us. As the network goes to a commercial, a Tahoe with blacked-out windows, carrying my husband, pulls in and parks under the carport in the backyard, well out of sight of the cameras. I watch him get out, his briefcase in one hand, my pride in his other.

The earlier look of defiance has been replaced with fatigue, worry, and maybe a little fear mixed in for good measure. He's at the kitchen door within seconds. A two man security detail is right behind him. I stand up when he walks in. We make eye contact. But no words pass between us. He turns to the men from the private security firm, "Thank you. Feel free to take a break. I understand the guest house has been opened for you with refreshments and the like. If I need you, I'll let you know." Both men nod. The older of the two turns and walks out first. The second guy hesitates a moment.

I make eye contact with him and then it comes out, faster than my filter can stop it, "Don't worry. I won't do any physical harm. He's safe. For now." Burns looks down at his shoes and then up at me. The defiance isn't there. At the moment, it's utter embarrassment.

Burns turns and says, "Chris, you can go. She was kidding." He slaps the guy's back like they're old buddies.

Chris nods at Burns. Then at me. "Ma'am," he says as he heads out the door. Burns turns back to me as the door shuts. He sets his briefcase on the table. He's still holding onto my pride.

"Ava, I - "he says and then stops when he realizes the TV is on, back to news coverage of my whoring husband. "Have you been watching that all afternoon?" he says pointing to it over my shoulder.

"Yep. I sure have. I watched the whole thing unfold live."

"Where? I mean, what?" He looks around the room, probably wondering where the kids are.

"Can you be more specific?" Never known for being a witch, it feels good at the moment.

He winces and then closes his eyes for a second. When he opens them, I am standing next to the TV, as if it's on my side in a battle for our marriage. There might as well be the Grand Canyon between us. "Did the kids see it? Where are they?"

"No they didn't. But you're one lucky SOB, Burns." He winces again, and takes off his suit jacket. "Will was in here watching television, flipping through the channels. He saw your picture on a teaser. He called me to come in here. I thought he'd hurt himself or something with all the racket he made."

The look on Burns' face tells me a story I'm not ready to hear. There's something there I can't entirely put my finger on. I know he's embarrassed. But I'm starting to wonder if there's even the slightest hint of repentance. Embarrassed he got caught? Yes. Convinced he's wrong? I'm not so sure.

"I had a sick feeling in my stomach. I can't explain it really. It was a stroke of dumb luck that they didn't use one of those pictures of you with her. I mean, who does that? Every other show or network would have. But somehow I still knew it was bad. I told Will to go outside with his skateboard. Which he did.

You know how he is. Happy go lucky. Didn't even ask me when he left why it was they were talking about you on the news." I look up from the tissue I've been worrying in my hands. "Ellie was here with me however." Burns shakes his head. He pulls out one of the kitchen chairs and sits. "As soon as I saw the photos, I told Ellie to take Will and Harper to the country. That's where they are now."

Burns runs his right hand through his thick, silver hair. He unbuttons the top buttons of his dress shirt. And then wipes a bead of sweat from his forehead. I continue, "I'll be driving down there in an hour or so," I continue. "I asked Ellie to keep the televisions off. Since the press is pushed back pretty far, I'm hoping the kids haven't figured it out. Ellie has good instincts. She's been with us long enough to know how to handle something like this. I talked to her about a half hour ago. She said she took the long way around to get to I-81 so the kids didn't see anything going on here at the house. I don't know what I would have done without her today. You'll be giving her a raise effective immediately," I say to my husband as he shakes his head in agreement.

And then I stop talking. And wait. From outside, several of our security detail are talking, their voices just audible over the silence between us. The television continues to chatter. But otherwise, the house and Burns are silent. I stare at him, willing him to speak. He doesn't. His silence is all I can handle for the day. "You bastard," I say, as I run out of the kitchen and up the stairs to our bedroom. He follows close behind. As I reach the bedroom, I look back. He's on the landing. I slam the door and unzip the luggage I've already laid out on the bed, empty. I open drawers and throw clothes in, panties and bras dropping to the floor as they fly toward the open bag.

He opens the door and stands still. "I know you're angry," he finally says. "And I don't blame you. I'm sorry. I'm sorry, Ava."

I continue opening drawers, throwing clothes into the bag. I walk past him, to the closet and shove him, my small hands barely enough to move his 6'2 frame. "You're in love with her, aren't you? It's true, isn't it?"

"What's true?"

"You were with her the night of Katie's funeral weren't you? Work was an excuse, an easy one, wasn't it? You knew I was too damn tired to even double check. How could you?" I scream from the inside of our walk-in closet. My breathing is so hard and labored, I tell myself to breathe deeply, knowing I'm moments away from hyperventilating. I take a deep breath and then grab two pairs of shoes.

I throw the shoes in the suitcase as Burns says, "Well what do you expect, Bennett?" He's forever using my maiden name, in heated arguments, as an epithet. I never have understood why he does that, unless it's a warning that I'm always this close to being yanked from my status as a Cooper.

"What do I expect?" I ask just above a whisper. I shake my head and then the tears come in a flood. "A. Faith-ful. husband," I say between gasps and body racking sobs.

"You might as well have walked out on me when Katie got sick the last time. You were always focused on everything else but me. I had no choice but to look elsewhere," says Burns.

"Oh this is *my* fault?" I shake my head in disgust. I look up at the mirror over my dresser. My makeup is running down my face, black pools of mascara are gathering on the edge of my eyelashes. My vision blurs when I open my eyes after blinking. I wipe my eye with the back of my hand. "How dare you? Six weeks. She was sick for six weeks. You take that to people of Virginia and we'll see if that excuse holds up. You don't stand a chance!"

"That. Is. Enough!" He yells, anger, bordering on rage, in his eyes.

"My career is not over," the defiance returns. His haughty, arrogant smile forces me to turn away – I can't even look at him. "They'll forgive me. You should too. I apologized. What more do you want from me?"

"What more do I want? A promise that you'll never see her again. An *I love you*, Ava. Or how about, *I want this marriage to work. I'll do anything*. How about that? How about begging for forgiveness?"

The defiant look remains. In a dark corner in the back of my mind I know my marriage is over. "I'm sorry Ava. I've already said it and I'll say it again. I didn't mean to do this to you and the kids. I really didn't. But it has happened and now we have to come up with a plan."

"A plan? A plan? Are you serious? You've got to be kidding me! I have no intentions of helping you recover from this. None. You're on your own buddy. You made this bed and you'll lie in it."

"Where are you going?" Burns asks.

"Ridgemont. Where do you think?"

"What are you going to tell the kids?"

"I'm not telling them anything, Burns. You're following me in the Tahoe and you'll be telling them yourself. You got me?"

I stand up, shoulders back and stare Burns dead in the face, with an I-dare-you-to-defy-me, look.

"I - "

"What? You want me to tell them? By myself?" I ask.

"No."

"Well then I highly suggest you follow me there and tell the kids so they understand. And make sure they feel your regret and repentance even though it's clear you'll be lying through your teeth."

"Okay," he says, walking out of the room.

I slip to the floor, my back against our bed frame. I cover my eyes with my hands and let my head hit the wood. Never one to use the word hate or to even feel it, the intensity of my anger boils into hate in that moment. And more than anything, I hate Burns for leaving me alone in my darkest hour.

~ ELEVEN ~

Present Day

It has been three months since Hope entered my front door. She is growing by leaps and bounds. She has steadily gained weight. She is never far from either Ellie or me - just how she likes it. After weeks and weeks of baby hogging, I gained enough confidence in her steadily improving health, to let others join in on the holding, too. You can't spoil a baby, right? Well, if you can, Hope is going to be spoiled. I'm okay with this. With Hope's parent's rights terminated, and a routine that we fell into easily, I am convinced that God knew Hope would always be mine.

There I said it. She's my girl. I am her mama. And no one could tell me otherwise. Ellie lives in the guest house and comes over every morning at 7:00 AM, like clockwork. I make enough coffee for the both of us and we sip coffee and read the paper, like an old married couple. Hope sits in her high chair babbling in her Hope way. I start her day, getting her dressed as often as I can. Ellie takes over when I walk to the office at 8:30 AM. I come home for lunch as much as possible, smack dab in between the baby's naps, of which she is still quite serious about.

A couple of months ago, sitting on the porch, with Hope in my arms, I thought back to the night Katie died. That's when the memories came. I remembered the day Burns left me, too. There were a few moments that night when I thought I'd never recover. The devastation left behind, after Katie died and Burns' affair became public, changed me forever.

But as Hope drank from her bottle and the night grew even quieter on Front Street, the despair that used to sit at the bottom of my heart, always riled up and waiting to rise to the surface, turned instead into determination for the first time since Katie's death and the end of my marriage. That week, when I didn't get to talk the kids, yet again, I called my lawyer. Needless to say, Burns hasn't let the kids miss a phone appointment ever since. Talking to the kids through some long hard days in the Jenny and Burns Cooper household has been harder than I'd imagined. But I'm grateful for my lawyer who ensured I would at least be able to encourage them over the phone while we worked toward a better custody arrangement.

All told, life started making sense, which is why I knew that I wanted to adopt Hope. After jumping quickly through the county's hoops, I became a licensed foster parent, specifically for Hope. Proving that bureaucracy doesn't always move at a snail's pace, they allowed me to take classes and complete the home study process concurrently. The state quickly approved my license, all with the goal of keeping Hope in a stable environment. The plan had been that I would be her caregiver while she healed from her surgeries, gained weight, and strength. But within a few weeks of Hope's arrival I decided she wouldn't go anywhere.

"So I hear you're going to the pig pickin' tomorrow," Carol said after I'd walked a patient to the front desk.

"That I am. Anything I need to know before going to my first pig pickin'?" I ask.

"You've never been to one?" Carol asked as if I'd just told her I thought the world isn't round.

"There's not much opportunity for pig pickins' in D.C. or Malibu, Carol," Jamie says rolling his eyes.

"You hush!"

"No, I haven't been to a pig pickin' before. Let alone a pig cooking contest."

"Well. You are in for quite the treat! You're gonna love it."

"You might enjoy it," Jamie quickly adds. "I'd rather pick up trash on the highway with my bare hands, while wearing a Speedo, and high heels."

"Weirdo," Carol says, probably horrified at the thought.

"Now you have me worried, Jamie. Is it really that bad?"

"Yeah," he says, wandering down the hall.

"It ain't that bad, Doc. You have to at least give it a shot. And besides, if you are keeping that baby, you have to understand her culture. And well, this is it," Carol replied, shaking her head at Jamie.

"Good point. We were invited by the Thompsons. And you know how it is, you can't turn them down. No matter how hard you try."

"They are a little pushy, aren't they?"

"Sometimes. But they also like hanging out with me and the little one. What can I say? I'm that awesome."

"Well that is true. Have a good time is all I'm sayin'. My beau and I are going tomorrow. You heading out now?"

"I think so. Ms. Kendall was our last patient, right?"

"Yes, ma'am. I'm ready to close up shop and head home, myself."

"Sounds like a plan." I call out to Jamie, "You heading out soon, J?"

"Yep. I'm right behind you."

"Good week, ya'll. Thanks for all of your hard work keeping this place running and me in line. Enjoy your weekends!"

"Thanks, Doc! You too!" Carol says grabbing her purse and homemade lunch bag and heading out the back door.

Jamie follows Carol out the back and waves as he goes. "You enjoy your weekend, too, Miss Ava. See you Monday!" I wave back and then gather my own things from my office. I walk through the practice and out the front door, locking it. The comfort of this routine suddenly strikes me as odd. How quickly life can change.

***

Not surprisingly, the Thompsons magically didn't have a space for Macon, so he had to ride with me and Hope to the pig pickin' contest. Weird how that seems to happen anytime we caravan to some party or event they invite us to. In that way he does, like we are a couple, he held out his hand for the keys when he came by the house. I handed them over, feigning annoyance when in reality he is another comfortable routine I've slipped into in the last couple of months. When we aren't spending time with his parents and his siblings, he is at my house. Hope and Charlie forget I'm alive when he's in the house.

Hope, known as Hope-ster, by Macon, has him wrapped around her finger. I sometimes wonder if she knows that, even as a six-month old. There are times we see him nearly daily. Sometimes when he runs through town, he stops for a few minutes before running home to his townhouse on the far end of Front Street. I regret on those days, when he stands in my kitchen, all tall, hunky, and sweaty, that I told him I can't date right now. Oh how I regret saying that. No matter what I do, I can't escape him.

"Earth to Ava," Macon says from the driver side of my truck. I look over at him. He smiles. If my knees could go weak while sitting, they just did. "You're a million miles away."

"I know. Sorry. What did you ask?"

"I asked if you have a new court date yet. I hadn't heard an update since your last convo with the lawyer."

"Sort of. We don't have an exact date yet but he's anticipating late June. I wish it were earlier because I'd like the kids to be with me all summer. But if things go my way, at least we'll have the majority of the summer. I honestly thought Burns would budge before this. This isn't exactly what he wants to step into while he's trying to recover from his constituent's hate for him. But he's hanging on so far."

"Weird. My guess is it's the wife."

"You nailed it."

"What's her deal?"

"She's young and dumb. But she is also jealous. She got the man but she didn't count on the consequences of their actions. Burns won't be re-elected. And he can't run for President. Me on the other hand? I could run for his seat and would win. But there's no way he can. She thought he was her meal ticket to power. Now all she's got is two step kids that see through her and misbehave constantly these days, constituents that can't stand what she's done and won't re-elect her husband, and the real kicker is, she didn't even end up with a good man."

"Yeah, well, I could see how that would make one cranky. To say the least."

"You make your bed . . ." I say and then look out the passenger side window. I found myself lost in thought for the first half of our drive because something is off. It's like the world is slightly off-kilter and bad news lies ahead. I can't shake the feeling. Talking about Burns and Jenny isn't helping. But I don't blame Macon for asking, or attempting to get me talking. I should probably just tell him about this foreboding feeling hanging over me, but he'll probably tell me it's all in my head.

Highway 101 whizzes past as I sit quietly, trying to shake anxiety. From Beaufort to Ula it's a two-lane highway that winds through farmland and swampy forest. It's a gorgeous spring day. Eastern Carolina is showing off today. The sky is the deepest of blues with fat, white clouds dotting the sky. The temperature is perfect and our first warm day in weeks. The weather does not match my mood.

The closer we get to Ula, a small town on the banks of the Neuse River, the more the Loblolly pines seem to grow together, they're packed into rows so tightly - with kudzu winding its way through more than half. In the fall, cotton fields dot the highway, in between thick pine forests. We turn right off the highway on to a road that looks like it leads to nowhere. But instead of nowhere, we're going to a quaint enclave on the river that's home to a few hundred permanent residents and a few hundred seasonal residents.

After driving another fifteen minutes we arrive in the center of Ula, which is a town park on the river. There are people everywhere and parking is tight. Macon loses his parents in the hunt for a space, after following his father since we left Beaufort. After winding through several narrow residential streets, we park in front of a brick ranch. A group of people sit on the porch, with wine glasses in hand. They wave when we get out. Macon and I wave back.

I grab the stroller from the back and before I can get it completely open, Macon steps in and helps. Another sign I'm not in Kansas anymore. It never would've occurred to my ex-husband to help me with something like that. After getting a babbling and suddenly excited Hope into the stroller and storing the diaper bag, which has become my purse too as of late, we head back to the river and park. We meet up with Charlotte, Beau, Grace, Grant, and Kenly a few minutes later. "So this is a pig-picking," I say.

"You don't sound excited. This is a great eastern North Carolina tradition here - a pig pickin' rolled into a contest. I mean, it doesn't get better than this," says Beau Thompson, never one to pass up an opportunity to eat.

"I'm excited!" Kenly says. "Mmm…pork." Everyone laughs at Kenly, as per the usual. In the two months since her official Juvenile Rheumatoid Arthritis diagnosis, she has steadily improved with treatment. Her pain is nearly non-existent and it's likely that the chances of major joint damage may be reduced significantly. Like all other autoimmune or rheumatological disease, there is no cure. But advancements in treatment, when diagnosed early, reduce joint damage in impressive ways.

While there is still a sense of sadness and shock for parents, that comes from a diagnosis of an incurable condition which causes joint deformity, treatments over the years have morphed into successful management of a disease. A disease that once led to multiple surgeries and deformity for patients is sometimes kept at bay, now. I'm thankful they paid such close attention. It's possible that the RA diagnosis would have been much delayed had the family not been so certain that something was very wrong. Kenly skips ahead of us. I smile.

"What a difference a couple of months make, right?" Macon asks pointing at Kenly.

"I literally just thought that myself. She is doing great."

"That she is. Thanks to you."

The smell of barbecue, eastern NC style, overtakes me the closer we get to the park. It's not the first time I've had eastern NC pulled pork, which is a vinegar and pepper-based sauce, unlike what I grew up with. But this shindig on the river, however, is new. The mix of people here is one of the things I love most about this area. Farming communities, those who make their living from the sea, affluent retirees, natives like the Thompsons, active duty military and their families, make up this strange and beautiful place. I used to think cities like L.A. and D.C. were melting pots. I realize now that most of America has no idea how much semi-rural America reflects our greatest values. "Well if it ain't the Thompson clan!"

Macon elbows me. "That's Hattie Robertson, mayor of Ula. We pointed her out at the church - Campbell's aunt."

"Ohhhh . . . right. I'd completely forgotten about that." Hattie Robertson bridges the distance between us quickly.

"Ava Cooper, this is Mayor Hattie Robertson," Charlotte makes the introduction first. "And this little pip is Hope."

"Well it's nice to meet ya," Hattie says, reaching for my hand. "I understand you know my niece. She'll be happy to see a familiar person. She's around here somewhere, stuffing her face. And look at this little thing! She's cuter than a speckled pup in a red wagon. What's her name again?" Hattie asked.

"Her name is Hope. She certainly is precious," I say. "Thank you," as if I had something to do with it.

"Well, duty calls," Hattie says. "I have to run. But do enjoy and try to find Campbell," she says to me, embracing me heartily. "My Precious, my Bird, I know you probably don't remember, but I was at your wedding with Blaine and Campbell. I was a wedding crasher. You are more beautiful today than you were that day, my dear. I hope you'll consider the NC Robertsons part of your family, too."

"Why thank you, Miss Hattie. I appreciate the welcome and compliment. Although you may be going blind. I will keep an eye out for Campbell."

"Oh I'm not blind, child. But I will see you all later I hope," she says as she struts off, with more sass and attitude than a famous model or movie star. Except instead of designer labels this tiny human is wearing an emerald green 70s style pantsuit. It would be hideous if it weren't for the fact that it's actually in style again.

"She's a trip," Macon says.

"Clearly." He places his hand on the small of my back and we move forward into the throng of people. If it didn't smell so good, I might be amused at the thought of so many people stuffing themselves with pulled pork BBQ and nothing else. After finding our way through the crowd and standing in line for food, we found an open picnic table and with our overloaded plates, sat down. Hope fell asleep like clockwork. I don't know how she falls asleep anywhere but it probably has something to do with the noise of a NICU that became a constant lullaby during her first three months of life.

Country music - the classics and the new stuff, plays through loudspeakers throughout the downtown area. Crafters and tchotchke sellers try to attract customers with their wares. It's quite the scene. My plate is piled high with hush puppies, baked beans and coleslaw piled up on top of the pulled pork BBQ. I'm not going to lie, my inner fat girl is pretty excited. Mid-bite, as I am about to shovel baked beans in my mouth, I look up to see a group of five people staring me down. And I do mean staring. I quickly run through patients I've seen wondering if anyone in the group has been through the office recently.

Occasionally, I deal with patients seeking pain meds. Opiate abuse is a problem everywhere, but sometimes seems worse here. By the looks of the group, I'd say there's at least one of them doing meth, judging by the sores on her face alone. There's one older woman in the center of the group. The ages of the other four are nearly impossible to discern. The older woman is Caucasian and probably in her 50's, dressed much better than the other four. The four younger people are wearing disheveled clothing that has seen better days.

The older woman maintains her stare while the others talk at her. She shushes them and walks toward us. It's then that I know. I instantly connect the African-American male that stands next to the older woman, to the photo I've seen of Hope's father. It's clear now that these people are related to my baby. I get up suddenly and pick up a sleeping Hope from the stroller.

"You can take that baby out of the stroller now but it ain't gonna stop us from getting her back," the older woman says. "That's my great grand baby and I don't intend to lose her," she says. "This here," she says, pointing to the young African-American man, "is her Uncle Christopher. Her daddy is Adam" she says pointing to Hope, "and this is his brother. We don't intend to let strangers raise her. The state can try but it won't win. This family does not give up easily," she says. So far she's talked the whole time and I've had no opportunity to respond. Not that I would know how to if I could. Before I have to think about what to do next, Macon stands up. He's closest to them. He towers over all of them.

"This isn't the time or place," he says, commandingly. "No one at this table makes decisions about who has custody of Hope. If you believe Hope should be living with you, then you should handle this matter through the county and courts. There is not a single good thing that can come from this conversation continuing. Once more, there is a no-contact order, right Ava?" he asks me.

"Yes," I say. "Please discuss this matter directly with the social worker assigned to this case. It's not appropriate to approach us in this setting."

"What's not appropriate is a child being taken from her family. But we'll leave you be. Just be forewarned, this baby ain't yours and you will not raise her," she says, so angry her face turns red. Without further confrontation, they all turn and walk away. Christopher, Hope's uncle, turns and looks back. We make eye contact and for the briefest moment I see regret.

Macon turns to face me. I realize now that I'm shaking and probably have been the whole time. He takes me in his arms, Hope between us. "It'll be okay," he says quietly. "There's not a chance they'll be able to get Hope back."

"That's right. It won't happen. I didn't realize Hope was related to *that* Brown family. The county won't do that to this sweet babe. They won't. Besides, I thought her parent's rights were terminated," Beau says.

I pull away from Macon and turn around searching for the Browns – who have disappeared into the crowd. "That's not how this works. After termination, there is a ninety-day waiting period. That's why even though you're on the course to adoption you could be stopped suddenly in your tracks. It's possible they didn't understand the process. Or her family hadn't made up their mind until now, or who knows. All I know is they can petition the court for custody. Hope is my girl. In my heart, I'm her mom. But she still technically is in the custody of the county. If they find a relative and can prove that this relative is fit, Hope will be given to a family member."

"That can't be. Plus, we're talking about the Browns. I know you don't know what that means, Ava, but we do," Charlotte says. "I don't think you have a thing to worry about. Not a thing. Just put this right out of your mind and hold onto hope - literally and figuratively."

I sit down with Hope in my arms and kiss the top of her head. Of course I knew that Hope was at least half African-American but until this very moment, I didn't think twice about the potential that maybe I'm not prepared to raise a child with a different ethnic background than me. Somehow, seeing her Uncle connected me in a way, I hadn't before, even after seeing her father's photo, to this truth.

The anxiety that slowly bubbled to the surface the closer we got to Ula, is now a full-blown panic. Thoughts race through my mind. Maybe I don't have a right to raise this child. Maybe I shouldn't have thought I could do this. What makes me think the court will let me adopt a child I have no connection to? The fears tumble around like rocks in my brain, bumping up against the pain of recent years. Macon touches my elbow as he sits down beside me.

"Stop thinking about it. I know you're analyzing this but it's not going to do any good right now. You can call the social worker on Monday and we'll figure out what to do from there." I note the "we'll" and then shake my head in agreement, as if I can quickly put this mess from my head. I know full well, I'll spend the next forty-eight hours in fear and panic.

Needless to say, I wanted to go home as soon I finished my plate of food. We said our goodbyes to Macon's family and headed back to my truck. As we make our way through the crowd, I see Campbell Robertson. She notices me immediately and waves, "Ava!" she says, quickly heading in our direction, with a plate full of food and a blond-haired little boy in tow. "It's so awesome to see you! You too, Macon. I haven't seen you since before your last deployment." She says as she reaches us.

"It's great to see you. So crazy that you live here. What a weird coincidence. How long have you been here?" I ask her oblivious to what happened to her after her father passed away.

"I moved here a few years ago now. I came down after Daddy's funeral to stay with Aunt Hattie. I fell in love with this place. Never mind the fact that I met my husband here."

"Oh wow. I didn't know. I have been in my own world. I hadn't heard you'd gotten married. Where is he? Do I get to meet him?" I ask, suddenly wanting more time with Campbell to hear the whole story.

"His name is Jack. Maybe we can catch up sometime in the next couple of weeks. I would love to have you over to our house. We live here in Ula - though we're a little out in the country. What do you say to lunch? Maybe next weekend? "

"That sounds perfect. Let me give you my card, I say, as I scribble my cell phone number on it. "Call the office or text me and we can figure something out. I would love to catch up."

"Perfect," she says, hugging me tightly, expertly holding on to her plate full of food. "See you soon!" We wave our goodbyes and Macon and I resume our trek back to the truck. Unexpectedly, seeing Campbell lifted my spirits in the same way seeing Jules did. Maybe because both are reminders of the good parts of my old life. I get Hope settled in the truck when we finally reach it and Macon puts the stroller in the back. These simple moments have built up over recent months. I had begun to believe that maybe I'd finally turned the corner.

But the panic floods me again when one of the girls, meth head girl, steps out in front of the truck without looking, after Macon pulls out on to the street. Luckily he is at a snail's pace with all the people around. She laughs. Laughs. She stands still in the middle of the street. Macon, normally a patient man, has become increasingly protective of the two of us. He clenches his jaw and takes a deep breath. I reach out and touch his arm, hoping maybe to steady what I recognized, from our first meeting, as white-hot anger quickly boiling to the surface. His hands grip the steering wheel tighter. We were in a stand-off with a woman, likely high as a kite that held a connection to the sweet baby in my back seat. Innocent and oblivious, Hope smacked the side of her car seat with her toy giraffe, like a drum beat, as if nothing in the world could be wrong. The irony of her innocence, compared to the angry and lost individual in front of me, reminded me of how weird life can be.

Macon laid on the horn. The girl jumped, practically out of her skin, as if she couldn't possibly have anticipated that standing in the middle of the street might not be the wisest idea. It struck me that she may have not even really been conscious of what she was doing. After flipping Macon off, she sauntered lazily across the rest of the street. "Idiot!" he said, the angriest I'd seen him yet.

"I have a bad feeling about this," I said, the panic taking root again.

"The crazier they are, the better it is for you. But man, that pissed me off. And by the way, let them come anywhere near my girls and they'll see how that works out for them." I note the "*my*," and in spite of the fear, I have never been more thankful for Thompson clan meddling.

When we got back to Beaufort and my house, Macon unhooked a sleeping Hope from the car seat and pointed upstairs. He had no intention of leaving anytime soon. He walked ahead, leaving me to grab the diaper bag and the few toys I'd given Hope for the ride home. I walked through the back gate as he stepped into the Carolina room off the back of the house, as if he lived here. Sometimes it felt like he did. I walked across the aged brick that lined the patio between the guest and main house.

Ellie, probably napping, would be furious when she heard about what happened today. While Macon took a protective stance that was sweet, nobody topped Miss Ellie in that department. I stood for a moment in the midst of my backyard. Surrounded by the thick overgrowth of so many live oaks, it could be hard to believe Front Street, with its tourists and looky-loos, is steps away. I took a deep breath and soaked in what was left of the sun that barely poked through the trees at this hour of the day. Macon had probably put the baby in her crib by now. I looked at my watch. She'd sleep for at least an hour and a half - maybe more.

I walked through the Carolina Room into my kitchen. Macon had already uncorked my favorite Pinot Noir. The man didn't waste a minute. He smiled when I walked in. I couldn't help but smile back. When did this happen? When did he become part of the routine that fit the way my favorite boots fit - lived in and comfortable?

He takes a beer from the refrigerator. I don't drink beer. I buy it for him. He takes a drink and then pours me a glass of wine. He steps toward me, his eyes never leaving mine and hands it to me. He's as close as he's been in a while, close enough to kiss me. He raises his beer bottle. "Cheers," he says meeting my wine glass.

With a clink, I reply, "Cheers. Now let's go sit in the sun room," suddenly longing to be away from the watchful eyes of those that pass by my home. I'm convinced that they wonder about who lives here and what possesses a person to buy such a large home. The answer is *I don't know*, by the way. I don't know why I bought such a large home. Except maybe an inexplicable longing to fill it with people who call me mom.

"Eh. I'm thinking the front porch. The weather is too nice to be inside. Come on," he says, with puppy dog eyes. It's impossible to resist his pleading.

"Okay. Fine. Whatever." He laughs and carries the wine bottle with him. Macon stops in my living room and turns on the sound system. As I step out onto the porch, he adds his phone to the docking station, setting it to play whatever playlist he's in the mood for at the moment. I never know what I'll get with him. Sometimes it's country and classic rock and then out of nowhere it's Vivaldi and Chopin.

I wait for the sound system to turn on. Ah, the Eagles. It's a classic rock afternoon. I sit at the far end of the porch, away from my normal spot that is hidden behind a massive azalea bush. Macon sits in the chair across from me.

He sets the bottle of wine down on the table and starts singing to "Boys of Summer." He does this sometimes. Usually when he's trying to get me to laugh. "Would you stop that?"

"What?" He says as he resumes singing.

"That!"

"You mean singing? Is that what you mean?" He says, immediately singing louder.

I roll my eyes and then lean back further, closing my eyes. The singing stops. He quickly loses interest when he knows I'm not annoyed. *Men.* With a warm breeze blowing in off of the water, and the sun still shining on us, I wonder if I can stay awake. Before I can fall asleep, the look of regret on Hope's Uncle's face, crosses my mind. The tears come fast and furious, before I can stop or hide them. Macon doesn't immediately notice but it doesn't take long. "What's wrong, Sweetness?"

I shake my head. I'm not sure if I'm trying to stop crying or answering Macon. Who knows anymore? "I don't know. I knew something bad was coming. I knew -" I get up and face the street, away from Macon. It wouldn't have been the first time he's seen me cry, but my weakness still embarrasses me. "I'm just tired. And I'm tired of the crazy."

"I know. But there's no sense worrying about it now. There's a fairly good chance that the lovely Mrs. Brown is bluffing. For all you know, DSS has already made a recommendation that additional family members not have custody. In a county like this there's no way that they're not aware of the rest of Hope's blood relatives. I'm sure there's an explanation. I think they were trying to intimidate you." Somehow, Macon's reasoning and logic calms me enough that the tears stop, at least for a moment. He stands up and walks across the porch. He's so close his arm brushes mine. "Hey look at me," he says quietly. I turn to face him. "It's going to work out. I know it will."

"I'm not sure I have your confidence. I knew something -"

"Don't even go there. I know the road you're walking down and I'm not going to let you. It's not going to do you any good to focus on all of that."

"I know but I don't have the strength right now. All I can think about is that sleeping baby upstairs. The first time I held her I knew. She is my baby. I didn't give birth to her and clearly I don't have a tie to her genetically but she is my daughter as much as Katie. Or William or Harper. There's no difference in the love I have for any of them. There's been so much loss in my life. I just don't have the strength to hope."

"I do. Remember I've been there. So I'll hope for you," he says, brushing a curl away from my eyes. In the quiet of the afternoon, with only a slight rustling of the Azalea bushes and oak trees, I've lost another battle, to keep Macon at arm's length. He's worked hard at finding his way in. Why fight it? Looking up into his eyes, I make an instant conscious decision to follow his lead for a while. What can it hurt? He smiles and my heart takes a step closer to trust. Before I know what's happening, Macon leans down and kisses me. A kiss is like a dance. And I'm a picky dance instructor. Highly critical. Difficult to please - able to teach but typically unwilling to do so. Macon doesn't need a teacher.

~ TWELVE ~

Three weeks ago, I decided to kick a couple of hornet's nests. If it hadn't been so scary, it would have been a hell of a lot of fun. My lawyer, at my request, filed for full custody of the kids. We filed for full custody, as in Burns gets holidays and school breaks, not the other way around. Instantly furious, he called me cursing and behaving ridiculously. It stopped when I told him I would use every word he had just said, in court. Not surprisingly, his tone changed. I hung up the phone with my confidence bolstered ever so slightly.

Hope's case, however, would not be as clear. The social worker had reached out to members of the Brown family and no one stepped forward to take custody of Hope. In fact, DSS had tried on more than one occasion. However, now that they had, and they were within the ninety-day window, they had to pursue it as a possibility. For the last couple of weeks, Hope has had weekly visits with Mrs. Brown.

It is the worst day of my week. The judge ordered supervised visits so at the very least I have the confidence that there isn't too much harm coming from her time away from me. But I'm that much more confident my girl belongs with me. If she lives with the Browns, she will end up in the system for the rest of her life, I am certain. All told, 90% of the children on both sides of her family have at some point or other. Those are terrible numbers. Mrs. Brown herself was investigated years earlier for child neglect. The case had been dismissed because of a legal technicality.

Her granddaughter, Hope's birth mother, had been placed in foster care as a result of the investigation. She was returned to her grandmother after the case was dismissed, only to run away, quit school, and get pregnant at thirteen for the first time. She had three more children after that pregnancy, including Hope. It's amazing what you can learn in this town without people even knowing that you're fishing.

On one hand, that made it seem more likely that reason would be on our side. But the courts here lean toward birth families even when it would not always be in the child's best interest. Why? It's not clear to me, even still, after hearing it said many times. Hope's GAL is firmly in my camp and has spent far more time with the Browns than I have. That's something, right? But a nagging fear sits like a rock in my stomach. I can't eat. I spend hours worrying that I'll win one fight and lose the other.

***

After struggling to find a good date to meet up with Campbell, we finally settled on a Saturday afternoon BBQ. Macon and I drove out to Ula to the home that Blaine Robertson had built years before. As a Senator from Virginia himself, sharing the same party and ideals, we spent a great deal of time with Blaine and his daughter Campbell, socially and personally. When Blaine passed away and our life fell apart, I let the tie between Campbell and me slip away. Macon knows Campbell's husband through their Marine Corps circles.

The way lives can be tied together in ways that one never expects, amazes me. To think that a tie I had to Campbell, through my husband and her father, would later tie me to Macon and the Thompsons an entire state away, blows my mind. We enjoyed a quiet BBQ on their expansive back deck, overlooking the Neuse at one of its widest points. The afternoon, warm with slightly rising humidity could not have been more perfect.

After general talk and laughing over old stories about all four of us, Macon, Jack, and Campbell's stepson, Ian headed out for a hike along the river. Campbell and I cleared the lunch mess and then sat, with margaritas in hand, on the back deck. With our feet on the railing and our eyes locked on the river, we talked about light topics until Hope cried out in the middle of a dream. She quickly settled back to sleep without so much of a word from me. But that opened the door for more serious topics.

"So where do things stand with custody of Hope?" Campbell asked.

"We go to court on Monday morning. I have her social worker, the Guardian Ad Litem, and of course my lawyer, behind me. No one wants to see Hope end up with her biological family, based on their history. But it's hard to know how the judge will look at this case. Hope's great grandmother doesn't appear to have a drug problem herself. While all of her kids have been in and out of jail, she has basically remained above the fray all of these years."

"But don't you think the history of instability with her kids, and their kids, is enough to ensure you are able to adopt Hope?"

"You would think. But there is a precedent lately for the courts to rule favorably for the bio family. Even when it seems unlikely. I really don't know what to believe."

"How are you doing with all of this?" Campbell asks.

"I'm dreading Monday. I have never been more confident about getting custody of Harper and William. Things have taken a turn there and at the very least, I think we'll share equal custody. So obviously, I'm happier than I've been in a few years, about that. With the kids acting up, Jenny isn't holding on as tightly. Burns is more removed now from all of the anger between us which means he's not holding on out of spite, either. With the threat of losing the kids entirely, his stance has softened. As much as he can soften. I mean, I don't have to explain to you, you know how he is."

"I do. I still can't believe any of that happened."

"Me either," I say.

"I sense there's a *but*."

"Oh yeah. It's a big one too. Since the day we ran into Hope's family I've had a rock in the pit of my stomach. I think I'm going to lose this sweet thing," I say, kissing the top of her head, as she sleeps in my arms. "Making the decision to bring her into my home was the biggest leap of faith I could have made after all of this pain. And now? Now I may be giving up another child? Will I ever catch a break? I mean it's not even about me. I want my sweet girl to have a chance. I fear what will happen to her. I fear her future will look like all the others in her family. Maybe I'm cursed?"

"I highly doubt that. But we do live in a pretty messed up world. When people have the free will to choose their path, it's going to mean hurt and loss sometimes. And of course there are the terrible realities like Katie's death, which have no explanation."

"I'm glad you don't think that is somehow God's will. I still cannot handle the insinuation that God somehow ordained that all of this happen."

"I absolutely don't believe that. After what I learned about my own family after moving here, I definitely can't look at life like that."

"What do you mean?" I ask, again reminded how far I let some relationships slip from my life.

"It's a long story. One I want to tell you. But if we go down that road, it will take a while. Maybe we can get together sometime soon and talk? The bottom line is that I too thought I'd lost everything, except my Aunt Hattie, when my dad died. Things got a little worse when I got down here. Those stories are for another time. That said, what I gained, what I have now, is a beautiful gift. I have a family restored to me. I have a family I didn't know existed, I get to be a wife to the greatest man I know, and a mom to the smartest kid I know. The pain of loss is real. But there is restoration and beauty beyond the pain. It's amazing what can be built from a pile of rubble."

"Thanks. That's encouraging. I will try to hang onto that over the next couple of days."

"I will be praying the Judge makes the right call. He would be crazy to let Hope go back to that environment. Crazy. Between Havelock and Beaufort, we all know around here where the drugs come from and the Browns are right in the middle of that."

"If only logic and common sense ruled, and bad things didn't happen to good people," I say, facing the choppy Neuse as the sun sets lower in the sky. I've discovered in recent years that common sense and logic are often missing from much of life.

***

The day of Hope's hearing came earlier than I planned. Hope had been up half the night with a fever. By 4:00 AM, the fever had broken and I didn't have to call the hospital. I tried to go back to sleep but tossed and turned. I got up at 6:00 and was ready to leave the house by 7:00. With the hearing at 9:00, those two hours were torture. I arrived at the courthouse, just a couple of blocks from home, to a crowd of Thompsons. They wouldn't be able to come in with me. But I appreciated the sentiment. "You know ya'll can't come in, right? They're pretty picky about that."

"That's okay. We'll be here when it's over. We intend to wait," Beau said.

"And I am coming with you," Macon said, his arm around my waist. "There's no way you or anyone else is stopping me."

"Got it, Boss," not feeling the least bit like arguing with him. The thought of his steadying arm is comforting in a way I would not have imagined just a few months ago.

"Everything is going to be fine. There's no way the judge will let Miss Hope leave your care. There's no way," Charlotte says.

"I know the man. I agree," Beau adds.

"I wish I had your confidence. These things aren't black and white. There are a lot of reasons judges side with blood relatives over foster or adoptive parents, even if the children are better off." I know this better than anyone. The Thompsons have been through their fair share of pain. But the one thing they don't have to worry about is being on the wrong side of power and position. In the ways that count, I'm an unknown entity to the court. That thought alone sends a shiver down my spine and I shake a little.

"You okay?" Macon leans in and whispers quietly, near my ear.

"Maybe. Or not. I don't know." I don't make sense because I don't know.

He kisses the side of my head, his face buried in my hair. Maybe we can just stand here like this and not face the rest of the day. When my lawyer arrives a few minutes later, I'm relieved to see him in the same way I'm tired of seeing him. Soon we'll be tackling custody of Harper and William. How did I get myself into this mess? "Good morning, All," he says soberly when he reaches us. "You ready to go in?"

"As ready as I'll ever be."

***

"Where is the child?" The judge asks in the midst of the hearing.

"Your Honor, if I may?" The Judge motions for Hope's GAL to stand.

"Hope is with a nanny. She has had full background checks and more than twenty years of experience as a nanny, including raising her own children, whom are all adults now. I felt it was best for Hope to maintain her normal daily routine."

"Thank you. Now, let's discuss the matter at hand . . ."

***

After a brief recess, we received word that the Judge would return with his decision at 10:30. Macon sits next to me, his arm around my shoulders. The judge, already seated, begins by thanking all parties present for passionately advocating on Hope's behalf. Something about that statement scares me. A flashback of a fall afternoon comes quickly to mind in that instant. A different man had his arm around me as we buried our daughter. Then, I had no idea what would meet me beyond the pain of that moment – least of all what my husband would do.

Now, I'm already resigned to Hope's fate. She will be raised by Mrs. Anna Brown and I will never see her again unless by accident. Her fate will be what her mother's was and what her sibling's fate will be. I know the Judge will not side with the county or state. But this time, the man next to me is focused on me, rather than the press that attended our daughter's funeral. Macon, unlike Burns, never takes his eyes off of me. I close my eyes and he squeezes my shoulder. I look into his eyes and I know, he knows what I'm already certain of. Hope will go home with Anna Brown sometime today or tomorrow.

"Dr. Cooper, you have a done a phenomenal job caring for Hope in recent months. You have nursed her to better health. She has gained weight and according to her medical team's testimony, is reaching developmental milestones ahead of schedule. She is no longer in the same medically fragile state she had been, though we know risks still exist, particularly with another surgery ahead. From all accounts, you have loved her as your own and between you and Miss Eleanor, she has thrived."

I wait for it, knowing more is coming. "However, the goal of the Department of Social Services is to ensure that a child is reunited with their parents. If parents are not fit to raise their children, the next best goal is to ensure that the child is raised by his or her kin." The tears begin to flow. There's no point holding back the ache. "Mrs. Brown is a long-time resident of this community and is the maternal great-grandmother of Hope Ann Brown. It is this court's opinion that Hope Brown will be best served by being in the care of her maternal great-grandmother. DSS is hereby ordered to ensure the safe transfer of custody of Hope Brown by 6:00 PM today."

The tears silently fall down my face. Macon wipes a tear from his own eye with his free hand. He squeezes me a little tighter. He leans in and kisses the side of my head. "I won't say it will be okay. I know it will not be okay for a while. But I love you," he says. I cry a little harder and he kisses me again. While I claw desperately to regain some composure the judge concludes the hearing and leaves the courtroom, as if he just decided where to get a burger tonight – without emotion and seemingly nonchalantly.

I look up to see Mrs. Brown embracing one of her adult children. She looks to me, on the opposite side of the courtroom, in the third row. Hope's medical team, the GAL, social workers, and a few additional witnesses take up the first two rows. No one charged with caring for Hope since the day she was born, wanted this. Mrs. Brown smirks and doesn't divert her eyes, staring me down. Instead, I divert mine. Let her think she has the power. It only proves this has never been about the welfare of that firecracker of a girl I've been raising the last few months.

My lawyer, on the other side of me, puts his hand on mine and says quietly, "Wait until they leave the courtroom." And then when I shake my head in agreement, he says, "This is not over. We may not have much of a legal fight but this is not the end of this story."

"I wish I could say I had any hope that the end of this story results in what is best for my sweet girl."

***

The hours between 10:30 AM and 6:00 PM passed far too quickly. My house, full of people, in the form of my staff, Ellie, and the Thompsons, did nothing to distract me from the heartbreak. How could I have let hope in? My girl's name had long ago stopped being ironic to me. How did I not prepare myself for this? I should have known.

I've kept her routine as close to normal as possible, except for one difference. Her afternoon nap, usually in her crib, is next to me. She sleeps soundly in my bed, not having any clue, in the way a child trusts simply and easily, that the world she knows is about to change drastically. Hope stirs fitfully. I reach out for her hand and stroke it gently, remembering how wonderful it has been to watch her tiny frame plump up – the slightest little dimples now indent her fingers. She curls her fingers around one of mine and settles back into a peaceful sleep.

My bedroom door opens quietly and slowly. Macon peeks around the corner of the door, and mouths, "Can I come in?" I shake my head yes. He stands next to my bed, closest to Hope and smiles at me. It's not a happy smile. Not really. His love for me is plain as day in his eyes and every line in his face. His smile is there because he loves me. Me. He loves me. But I also see grief. He knows in ways I'll never have to explain, how deeply I ache.

He takes off his shoes and walks around to the other side of the bed. Before I can resist or protest, he climbs onto the bed and lays down, next to me, wrapping his arm around me as I lay on my side. The tears, as they've done on and off all day, flow again. He pulls me closer, spooning me. To stifle the sobs that I know are coming, I focus on his breathing and the beat of his heart. As he breathes in, I breathe in. I close my eyes and pray the only words I have left, "Protect my baby girl."

Autumn 2013

"Mrs. Cooper? Did you want a pink rose spray for the casket? Or were you thinking of going with white?" I hear Connie Hamner. Loud and clear. But the answer is stuck somewhere between my heart and my voice box. Connie has asked the question twice. I still haven't found the words. "Would it be easier to wait until the Senator arrives to make these decisions?"

"My husband won't be coming. Pink roses," I say. The words slip off my tongue sounding foreign and unfamiliar. Since Katie died, I've been dizzy, disoriented, and perpetually nauseous. Words escape me.

"I know this is difficult. Would you like me to call someone to be here with you?" Connie's voice is draped with compassion. Her Virginia drawl makes a person want to climb into her lap and sleep like they would a hammock in the backyard. It's sweet like the jasmine that blooms in our yard. "I can call Miss Ellie. Would you like me to call her?" Connie continues.

"No. She's at the house with Harper and William. I want the pink rose spray and a wreath of white and pink roses." The tears flow down my face now, carrying my mascara with the tears. I look up at Connie whose lack of professional distance in this case, is etched all over her face. My husband, Burns Cooper, is this town's most famous resident. Our dying baby became its most cared for citizen.

"Mrs. Cooper . . . I"

"Ava. Please don't call me Mrs. Cooper."

"I'm -," Connie pauses and looks down at the paperwork on her clipboard. "I'll be right back." She walks away. A trail of her perfume wafts up after she's passed. Lilacs. Connie pulls her wool sweater tighter, her arms now cradling herself like she needs a hug. She slips through the door to the back office but first turns and looks back at Ava. A slight, contrived smile stretches the corners of her mouth. Classical music plays quietly, just barely audible above the heater running. The air blowing from the vent, on this cold autumn afternoon, stirs the pages on the clipboard she's left behind. They flutter up, dancing in the invisible breeze that moves them.

I close her eyes. Connie calls out from the hallway. "Can I get you something to drink? Coffee? Tea?"

"Yes, coffee please, black."

"Sure thing. I'll be back in just a minute," she says.

"She's stalling," I say out loud. I walk across the room, staring at the family photographs that line the wall. The Hamner family has been in the funeral business since Thomas Jefferson was running around the county in short pants. This wall of memories is like a who's who of polite, southern Virginia society. Speaking again to the wind, as all of my words belong to the wind these days, "I don't know how they do this."

Connie reappears at the end of the hallway, heading toward me with a tray, a carafe, and two china cups. "I brought some scones. I just made them this morning. Will you have one? I'd be willing to bet you haven't had anything to eat today." She breezes past me, her lilac perfume mixing with the scent of the coffee. Connie sits down in a leather wingback chair and reaches for a small plate, placing a scone on it and then setting it on the side table between us. I take the hint and sit down, accepting a coffee cup with the Hamner logo on it. "I hope you like the scones. It's my Grand's recipe."

"Thank you." The coffee, earthy and bitter, provides a brief moment of comfort.

Before the conversation resumes, the bell on the front door jingles as the door opens. The old wood floor creaks, as heavy footsteps lumber across them. Before we have to guess, a familiar voice says, "Connie, good to see you this morning."

"Good to see you too. Is Maybelle here with you?"

"She is. She stopped on the front porch to chat with the dog. She'll be in shortly."

"How are you?" Pastor Jim asks. I stand to accept the hug for which I am about to receive. Pastor, a bear of a man exceeded in girth only by his house, has a good soul, as good of a soul as his wife's is questionable.

"I've been better," I say. As I do, Maybelle Lynch breezes through the door. His eyes look like a doe's and fill with tears. It's like an apology for bringing his wife.

"Sweetie Pie, let me give you a hug," Maybelle says, her voice dripping with sugar. She gives me a Maybelle-style pat, complete with air kisses, as if she's a Hollywood starlet. "My heart is just aching for you and the Senator, and the children of course. When Connie called to tell us you could use some support here, well, there's no way we wouldn't race right over here to be right by your side."

"Well, my thanks to Connie then," I say, with the graciousness expected of me. I look over at Connie. She mouths, *I'm sorry,* from behind Maybelle. The pastor, known for his sweet spirit and general love of every living thing on earth is the near opposite of his social climbing, gossip-loving wife, whose likely motive for stopping on the front porch was to be seen by the national and local media there. There's a not a soul in three counties who understands this match.

Pastor Jim sits on the couch, Maybelle follows, looking positively excited to help plan a baby's funeral. Before Maybelle can take over, the pastor says, "Connie mentioned a bit ago that you were here and I figured we could come and meet up with you here to talk about the funeral. I know this is hard. So I want to make this as easy on you as possible. Burns has mentioned a few things he would like to happen during the service but was clear that everything else should be to your specifications," Jim states matter of fact like we're picking out cabinets or bathroom fixtures.

"What did Burns ask for?" I ask, unconcerned how it appears. Had my husband been here I would have paid dearly for a comment like that. He always wanted it to appear as though they were on the same page, at all times. We rarely were these days. But God forbid anyone should notice even the slightest hint of that.

"He said that he planned on speaking briefly and that he wanted your minister from McLean Episcopal to officiate," said Pastor.

"Oh. That. Yes, he did tell me about that." Burns Cooper had not told his me that. In fact, they'd barely spoken for weeks. But ever the dutiful wife, I think I made a fairly convincing recovery.

"We can tie up all the details this morning and I'll pass along the information to Father Charles so you don't have to worry about that. We can just focus on the important stuff and then you won't have to think about another thing," he says, reaching over, patting my knee, like I'm six.

"Thank you. I appreciate that. I sit back further in my chair and grip both arms, as Maybelle, Connie and Pastor Jim talk about my daughter's funeral service as they might the church's Easter Cantata.

***

In the late afternoon sun, Yellow Birch and Dogwood trees shimmer in the light. The golden glow of a Virginia afternoon, in the midst fall, is a sight one should never grow accustomed to witnessing or feeling. If it weren't for the fact that my baby's funeral has begun, the day might even be beautiful. A slight breeze jingles the leaves of the trees. The world looks exactly like a fall day south of the Mason Dixon line should look like: spun gold stretched over the rolling hills of the Virginia countryside. It's all I can think about – how gloriously beautiful this nightmare looks.

Burns has been in control all day. He has guided me through the day with ease and precision. There's not been a moment when I've had to think about how to act or what to say. It's like we're at a cocktail party in Georgetown. The irony is not lost on me, now that all eyes, including his staff, and handpicked reporters are watching, he takes a protective stance. When all eyes, except those who are closest, are on us, and when I need it most, he is nowhere to be seen.

The hole in the ground awaiting the tiny teakwood casket is covered by fake green grass meant to disguise the gaping black. The clumpy mounds of musky dirt and green grass, off to the side of the gathering, are telling the real story. My Katie Cooper's tiny casket sits atop the artificial turf that's meant to hide its eventual fate. Burns his hand, manicured and soft, is on mine.

A shiver races through me, he squeezes my hand tighter as tears finally escape and begin flowing. He puts his arm around my shoulder, pulling me closer like he's folding me into himself. My head rests on his chest, my body turned now, away from the casket and priest. Father Charles' voice, soft like cotton, reads the final verse of the 23rd Psalm, "Surely goodness and mercy shall follow me all the days of my life: and I will dwell in the house of the LORD forever."

***

Present Day

After Hope's nap, we stood or sat in the kitchen and family room, waiting. Beau and Grant were grilling the steak that Charlotte and Ellie had bought earlier. The sides and desserts prepared, waited. They made a feast fit for a King. Other than the scent of the grill in the backyard, the huge amount of food reminds me of a funeral. It reminds me of the food that filled my kitchen, family room, and our formal dining room in Ridgemont after Katie's burial. I don't want to draw parallels between that day and this one, but I fear for Hope's future. It might as well be a death.

As I fell asleep between Macon and Hope earlier, I remembered that day. The similarities between the two days are almost too much. Knowing Hope's mother's fate alone is enough to fear. It's not about money or status. Lord knows that hasn't stopped me from deep, soul-aching pain. It's something else entirely. I ache when I think about her future. I ache.

At exactly 6:00 PM, the doorbell rings. It's the worst thing I've heard in ages. I now hate that doorbell. I kiss the top of Hope's head and walk to the front door. Macon and Ellie follow, gathering up her bags, which have been packed with as much clothing and her favorite toys as possible, notes about her routine and medication schedule. They follow me out the front door. The social worker says, "I'm so sorry. We all are." I'm surprised by this but hold onto it because it's the only thing I have to prove that at least someone out there sees the injustice of this.

"We'll take her things to the van," Macon and El head down the steps.

"Can I carry her to the car?" I ask.

"Yes, of course."

We follow Macon and Ellie. Hope says, out of nowhere, "Ma - ma?"

I say, "Yes, baby," through tears that have begun to fall. "I love you, Hope-baby." I kiss her on the cheek and then on the top of her head, again. We are at the van now and I know it's time to let go. I can't drag this out any longer. "Mama loves you, Hope," I say as I hand her to Ellie. I turn and walk away. I can't watch.

Macon says his goodbye to Hope. I hear him say, "Bye sweet girl." And within moments, he's at my side, taking my hand in his. When we reach my porch, I look back as the van door closes. Macon puts his arm around my waist. I can't decide in that moment whether I want to watch them drive away or not.

Macon, reading my mind like always, says, "Why don't we go inside?" I shake my head, yes and let him lead me by the hand, inside. After Ellie follows, he closes the door before the van drives away. Expecting everyone to be where we left them - in the kitchen and family room, my new extended family has gathered in the foyer. The tears spill down my cheeks. They have become family, though I feared letting them in.

After a few hugs, I say, "I'm going to go lay down. Please stay everyone. I'll be down soon."

Macon, never far from me, leans down and kisses my head. "Do you want company or do you need to be alone?"

"I think I need to be alone for a little bit."

"Okay, Sweetness," he says, as I head upstairs.

***

After an hour of crying, I decide that I've had enough. I get up and splash my face with water. When I get downstairs, I see through the kitchen to the backyard, that everyone is still here sitting on the deck, including Jamie and Carol. But now Carol's husband has arrived. On my way out, I stop and pour myself a glass of the open bottle of Pinot Noir. When I get outside, Ellie hugs me tightly. "Ready to eat?" she asks.

"Yes. I'm starving."

"Well you came to the right place because we have food and more food. Have a seat," Charlotte says, pointing to one of my Adirondack chairs. "I will get you a plate."

I sit down with my wine glass and the conversation that they were in the midst of when I walked out, resumes. The guys are talking basketball, of which I know nothing about. Charlotte returns with a plate full of food. Way too much food. "Thank you," I say, taking the plate from her. She hands me silverware and then takes a seat next to me.

"You're welcome, Sugar. You are welcome." I wolf down my food while the conversation continues around me. Like he usually does, Macon has turned on music. It quietly plays in the background. Tonight it's country.

Though I wish it didn't feel this way, it's like a death in the family. I have lost another child. But the difference between losing Katie and losing Hope is what is left behind. On the night I lost Katie, I sat alone on the back deck of my home. Tonight, except for Ellie, I'm surrounded by people I didn't know a year ago. Jamie and Macon are now arguing about something sports related. I stop eating and watch Macon for a moment. He has my heart. He has for a while. I'm just better able to admit it now. I smile. He's ridiculous sometimes, especially when trying to win an argument. He looks over at me and catches me smiling. He smiles, too. My heart. He is my heart. He gets up and cross the deck. He leans down and kisses me.

"I love you," he says.

"I love you, too. I don't know what I would do without you."

"Ditto," he says.

~ THIRTEEN ~

Two months later

Since Hope left, the Thompsons have rarely let me have a moment to myself. Though there are moments I feign irritation, the truth is, I'm grateful for their constant presence in my life. Macon had to go to a work related conference a week after Hope left and they filled my time as often as they could. I still have trouble computing that this is my life now. Where once I felt alone, the most alone one could possibly feel, I now have a family.

The emptiness is there. It's a gaping wound. Hope had been quite literally attached to me for months. There is an actual physical emptiness. It's like what I imagine a phantom limb feels like after an amputation. She's there, wrapped up next to my heart, like she had been while she lived with me. But she's not there. I feel her presence so absolutely, that I could reach out and touch her. People who haven't faced much loss in their lives don't understand that the difference in my heart between Katie's death and losing Hope is, well . . . there is no difference.

In the middle of my introspection, the phone rings. Grace called in the big guns. Kenly. It's impossible for me to say no to that child. When she asked me to come to church to hear her sing for children's Sunday or some such thing, I couldn't say no. So here I sit with every other Thompson on earth. Grace is on one side of me. Charlotte is on the other. Macon is sitting two down from me, next to his father and Grant. Every so often, as we wait for church to start, I hear pieces of their conversation or Macon's laugh above the others. I listen and nod as Grace and Charlotte chatter about who knows what. You'd never know that Grace wasn't born right into this family. She's as much a part of it as Beau and Charlotte's own children are. Frankly, I'm beginning to feel like I am, too. This family loves well.

***

The Thompson clan and I have taken over the top floor balcony of the Dock Side restaurant on the waterfront. Somehow we managed to beat the rest of the after church crowd for this prime piece of waterfront real estate for Sunday lunch. I'm picking at my food, while they talk, often all at once, about the most random stuff. They always find ways to entertain themselves. In my mind, I'm still stuck in the third pew from the front, in a white clapboard church, in the center of town. I've been there since the pastor said, "the God of creation is also in the restoration business."

Macon, sitting next to me says, just above a whisper, "Where have you been? You're obviously not here with the rest of us."

"Just thinking."

"What are you thinking about?"

"I'm thinking about how impossible it is to be left alone with one's thoughts in this town."

"Well excuuuse me," he says.

"I'm joking."

"I know," he says, smiling.

"I'm thinking about the sermon if you must know." Before he can respond, Kenly chirps up from across the table.

"Miss Ava?"

"Yes, Kenly."

"Did you hear about where I'm going this afternoon?"

"I didn't. Where are you going this afternoon?"

"Uncle Macon and Daddy and Mommy are taking me to Mee Maw White's so I can ride my horse."

"Is that right? Awesome!"

"I know. It's the best thing that's ever happened to me. I can't wait to ride him. Will you come too?"

"Oh I don't know Kenly. I have a lot of things to do before work tomorrow." The entire table quiets down now as the rest of the Thompson clan listens in.

"Please? Pretty please? It will be so much fun. And you're my favorite person that's not in my family and I want you to come."

"How long will you be there?"

Grace answers, "A few hours. We're keeping our horses there until the house is finished. Won't you join us?"

"Please?" Kenly asks, drawing out the "e" as long as she can and then starts over again, "Please?"

"Okay," I say as if I just agreed to have bamboo shoots shoved under my fingertips. "I'll come. What time should I be ready?"

"We'll pick you up at 3:00," Grant says from the other end of the table.

"3:00 it is," I say, trying to act indifferent though the thought of being on a horse again makes me nearly apoplectic with excitement. It's been a long time.

"I bet she can't keep up," Macon says.

"We'll probably have to go really slow so she doesn't get freaked out," Grace picks up where Macon leaves off.

"Yeah, you know how the city folk are. She probably doesn't even know you can ride a horse."

"Go ahead people. Make fun. We'll see how I do when we get there. You'll be eating your words and my dust."

"Ohhh big talk coming from the city slicker," Macon says.

"It's not talk. You'll just have to see."

"What horse should we let her ride?" Beau chimes in, never one to miss an opportunity to tease me.

"I think . . . Spot," Kenly says. They all laugh. I have a feeling my closest ally just betrayed me.

"Go ahead, make fun. Just remember this moment when y'all are embarrassed later."

The conversation returns to normal just as quickly as it stopped earlier. Everyone talking at once. Macon leans in again, "This mean a lot to Kenly."

"It's impossible to say no to her."

"Don't we all know it. We'll have fun today. But you have to promise me something?"

"What's that?"

"You won't get too upset when we leave you behind on the trail. We're pretty serious about riding."

I turn and face him, his brown eyes, like one of the missiles on his Harrier, are zeroed in on me, right on the target that's over my heart. There's heat in those eyes. I smile, returning the eye contact with the same intensity as his. "We'll see about that Cowboy."

***

"I'm coming! Keep your shirt on. Sheesh." I run down the stairs to incessant knocking. I arrive on the landing to see Macon standing there in all his hotness.

I take my time on the second flight of stairs, opening the door in my own sweet time. "You ready?" he says as soon as the door opens.

"Yep! Just let me grab my boots." I turn and walk to my hall closet where a box sits filled with boots and extraneous pairs of shoes. After all these months, I haven't even touched the thing. I shoved it in the closet when I got here and forgot all about it.

I throw shoes from the box, creating a small pile next to me. Macon sits on the bottom stair step. "You keep your shoes in your downstairs hall closet?"

"Yeah. Doesn't everyone?" I ask, still dropping shoes in a pile. I finally find my favorite boots – which haven't been worn in ages. "There they are," I say, suddenly thankful I decided to search for these rather than wearing a newer, brown and turquoise pair of Justin boots I bought a few months ago.

I sit on the hardwood floor and pull them on. "What?" I say to Macon who is looking at me his head cocked to the side as if he's surprised at something.

"Those boots look pretty lived in."

"They are."

"Well now. Not what I expected from a fancy, Malibu born, Boston-schooled, D.C. socialite type."

"I, my dear, have many more surprises up my sleeve. I know how to muck a stall with the best of them. You can't judge a book by its cover or where she was born or lived. Or who she was married to. Didn't your parents ever teach you that?"

"Sure. Just not about Yankees."

***

Funny how you can ache for something as simple as a quiet morning when it's filled with the sound of hip hop from your daughter's room, your husband yelling for her to turn it down, and the sound of your son bouncing a basketball in the kitchen. Funny how life can change and you curse the day you ever wished for silence. My new life with a family full of wise crackers, is thankfully filled with commotion and noise. When we arrived at the stables, I got on my horse and took off. Just to prove a point. Macon tried to offer his assistance to get my horse saddled. I bristled, did my thing, mounted my horse, and literally left them in my dust like I said I would.

In my wake, I left them laughing. I've slowed down since then, waiting for them to catch up a bit. Their conversations filter through the sounds of the forest all around us, in between the wind rushing through the trees, the birds squawking and the sounds of the jets flying overhead from time to time. Not even Sunday's are safe from jet noise I guess. When I took off, leaving them behind laughing brings a joy to my heart I didn't think possible after so much loss. I turn around and head back in the other direction, toward this family that has adopted me.

***

The doorbell chimes ring throughout my house. Macon is not supposed to be here for a half-hour. Figures. Who knew Marines were so anal retentive about schedules? I race downstairs more excited than I would have thought possible, when I moved here, to see him. But as my feet hit the floor, it's not Macon waiting for me on the other side of my front door.

It's Burns.

I open the door though it's the last thing on earth I want to do. Other tasks that rank higher? Emptying porta johns, being the pooper picker upper at a dog park, etc. Seeing Burns on my front porch ranks far below these. Come to think of it, there are similarities between these things and Burns. I stand there in my bare feet, jeans and tank top, no makeup, and my hair in the unkempt way he hated and stare at him, full on in the face through the beveled glass of my door. How good would it feel to turn around and walk back upstairs?

He waves at me. My ex-husband, the father of my children, who abandoned me by the way, is standing on my porch waving as if he's sixteen and here to pick me up on a date. Charlie decides for me whether or not to open the door. I hear his tags jingle as he trots from the kitchen to the front door. Burns mouths, *please?* I see Charlie from the corner of my eye. He stops for a split second, long enough to register that it's his former master outside, and then takes off for the door. He paws at it, nails clacking and scratching at the wood and glass.

Burns bends down so that's he's face to face with him. He taps on the glass. He becomes human again then. I bridge the distance between us and open the door. Charlie is beside himself.

"Hi there, Boy," he says, rubbing his special spot behind his ears.

"What are you doing here?" I ask, leaning against the door frame.

"Hiya Bennett." He stands and looks me in the eye.

He looks old. Worn. He's gained weight around the middle. The lines around his eyes that he had done such a good job at beating back with a stick, have now run all over his face. He looks defeated. But he's dressed appropriately as always. He is dressed as though he's ready to board a yacht. His signature cologne, heavy and dark hangs in the air around us. I used to love this scent. Now it's like noxious fumes and makes me miss Macon.

"I know this comes as a surprise."

"I'd say so," I say flatly.

"I am sorry for showing up like this. Unannounced. But I knew you wouldn't see me if I told you I needed to talk to you."

"What is there to talk about?" I ask, sarcasm dripping from my voice. I let the question hang in the air and then go in for the kill. "No wait. Let me guess. You need my endorsement? You want me to make some campaign appearances for you? You need me to teach your Legislative Assistant how to diaper a baby? What? What could you possibly have to say to me after everything?"

"First of all, I deserve everything you just said. Second, can I come in? I'd like to sit down and talk."

Because this can't possibly get any worse, "Sure why the hell not?" Should I be surprised by anything Burns says or does?

I let him inside, Charlie following close on his heels. He waits for me to direct him. I wave him into my formal living room to the left of the entryway. He's not getting any further than the front room.

"Sit," I say.

"Thank you."

"Can I get you something to drink?" I ask, remembering my manners for the briefest flash.

"As long as there's no rat poison in it," he says, smiling.

"Good one. Cognac?"

"Sure," he says, patting my couch, enticing Charlie to join him.

"He's not – oh never mind," I say turning to see my traitorous dog looking at my ex-husband as if he's a huge piece of steak.

I pour Burns a drink and then hand it to him, putting my index finger under my nose as he takes it. His movement sends a waft of that Burns scent upwards and it swirls around me. It makes me want to hurl, violently. It wasn't so long ago that his cologne made me want to be the mother of his children.
"Allergies," I lie. "So what are you doing here?"

"I'm going to cut to the chase."

"Okay. I think." I say, nervous.

"I need your help." I cough. And then laugh. "I know. It's absurd of me to be so presumptuous."

"You got that right," I say.

"The thing is I have a problem. Of my own making of course. Jenny and the kids are not doing well together, to say the least. I know I fought you on custody and we are just a few weeks away from the new hearing. But things are bad right now."

My heart fills with regret for my attitude when I realize this is about my step-children. "Are you surprised by this?"

"I guess not," he says and then continues, "I've made a lot of excuses for my behavior, as a way to make me feel better about what I've done – who I've become. I thought the kids would adjust because I didn't want to admit that I'd ruined their childhoods and destroyed our home."

I sit all the way back in my chair. Stunned into silence. I look up and past Burns, through my enormous picture window that looks out to the water of Taylor's Creek across the street. The diamond sparkle on the creek puts me in Beaufort. But inside I'm sitting on the floor of my kitchen in McLean, Virginia, hearing for the first time, about my husband's dalliances with a twenty-three year old staffer.

"I know I ruined everything. Me. I did it."

"And why are you telling me this now?" I ask. I'm overwhelmed by the weight of what he's saying. It's the first time he's even hinted at wrong doing let alone fully at admitted that he's ruined our family.

"Jenny has given me an ultimatum."

"Is that right?" I ask. Not surprised.

"The kids have been out of control. I don't blame them. But let's just say that you take the worst fight that either of us ever had with Harper and multiply it by a million. That's Harper and Jenny. William was suspended from school last week. He's taken to throwing things at her, yells at her - calls her horrible names."

"Again . . . you're surprised?"

"No."

"What is the ultimatum?"

"Jenny told me I have to choose between her and the baby and the kids." He says this thing that skips off his tongue like he's telling me the sky is blue, so easy-breezy like. Yet my insides are churning inside me and I am instantly nauseous. I hurt that my kids are in pain. And I long for them.

"And what are you going to do about that? Because I'd tell you what I'd do."

"What?" he asks.

"I'd help her pack," I say, my voice cracking.

Burns has been looking at his hands but now looks up at me. Shocked, I suppose. "I . . . I . . .I can't do that."

"I see," I say, not surprised. "So what are you here for? To ask my permission to send our children off to boarding school or?"

"Will you take the kids?" And there it is. A question I wanted him to ask but didn't dare hope he would.

"So let me get this straight . . . you put us all through this hell after we lose Katie? You bring that woman into our home. And when things get challenging, after she's, she," I say again, raising my voice as I say she, "cuts off contact between me and the kids that forces me to take you to court? And you want me to save your ass?"

"It's not about me."

"Oh it's not? Could have fooled me."

"So are you saying I should abandon another family after destroying the first one?" The tears rise in my eyes and sit there. And then when they can't wait any longer, brim over and spill down my cheeks. Through the blur I know I need to respond but I'm still trying to figure out if this is an apology.

"The kids can live with me. I want them with me," I say, my heart rate quickening, the knot in my stomach, untying. I sigh deeply, letting out the years of sorrow.

"They can?"

"Yes."

"Thank you. This is best for them," he says.

"No Burns. Make no mistake about it. What is best for Harper and Will would have been that the four of us were still a family."

I watch him – like a hawk. He closes his eyes and runs his hands through his silver hair. "You are right. I am sorry. I'm sorry for what I've put the three of you through." We sit there in the silence of loss and regret. For the first time since his affair, I can feel his repentance. It's hanging in the air like the humidity of a mid-August afternoon. Burns picks up his cognac and takes a sip.

I begin to figure out how to broach the topic of details when the front screen door opens and shuts, followed by Macon's voice, "You'll never guess what I just heard at –" he says, coming around the corner. "Oh. Sorry," he says seeing Burns seated on my couch.

"It's okay." I say standing and walking to him. Charlie remains in his position of adoration, forsaking Macon for Burns. Usually he's forsaking me for Macon. I hug him, letting his embrace soak into my bones before attempting an explanation.

He whispers, "Are you okay?"

"Yes. I will explain."

"Okay," he says as I pull away.

"Let me introduce you." Macon takes my hand as I head into the living room.

"Burns, this is Major Macon Thompson. Macon, this is Burns Cooper."

Macon reaches out first. Burns responds. They shake hands. "Nice to meet you, Major," Burns says sounding suddenly like a United States Senator.

"Likewise," Macon replies with uncharacteristic terseness.

"Burns is here to discuss some issues about Harper and William," I say, looking at Macon, hoping he understands the look in my eyes, what I'm certain is a mix of hope and peace, something he's not seen much of in me.

"I see. Well, our plans this evening are an easy change. Would you like me to wait here for you? Or meet you at Mom and Dad's?"

"How about I meet you there?"

"Okay." He nods at Burns, "Nice to meet you, Senator." Macon turns to walk out and then turns around, looking at Burns. I know Macon is not prone to outbursts but something in his eyes tells me he'd like to take Burns outside and turn him inside out. I shake my head no. He clenches his fists. Burns looks up and away from the bookshelf he's been staring at, in the most humbled state I've ever seen him in. Fear registers in Burns' eyes.

Macon says, his voice steady but firm, "Let me make one thing clear. If you hurt her, I will introduce you to an ass whopping the likes of which you've never seen. Got it?"

Burns shakes his head, "I won't hurt her. I've already done enough of that."

"Good," Macon says. He turns then and walks out of the room. I follow him to the porch. We stand there in the doorway. He brushes a lock of hair out of my eyes and then runs his finger down my cheek.

"Are you really okay?"

The tenderness in his eyes is what I've always wished I'd had with Burns. "Yes. Promise. It's good news. I'll be over soon with all the details."

"Okay," he says.

"Okay," I say back, smiling. He kisses my forehead and then bounds down the stairs. I walk back in the house. Charlie meets me, wagging his tail. "You wanna go?" I ask. He barks. I open the screen door and call out, "Mac!" He turns and smiles as I wave. Charlie, my forever fickle dog, races after him.

I walk back into the living room. Burns looks humbled again. What an hour ago I believed was impossible, is now very much a reality. "I'm glad you found someone to take care of you," he says with more sincerity I've heard from him in ages.

"Thanks. He is the best man I know. And he's my best friend. But we're not here to talk about Macon now are we. We have some details to iron out."

"That we do," he says as I sit down.

~ FOURTEEN ~

"So let me get this straight," Harper says, "there isn't a mall?"

It all comes back to the mall when you're twelve. "There isn't really a mall, no. At least not like you know a mall. There is nothing like Tyson's Corner, for example. But there are places to shop. And we can take some trips up to Raleigh."

"Is there a Starbucks?"

"What are you doing drinking coffee?" I ask, wondering what else my kids have been up to that I wouldn't have allowed had I not been pushed out of their lives for more than a year.

"Mom. Dude. I'm twelve. Plus they serve more than coffee."

Dude? "Yeah, there's a Starbucks in Morehead City."

"Is that close?"

"Yeah, pretty close." The questions have come on and off for the last couple of hours. Ellie is in the front seat, a Cheshire grin on her face. A couple of times, she's raised her eyes as Harper makes a pronouncement or uses a word that at one time, would have been forbidden in our home. My responses seem to settle Harper a bit. Will's nose is in his book. This is a development I'm happy to see.

Unlike the majority of the other baggage more than a year with Jenny has added to my kid's lives. I look in my mirror, Harper smiles, sticks in an ear bud for her Ipod and settles into her seat. Miss Ellie and I made a pact when we arrived in McLean to pick them up. We decided that we won't discuss Jenny at all in front of the kids. When she fired Ellie, the kids decided then and there, so I'm told, to ensure she regretted that decision.

While the pain of losing Hope remains ever present, this gift is not lost on me. In one fell swoop, I have my family back – the rest of my family. The icing on the cake is the house in Ridgemont. Jenny hates the country. Too many "rednecks" and not enough civilization she told Burns. So, he told her that he'd sign the house over to me, with the caveat it goes to Harper in my will.

When he told me, I asked him several times if he really meant it. The house in the country means that that we, the kids and me, have a piece of the old life. Their rooms. Their horses. It's where William's tree house is. It's where Harper's best friend lives. And it's where my baby girl is buried. Perhaps it's another way of Burns trying to make up for what he's done? Whatever the reason, I'm relieved. I'm relieved and grateful in spite of the circumstances that brought us here.

"Mom?"

"Harper."

"Where are we going to school again?"

"St. Egbert's."

"Is it a Catholic school?"

"Yes. It sure is."

"Isn't there a school like Sidwell?"

"Nope. Afraid not. You didn't even like Sidwell half the time."

"Because of all the snobs. But I still liked it there," she says, trying to sound convincing after spending the last five years of her life cursing the day we decided to send her there.

Will looks up from his book, "Are there nuns who hit you when you don't behave?"

"Of course not, baby. I have heard wonderful things about the school. It comes highly recommended by friends of mine. You'll meet them soon."

"Okay, but if we really hate it can we try another school?" Harper asks, nervousness evident on her face. So many changes in so little time. I'd be nervous too.

"We can cross that bridge if we come to it," I say. Slipping into our old roles is as natural as breathing.

"Cool," she says, going back to her music.

"Cool," says William, following his sister's lead. He looks back to his book, a smile crosses his face. Tears come quickly then. I've missed his sweaty head. He's a taller, year older version of himself. But still my little guy. The tears continue. Ellie reaches out and pats my hand that rests on the stick shift. I look at her. She smiles and squeezes my hand. It's almost too good to be true. But I'm not for a single second letting them out of my sight lest it all disappear again. I spent the week prior to my trip to McLean, shopping for furniture for the kid's rooms and filling the house with their favorite foods.

"I'm going to have to use my imagination to live here," Harper says, sounding so much like me it's hard to believe I didn't give birth to her.

I look at Ellie who shakes her head and says, "Hey she learned from the best."

"That she did," I say, filled in that instant with both awe and fear. Awe because my children are with me. Fear because I don't want to get cocky after what's happened the last couple of years.

***

The kids, Miss Ellie, my Beaufort friends, Jules, her husband, and my brother who is back in the states for a whirlwind vacation, fill my backyard. We are having a BBQ of gigantic proportions complete with fireworks on the dock when it gets dark, to celebrate my kid's arrival in Beaufort. I sit on the bottom step of my deck and watch as William chases Kenly around the yard, both with plastic light sabers drawn. Harper is on my white-washed, creaky old swing having a heart to heart with Jules and Grace.

Ellie is sitting with Beau and Charlotte laughing at Kenly and Will. Life is good. Again. The sun shines through the canopy of live oaks in the yard. It's a perfect day. The sun on my face, through the tree branches is comforting. I won't take this for granted. Not after where we've been. The losses still hang over everything I do. I have started to believe they always will. But I have the kids. And my heart knows a peace it hasn't in so long.

"Penny for your thoughts," Macon says walking up, a smile breaking out across his face. The way he looks at me reminds me there are more conversations left to be had between us. Conversations that I locked in a box the day Burns showed up on my porch.

"It's just – I can't believe they're here. I . . . it's just -"

"Freaking awesome," he finishes the sentence for me.

"Exactly. Freaking awesome."

"It's weird you know. I had no idea it would be possible to be this happy for someone else," he says sitting down next to me.

"Thanks. You're sweet, as always"

"I mean it, you know that right? Harper and Will are great kids. Funny as heck. Smart. In spite of what they've been through, they're quite respectful."

"Yes. They are. Thank you for noticing. There are scars. And Burns handing them over to me is one of those things that's bittersweet. But I found them a great counselor a few days ago. I hope that will help us all along in the healing process."

"I'm sure they'll be fine. You're an amazing mom," he says, reaching out and rubbing my back.

Will, as if my back has an alarm on it, stops what he's doing and races toward me. My protector. Before he reaches us, Macon says, "He doesn't feel very comfortable around me, does he?"

"It's not you it's me," I say, hoping he'll laugh.

He laughs. I try to ignore the way his laugh makes me feel like a new person, with all the pain of recent years a distant memory. "It's understandable," he says as Will reaches us.

Will eyes Macon like he's a dad with a shotgun, ready to send his daughter on her first date. "Hey son, watcha doin'?" I ask.

"I just came to say hi," he says, watching Macon until he turns and plops into my lap.

"Well hi there."

"Are we going to eat soon?"

"Yep. The guys will put the shrimp on the barbi soon."

"I don't like shrimp."

"I know. It's just a saying."

"Oh. Well I don't know any North Carolina sayings. What's that?" he asks, changing the subject at the sound of a helicopter's approach.

"That's an HH-46," Macon answers. "It's called PEDRO. It's a rescue helicopter."

"How do you know that?" Will asks, suddenly interested in what Macon has to say.

"Because Macon is a Marine – a pilot. I told you that."

"You are? He asks standing now to face Macon taking his sweaty boy smell with him.

"Yep. I fly Harriers. It's a jet that takes off and lands vertically like a helicopter. Do you want to go see if we can catch a sight of PEDRO?"

"Yeah. Cool." Macon gets up and the two of them race through the yard, around the side of the house, as the heavy whir of the rotors approach.

I wait for their return, hoping Will might become fascinated enough with Macon's career that his protective ways chill out a little. I hear Will before I see them. "So do you have a gun?"

"I do at home. For work, when I deploy overseas, I have a gun on me all the time."

"You do?" William asks, his eyes wide.

"Yep."

"Do you fly the Harrier every day?"

"Nope. Not every day. I have to fly a set number of hours every month though."

"That's sick."

"That it is," Macon says, "Would you like to take a tour of our squadron one day soon?"

"Oh man!" Will says, sounding like he's found the Holy Grail for ten year old boys.

"Is that a yes?" I ask, raising my eyebrow at my son.

"Yes, sir. I would like to go and see it."

"That's better," I say. I feared that there might be walls between me and the kids. There were walls. But they were erected by their step-mother. It took a matter of hours for the shyness of the many months that have passed, to disappear. The kids made it easy.

"Well maybe this coming week, since it is Spring break, we can do that. Your mom and I can figure out a good day," Macon says.

"Okay. Cool," William says, racing off, having long forgotten that Macon had his arm around me a few minutes ago.

"Is that what you'd call bribery?" Macon asks, winking at me.

"Could be. Whatever it is, it made my son happy, so thanks."

We watch and listen as Will tells Harper, "Dude's a Marine. A pilot. He's going to take me to his base and show me his jet. Dude."

"Great. That's great," Harper replies. Her face shows a total lack of interest but I know she's trying to figure out how to join the fun.

"Do you mind if Ellie, Harper and I join in the fun? I think it would be fun," I ask.

"Sure. We can do that. I'd love that actually."

"Me too," I say smiling at him and then looking to my feet, suddenly shy and unsure how to get us back to the spot we were in before the kids arrived.

After dinner we all walk across the narrow, two-lane Front Street to my dock. Rarely used, the kids have made me promise to buy a small fishing boat before summer. Most of the guests are crowded onto the dock. But a few others are sitting on the grass, just the other side of the long sidewalk that runs through downtown. The air is warm enough that we don't need our sweatshirts and sweaters.

Macon, Beau, and Grant have gotten the festivities underway and light fireworks they bought along Highway 17 in South of the Border, South Carolina. Harper is still pretending to be disinterested. William can't contain his excitement. I sit back further in my beach chair and take a deep breath. The scents of a spring evening – blooming wisteria and daffodils -- combine with the marsh grass and the sticky, sweet mud from the creek's shore, combine to make one heady, earthy scent.

William, for the fifth time since we walked out here, has turned around, a look of panic in his eyes, until he finds me. He makes eye contact and then waves, peace returning. I feel the same way. More than once I considered quitting the practice and focusing solely on the kids, even thinking about home-schooling. Maybe I still will quit? Harper is a tougher nut to crack than Will. In many ways, I'm more worried about getting through to her before she hits too far into those terrible teen years. But the truth is, it's always been that way with Harper. I'm the only mom Will has known so his allegiance has never been stretched or pulled. Harper has memories, though fleeting, of her mama, the woman she's named for. She's too cool to need us, but desperate for her parent's approval. The time with Jenny running the Cooper household has been cruel to her. She never got Jenny's approval. And after last night's heart to heart, with my stubborn girl, I know now that she also bore the weight of rejection.

It's not just that my ex-husband's new wife couldn't handle my misbehaving children. It's that she couldn't understand it was a cry for love. Harper told me that she knew things weren't going to get better when last year's Christmas card was a picture of Burns and Jenny. And Jenny's dog. "From the Coopers" it said. Except the Cooper "family" was short two members. Harper lay in her bed last night and cried, soaking her pillow, while I rubbed her back and tried to breathe truth back into her. A truth I'm only now beginning to believe again myself.

It's moments like that that I hope I don't ever encounter that woman face to face, especially in a dark alley. Harper turns around and searches for me. The corners of her mouth go up a little, as if she's trying to suppress a smile, and then she does the unexpected. She walks over to me, bearing the weight of all of her losses in her eyes. She sits on my lap. I wrap my arms around her. "I love you, Sweet Pea. Always."

She whispers back, "I love you too, mommy." My eyes fill with tears. And for the first time since I packed my bags and moved out of the home we had all shared, I pray a silent prayer, "Give me wisdom. And please heal our hearts." With my girl sitting on my lap, and my son sitting on the dock next to Grant Thompson, I'm starting to believe healing is within our reach.

A few weeks later

We've found our routine. The kids are doing better than I would have imagined. I am doing better than I would have imagined. But when things are quiet, Hope seeps into my heart. I still miss her so much. My arms feel empty even though two of my four babies are with me again. While I still contemplate leaving the practice, I'm glad I haven't yet as it is a good distraction while the kids are at school. Carol and Jamie fight like my kids so actually, it's not all that different than being at home with them. Keeping the kids in school had been the right decision. Sitting at my desk after an insanely busy morning, I dig into my leftovers from last night just as someone knocks on my door. "Dr. Ava?"

"Yes, Carol. What's up? I just sat down to eat."

"I'm sorry. I am. I said I wouldn't disturb you. But I think you'll want to come out here. Now!" she exclaims.

Suddenly worried at her tone, I step out into the lobby. Jamie and Carol are both standing behind the counter of the reception desk, but they're facing a man standing in the doorway. His face is blocked from my vantage point. I walk quickly down the hall and know immediately why Carol was so insistent. It's Christopher, Hope's uncle. "Ma'am," he says.

"Hi Christopher. What can I do for you?"

"I'm here to tell you about some things because what happened ain't right. Hope is not being taken care of the way she should. She's been real sick lately and Miss Ann ain't doing anything for her. And here's the other thing, there are more drugs coming out of that house now than ever before. Miss Ann has somehow found her way out of trouble for a lot of years. My brother belongs in prison for what he done. And so does Janie. But the one behind it all is Ann. I paid for the dumb things I did when I was a kid. I have been clean for a year now and after I saw what happened there yesterday, I knew I had to do something."

"What happened?" I ask, unsure I want to know.

"Ann left the baby at the house with a guy that had only been out of prison for a few days. It's not the first time she's left her there with god knows who. But this time, knowing what that guy did, I couldn't take it no more. I stayed there at the house until she got home and told her that if she didn't call the county to say she was giving up custody I would report her. She said she would do no such thing. So I just came from the sheriff's. DSS is on their way to pick up Hope, with a deputy."

My heart sinks. Hope is sick and that's the least of my worries about her condition. "This man that Ann left Hope with, what did he go to prison for?"

"He killed his kid in a wreck. Drunk and high. Put him in the car, no car seat or nothin'. He's been away for a long time. The guy hasn't tried to get his life right. That's no one Hope should be around. When I got there, he had been drinking. Hope was in her crib, wearing a dirty diaper. She has a bad rash and a cough that doesn't sound good at all. I got her cleaned up and stayed there with her. I haven't always done things the right way and I'm not working because no one wants to hire me because of it. But Hope is my niece and I want her to have the chance none of us kids had. I know the difference between right and wrong and this is wrong."

"Thank you, Christopher. Thank you. You did the right thing. I know you're trying to make things right and I'd like to help you find a job. Come see me on Monday, okay? I have an idea for how we can find you a job. In the meantime, will you be okay since you've reported this?"

"Oh yeah. They all gettin' arrested right this minute. I told them a whole bunch of other stuff," he says, smiling. "The lawmen have been waiting for a long time for one of us to turn and I decided to be the one. They put me up in a motel. I'm going to be alright."

"Okay, good. Well, you come see me on Monday if you can."

"I will. Thank you, ma'am. Take care of my niece, okay?"

"Well I don't know what the plan is -" I say as he interrupts me.

"I do. I overheard. They're carrying her to the hospital and they're gonna call you."

"Thank you, Christopher. Thank you for taking care of her and watching over her."

"Well I wish I'd done it sooner."

"Let's not worry about that now. Thank you."

"You're welcome, ma'am. I better go now. I just wanted to come here and talk to you myself. Christopher waved a goodbye and then walked out the front door of the office.

I look at Carol, who is wiping tears from her eyes. "Well I s'wanee! Should we just drive to the hospital now?"

"I'll need you to stay here and reach the rest of the afternoon's patients. Can you do that for me?"

"Of course I can," she says.

And as she replies, my phone rings. I answer quickly. "This is Ava," I say, wanting desperately for Hope's social worker to be on the other end of the line.

"Dr. Cooper, this is Nina, I can't get into all the details now but we are the way to the hospital with Hope. She will not return to Mrs. Brown's home. We've already gotten a judge to grant temporary custody to you, if you are agreeable."

"Yes. Yes, of course! But is she okay?" I'm worried that her health has been compromised and wonder what else has happened to her.

"I hope so. I certainly hope so. She has a terrible, croupy cough. With her health being what it is, we were concerned. She's lost some weight, too. When I got to the trailer, she just clung to me. Can you meet us at the hospital?"

"Of course. I'm leaving now."

"We will see you in a few minutes."

My first phone call was Ellie. My second, Macon. He is flying. I knew this but forgot until his voicemail picked up. I left him a message and hoped he would get it soon. Ellie was picking the kids up and taking them back to the house. Until I knew more about Hope's physical condition, I didn't want the kids to come to the hospital. Seeing Hope a few minutes ago, for the first time in months, made my heart soar, in the same breath as it broke my heart. She had lost weight. Hooked up to an IV and a heart monitor, she was asleep when I walked in. In her room, like the first time I met her, was her social worker and her GAL, Toby.

"Hi," I say as I step into the room. "Long time no see."

"Yes. Thank you for coming so quickly, Nina says.

"Has the doctor been in to see her yet?"

"Yes, he walked out a few minutes ago."

"I'll be right back," I say, anxious and hopeful all at once.

***

When I return to the room, Hope is still asleep. I walk over to her bedside and kiss her head. The day she was taken to the Browns floods back in for a moment. "I'm so sorry I couldn't protect you, Sweet Girl," I say, kissing her again. I touch her hand and the weight of all that has happened to her in her young life, sweeps me under the crushing weight of the burden. What people do to children horrifies me. In the name of what? The tears flow down my face.

"What's the word?" The social worker asks.

Sniffling and trying to regain my composure, I say, "Well, her heart sounds good. They want to keep her overnight at the very least. They're going to give her a course of antibiotics and they're on the phone with her cardiologist to ensure that they know what to look for but right now, she's doing fairly well. All things considered. The fluids will help. She's pretty dehydrated on top of everything else. So are we officially past kinship placement now?" I ask, sick to my stomach at the thought that a judge actually thought Hope would be better off in that mess.

"Yes. We will begin the adoption process in terms of our side of things. You still want to adopt her, right?"

"Hell yes," I say. "There's not a chance this kid is going anywhere but home with me."

An hour later, when Hope wakes up from her nap, I am there. Her sleepy, take her time waking up style, is her normal way. She loves her sleep that girl. When her eyes focus on the person sitting next to her bed, they grow wide. "Did you have a good nap, my sweet girl?" I ask her.

Her smile lights up my heart. "Yes, baby. I'm right here. And you are stuck with me forever." I fiddle with her IV and scoot her over a little so she's closer to the side of the bed - an adult size bed. I climb in next to her and lay right down. "I've missed you so much! Mama loves you," I say to her. She settles right into my arms. She sticks her thumb in her mouth and wraps her other hand around mine. I don't know what she's been through in the months she was away, but she's safe now, and that's all that matters.

***

I should have known Grace and Charlotte had ulterior motives when they asked to take the kids horseback riding with them. Charlotte brought Ellie along so Hope went, too. Macon is standing at my screen door. In all his pink shirt glory. I'm not sure how such predictable people get away with this kind of thing over and over again. And yet, I miss it every time. "Hey there," I say as I open the screen to let him in. I've been avoiding him as much as possible since I brought Hope home from the hospital. Managing three kids, all of whom have major issues these days, has been exhausting to say the least.

"I was wondering if you would like to join me for a walk over at Ft. Macon?"

"Hmm. Sure. Why not?"

"Great," he says. "Should we take Charlie?"

"Is that a question or a statement?"

"More like a request."

"That's what I thought," I say. "Charlie," I call out. His familiar dog tag jingle comes toward us from the back of the house where he's likely laying in the swath of sunlight on the kitchen floor. I reach into the basket next to the door and grab his leash and then throw it to Macon. "Let me get my shoes. I'll be right there." I run up the stairs as Macon walks out with my dog. I'm pretty sure this is going to be the continuation of a conversation we have needed to finish for a while. Ready or not, it's coming.

***

We've climbed the steps that lead to the bathhouse at Ft. Macon. There's a slight breeze off the water. The sea oats are moving with it, I slow enough to catch just a bit of that sound that's so comforting to me. Macon turns and looks for me, probably wondering where I went. "Sorry. Just listening to the sea oats."

"Huh?" he asks, smiling like he does.

I catch up to him as we walk down the ramp to the sand. "The sea oats. I love the way they sound when the wind blows. I was just stopping to listen."

"You're cute," he says as we step into the sand. Another couple, with four kids and a couple of dogs, is headed our way, with one hand on the leash, he puts his right hand on the small of my back, steering me clear of them.

"Cute? Hmm. Don't think I've ever been called cute before." His hand is still on my back though we've already navigated around the family.

"How is it that no one has ever said that about you before?" He sounds honestly surprised.

"I don't know. They just haven't."

"Not ever?"

"I don't think I've ever heard that, no."

"Well you are. And you should have heard it."

"Thanks. That's not really Burns's style. He's not really the type to compliment much. My parents aren't either really." I walk over to a shell sitting alone in the sand, away from the thousands upon thousands of broken shells that run the entire beach. I want the shell. But I also feel the need to escape Macon's hand. I pick it up and wipe the sand from it. It's a sand dollar. The intricate lines and curves of the poinsettia-like design amaze me. Not so much as a blemish to mar it or a piece missing.

It's hard to imagine how it has survived the rough seas of the Atlantic and is still whole and perfect. Particularly for something as delicate as a sand dollar. Macon and Charlie continue to walk a few feet ahead of me. I put the shell in the pocket of my sweatshirt and wish I could have fared as well as the sand dollar. I've been tossed around in the waves and slammed into the shore more than a few times, I have more chinks and chunks missing than seems fair.

I catch up to Macon. He slows his steps. "Did you find something?"

"I did, a sand dollar. It's perfect. It blows my mind actually. How it survives in those waves and hitting a rocky jetty or being washed up onto shells and glass."

"Amazing, isn't it?"

"Yeah." We walk in silence for a few minutes. He hasn't put his arm around me or his hand on my back again. The Sandpipers run about the shore in circles searching for food. A line of pelicans is sitting in the water, bobbing along in the waves, waiting, though I'm not sure what for.

The silence between us doesn't last for long. "So how are the kids doing?"

"At times, things are good. Other times they are quite challenging. I think the big thing right now is that the kids are trying to balance this abandonment feeling with having me back. In a way, they feel disloyal to me when they acknowledge to the counselor that they feel abandoned by their father. It's so confusing for them. It's my job to let them know they can have those feelings and still be safe with me. It's not easy. And on top of that, I have to work overtime at keeping the things I'm struggling with to myself. Ellie helps with that. If she senses I'm having a rough moment she takes the kids out or sends me to my room to take a bath." I laugh. It's a nervous laugh. I fear when I say things like that I sound a little crazy. I laughed, trying to sound easy breezy, hoping he wouldn't notice that I'm still filled with fear that everything will change again.

"I'm glad you have Ellie with you. How has everything gone with turning the practice over?"

"Yeah, I guess it has been a while since we've talked about this. That's kept me pretty busy. But it's the right thing to do. The kids need me more than I need to be a doctor."

"So how is it going?"

"It's going. Pepper is actually coming back early. She called me a couple of weeks ago. I told her what was going on and that I was thinking about making changes. She's convinced me to hold onto a stake and work with her and the new doctor, on consults. She's also got some plan to open a clinic, a free clinic, and wants me to help her with that. Maybe volunteer some hours. I can do that while the kids are at school and still give as much time as I can to Hope."

"A free clinic, eh?" Macon asks. I look up at him. His countenance has changed. I don't know why.

"Yep. I think it sounds wonderful. Financially it's entirely feasible for me to do this. I like the idea of being able to help out at the kid's school and to know that I'll always be around when they get home. Hope needs the one-on-one attention but having Ellie gives me the opportunity to be at the kid's school when I need to or volunteer."

"Can you still afford to pay Ellie? I mean. Not that. Well, it's not really my business."

"No. It's not," I say, hoping to lighten his sudden crestfallen face. He smiles. I continue, "Burns is paying Ellie's salary. He's not going to care one way or another what I'm doing. He'll keep paying her."

"Well I'm glad everything is working out." We continue walking down the beach, headed in the direction of the Civil War era fort, next to what is now a Coast Guard station. Our pace has picked up though I'm not sure why. Macon's face is still serious, marked with emotions I don't fully understand.

"Is something wrong?" I ask.

"Yes. No. Not really."

"So which is it?"

"Nothing's wrong. But um . . ."

"What?"

"It's just that Pepper had been working with Caroline and Grace on opening a free clinic when Caroline died. It was on Highway 70. I didn't know she was trying to resurrect the project."

"Oh. I didn't realize. I – is it a bad thing that she's working on this again?"

"No. No. Not at all. I'm just surprised no one mentioned it to me. Though I'm sure there must be a reason."

"I can probably answer that. I didn't realize the connection. She didn't want to publicize much because she didn't know if we could pull it off yet. I shouldn't have opened my big mouth. She said there were other parties involved. I didn't ask whom. I should have known your family was involved. She really wanted to keep it hush hush until she got back into town and could analyze everything and look at locations."

"Ah. Makes sense now. Should I feel privileged that you shared privileged information with me?" He's not looking at me instead his eyes are focused ahead of us.

"I suppose you should," I say, and leave it at that.

"So can I ask you a question?"

"You certainly can."

"Are we ever going to get back to that conversation we were supposed to have before Burns showed up in Beaufort?"

"Maybe," I say. There's no sarcasm, or flirting intended. I don't know how to answer.

"Maybe? Is that all you have for me?" He asks, as if he's gearing up for our typical banter.

"I didn't mean it to be sarcastic. I'm not sure what to say. When it was me by myself, I felt more capable of having that talk – of figuring out what's next for us. But it's not just me anymore." I say it, what I've been afraid to say to him for weeks and weeks. I let it hang there in the air. A group of seagulls are standing on the sand in front of us, their squawking and high pitched near screams fill the sudden silence between us. "Listen," I say, suddenly uncomfortable with the quiet, "those kids are my priority. It has to be that way. We know what happened when Burns decided to bring someone else into our family. The problem is that these kids didn't ask for this mess. I can't bring someone else into our lives until I either feel comfortable with how they're dealing with everything or I know that that you can handle how things will need to be. Make sense?"

"It does." He's a man of few words today. I'm not sure what to make of it. We walk further, the seagulls are behind us now, their cries heard only through the sound of the waves and the young families that have pitched umbrellas and set up mini-day camps on this section of the beach. There was a time when a physical ache pounded in my chest when I watched families doing every day normal things. But now, instead of the overwhelming silence, the house will be filled with the sounds of a life I thought I'd lost.

Macon bridges the silence between us out of nowhere. "But," he says, as if we haven't been quiet for at least five minutes. "at the same time, it depends on the circumstances. I get where you're coming from. I know what it means to be a step-father, remember?" I nod my head yes, feeling another stake to my heart for forgetting what he's lost. "The difference between you, me and Burns and Jenny is that I won't ever ask you to make that choice. But there's only one way for you to know that for sure."

"What's that?"

"You have to trust me."

"Isn't there another way?" I ask, hoping again to lighten the mood. "Kidding."

"I know you're kidding but that's really our only option if there's any chance for us."

"You see a *long term* us, when you think about me and you?" I ask.

"Yes. After Caroline died, I wondered if that would be possible. When you lose everything at one time, you walk around like the living dead. Well, I don't have to tell you that, you understand." I shake my head. I wish I didn't. I wish we didn't share this thing in common. But in a weird way, I'm thankful we do. "Anyway, I went on a handful of dates in the six months or so before that last deployment. Because I thought I was ready."

"You weren't?"

"Well, honestly I was ready but that's all beside the point. I just hadn't found the right one. I am looking for someone to do life with. Whatever that means and wherever it takes us. The truth is . . ." he stops walking. He faces the water, looking out at the horizon but a determination in his eyes I've grown accustomed to submitting my heart to in small pieces.

He turns to face me, letting Charlie's leash drop to the wet sand. He puts his hand on my elbow, my arms crossed in front of me. I'm still trying to protect myself. "Ava, the truth is, I can't imagine wanting to do life with anyone but you. I know that it won't always be easy. I know that the consequences of living with Burns' choices will mean that our priorities will have to be different than other couples. But I don't want to live my life without you in it." I drop my arms to my side, releasing myself from my defensive stance. He takes my right hand in his, tracing the lines of my fingers with his. "I don't want you to say anything just yet, okay?" I shake my head yes. I sometimes see myself as a big knot of sorrow and grief. When he looks at me, it's like he's pulling one end of that knot, unwinding my big tangle of mess. He unties me. He awakens the parts of my heart I thought were dead.

"I have never fully bought into the belief that everything happens for a reason. To do so is to say that God willed for me to lose Caroline and my kids. And if I believed that for you, I'd have to believe that God meant for you to lose Katie and for Burns to have ruined your family. "I can't believe that. But here's where I think I've found peace. And I hope that if you're not there yet, you will be soon. He didn't intend for these things to happen. But He will make something beautiful from the ashes."

I bite my lip, trying like a mad woman to keep the tears back. He squeezes my hand and then laces his fingers through mine. "I don't understand suffering any more than you do. But I have a peace now I didn't dream would be possible after the accident." Charlie is walking in circles around us, sniffing the sand, digging here or there. Meanwhile, Macon is making quick work of breaking down the remaining, though crumbling, wall that is around my heart.

"I guess what I'm saying is, I love you Ava. I've said it before. I'll say it again. I am in love with you. I don't want to live my life without you. In fact, I can't imagine it any other way. But," he puts his finger to my mouth as I start to speak up, ready to remind him that it's not just me anymore.

"You wanna hear something crazy?" He doesn't wait for a response from me. I look up into his eyes as he smiles. "The first day I met you at my parent's house, I knew. I just knew you were the one. I prayed for you a lot – I prayed that you would get your kids back."

"You did?"

"Yes. I did."

"I couldn't ask that for myself," I say.

"I know. I understand," he says as he laughs. I'm certain he's remembering how I used to feel when he said he understood where I was coming from.

"Thank you for asking for what I couldn't ask for myself."

"You're welcome," he winks at me and then continues, "It's my pleasure. Now I'm just waiting for you to completely trust me. I know you sort of do. But you still have some wall up. It's the reason you've let the kids become an excuse."

In that moment, I know I have nowhere to go. I did use the kids as an excuse. "I think God is answering a lot of your prayers," I say, in a whisper, hoping he can hear me. I'm afraid to say it louder.

"You think?" he asks.

"Yes," I say.

"Which ones?" he asks.

"All of them."

"Are you going to let me love you?" he asks, kissing my forehead.

"Yes. But –"

"Uh oh," he says smiling, putting his arms around my waist. "There's always a but with you, isn't there?"

"Always. I only let you love me with two conditions." He knots his hands behind me, on the small of my back.

"Okay, let's hear them," he says, smiling the smile that makes me hope I'll wake up beside him for as long as I live.

"You have to agree to let me love you even if I fumble my way through for a while. And, you have to work with me, not against me, when I set limits on our relationship for the benefits of Harper, William, and Hope."

"Done. And done. Anything else you got for me?"

"Yeah. I do have something else," I say.

"Uh oh," he says again.

My hands on his chest and my eyes locked on his, I wait a second before continuing. I'm steeling myself, the previous two years and a lifetime of belonging to no one, are urging me to take the easy way out. But I beat the doubts back with a stick and let go. "I. Love. You," my voice wavering as I try to speak past the threat of tears.

"I love you too," he says. He leans in, this man I don't deserve but won't ever let go, kisses me. It's not the first time. But it's the first time in maybe my whole life, that I have utterly abandoned fear. For better or worse, I am trusting. For better or worse, I believe that the God I feared was absent, has filled my life with hope. He is the God of restoration.

***

The day I met Harper and William changed my life. I didn't have a story – only one written for me by parents who lived for image and status. Even with their father, the story written for the three of us was for the benefit of his career. Burns needed me, but only as an ancillary tool, to complete an image he needed the world to see. As if we're merely a means to an end. But with the kids, it was different. They needed me. Me. I floated through those early days, gauzy and light. I had been baptized in the living water of being needed. Not for anything or anyone but two babies who needed to be loved.

The thought that this man, standing at the grill in my backyard, my son at his side, talking a mile a minute, needs and wants me and my kids for no other reason than he simply adores us, has given wings to a heart that's long been tied up in the corner. He is the only one I know of on earth that dared ask the Creator of order for this outlandish thing – this gift of restoration. God answered his prayers. There is still the remnant of a wall around my heart, around the kid's hearts too. But that's the thing, it's a remnant. You know how there are old walls around ancient cities. Archaeologists work painstakingly to unearth these old cities, finding pieces of what was once a mighty wall protecting the city from impending invasion and war. But with the death of the old, the wall remains only in chunks and crumbling pieces.

We're like those ancient walls. We still have battles to wage in our minds and hearts. There are days and nights where if feels as though either myself or the children have returned to square one. But restoration, our friends, our new family, and my Macon, keep on loving us through those moments. We emerge on the other side, another piece of what was once a mighty fortress, crumbling in front of us.

In its place, are moments like this. A normal day, in the midst of a searing hot summer where we've done nothing but read in overstuffed chairs, the air conditioner, working overtime to beat back the August sun. There's been little conversation today. Nothing crazy. Nothing out of the ordinary: just five people and one Boxer, living life together. Sometimes I feel most blessed on days like this when what is normal for everyone else becomes extraordinary.

Made in the USA
Columbia, SC
15 February 2018